Night Roads

T0071175

》 》 》 》 》 》 》 》 》 《 《 《 《 《 《 《 《 《 《

Gaito Gazdanov

Night Roads

A Novel

TRANSLATED FROM THE RUSSIAN
BY JUSTIN DOHERTY
INTRODUCTION BY LASZLO DIENES

NORTHWESTERN UNIVERSITY PRESS
EVANSTON, ILLINOIS

》 》 》 》 》 》 》 》 》 》 《 《 《 《 《 《 《 《 《 《 《

Northwestern University Press
www.nupress.northwestern.edu

Printed in the United States of America

10 9 8 7 6 5 4 3 2 1

Library of Congress Cataloging-in-Publication Data

Gazdanov, Gaito.
　　[Nochnye dorogi. English]
　　Night roads : a novel / Gaito Gazdanov ; translated from the Russian by
Justin Doherty ; Introduction by Laszlo Dienes.
　　　　p. cm.
　　"Published in French in 1991 under the title Chemins nocturnes."
　　Includes bibliographical references and index.
　　ISBN 978-0-8101-2558-2 (pbk. : alk. paper)
　　1. Paris (France)—Fiction. I. Doherty, Justin. II. Dienes, Laszlo. III. Title.
PG3476.G39N613 2009
891.734—dc22

2008048255

♾ The paper used in this publication meets the minimum requirements
　　of the American National Standard for Information Sciences—
Permanence of Paper for Printed Library Materials, ANSI Z39.48-1992.

» » » CONTENTS « « «

On Gazdanov and
His Novel *Night Roads*

Laszlo Dienes

Gaito Gazdanov has become a classic of twentieth-century Russian literature. A minor classic, perhaps, but a classic nonetheless. At any rate, this seems to have been the general judgment, both popular and critical, in post-Communist Russia for the last twenty years or so, since this émigré writer's posthumous revival in his homeland in the 1990s, when his works were first allowed to be published after a lifetime ban on them in the Soviet Union. During these last twenty years Gazdanov has begun to acquire an international reputation as well: translations of his novels or short stories have been appearing in English, French, Italian, Dutch, Serbo-Croatian, and Hungarian, and interest in him is growing in Germany, Japan, and elsewhere. The present volume is a welcome addition and signals, I hope, a renewed interest in America, and perhaps in the entire English-speaking world, in making this writer more available in English.

And yet, as of now, to most readers, even educated readers and literary scholars, his name sounds unfamiliar in most of the world, except perhaps in Russia herself. So I need to start by asking, and answering, the question: who was Gaito Gazdanov?

Gaito Gazdanov was born in St. Petersburg in 1903 into a well-to-do middle-class Russified family of Ossetian origin. (Ossetia is one of the northern Caucasian republics, an area conquered by czarist Russia and still part of Russia today.) His father was a forester; his mother came from an aristocratic Ossetian family. His father's job took him and the family all over Russia, and Gazdanov spent large periods of his childhood and his schooling in various parts of the Russian empire. Gazdanov was a precocious child, reading serious fiction and even philosophy as a young teenager. His early maturity must have played a role in his being ready to leave his family and volunteer for the White Army at the age of sixteen, in 1919. He spent nearly two years fighting in the Russian Civil War that followed the 1917 Bolshevik Revolution. Defeat meant emigration through Constantinople into permanent exile: first finishing high school in Bulgaria, then on to Paris and hard physical labor at the bottom of French society until a relatively easy job (nighttime taxi driving) made life tolerable enough for writing. The young Gazdanov started publishing short stories in the mid-1920s, all in Russian and all in Russian-language journals published in the West, a pattern he kept to all his life. He also attended the Sorbonne for a while, and in the early 1930s he joined the Parisian-Russian Masonic lodge Northern Star, giving numerous speeches there and remaining an active member for about forty years until his death.

The turning point in Gazdanov's literary life came in 1929–30, when his first novel, *An Evening with Claire,* was published in Paris by a Russian publishing house. The novel was an enormous popular and critical success in the Russian émigré community. Gazdanov was seen (only partly correctly) as a Russian disciple of Proust and was compared to Vladimir Nabokov as the only other major literary talent among the young generation emerging in the emigration. *An Evening with Claire* remains his best-known, and perhaps best-loved, novel: it is fortunate that this novel has been well translated into English, so much so that the *New York Times* reviewer considered some of its passages to have "Tolstoyan power." The young hero of *An Evening with Claire,* clearly the writer's alter ego, meets his former sweetheart in Paris; from then on the novel is a voyage into memory, in search of their lost life and love back in Russia. *The History of a Journey*, his second novel, published in Paris in 1938, is a joyful celebration of life's sensual pleasures amid the difficulties encountered by émigrés, rich or poor. *The Flight*, his third novel, which remained unpublished in its entirety until 1992, depicts a complicated set of amorous relationships in a Mozartean blend of lightness and tragedy. But the 1939–41 *Night Roads*, his only book to deal directly with the Parisian underworld he was exposed to as a nighttime cabdriver for about twenty-five years, offers a mercilessly bleak vision of the debris of human society, without hope, forgiveness, justification, or redemption.

During World War II, Gazdanov joined the French Resistance and tried a new genre. Both *The Specter of Alexander Wolf* and *Buddha's Return* (his fifth and sixth novels, respectively) are "metaphysical thrillers" in which a criminal plot is combined with meditations on death, chance, fate, and predestination. After a French translation appeared in 1951, critics compared Gazdanov to Camus. The taxi-driving years finally came to an end in the early 1950s. In 1953 Gazdanov got a job as a writer-editor at the American-sponsored Radio Liberty in Munich, Germany, and remained with the radio station, either in its Munich or in its Paris bureau, in various capacities (senior news editor, correspondent, chief editor) until his death from lung cancer in Munich in 1971. Of his three post–World War II novels, *Pilgrims* (1954) and *The Awakening* (1966) are moral tales expressing his newly found "existential humanism": the meaning of life is helping others, even if chance and death render one's actions pointless. *Evelyne and Her Friends*, Gazdanov's last completed novel, serialized from 1968 to 1971, is a novel about the novel and about metamorphoses, including the transformation of life into art, which is realized vividly and convincingly in the pages of that work.

Although the Radio Liberty job came with an American salary (huge by European standards after the war) and Gazdanov, for the first time in his life, did not lack material comforts, the 1950s and 1960s cannot be said to have been successful for him from the point of view of literary recognition. The stirrings of the early 1950s (English, French, Italian, and Spanish translations of his works within a few years and the American television dramatization of *The Specter of Alexander Wolf*) did not lead to continuing international attention, and as far as I know, no Gazdanov novel or story was translated into any language between 1955 and 1981. The first changes started in the 1980s, in the West and in the former Soviet Union, in terms of both critical recognition (pioneering studies by the present writer as well as a few others) and reprints and translations of his works. One could say that Gazdanov the writer was reborn around 1990. With the collapse of communism, the writings of formerly banned émigré authors were finally made available to the people they had been written for. Since 1988, Gazdanov's novels and short stories have been published or republished many times in Russia, and a series of new translations have appeared in the West: four of his novels have been published in France, two in Italy, and one in the Netherlands. But Gazdanov's largest presence in any country after Russia at the moment is Serbia, where the only other multivolume edition of his collected works has been published, in the loving care of the brothers Duško and Zorislav Paunković. Also in Serbia a novel has been published in which one of the characters is based on Gazdanov and a film inspired by one of his novels has been planned.

A few remarks on the relative neglect of Russian émigré writers in the West and their total ban in their Soviet homeland may be useful. The latter is easier to explain, if not to understand: anyone who chose to leave (or was forced to flee) Soviet Russia was considered a traitor or an ideological (class) enemy, hence a threat to the Soviet way of thinking and therefore was deemed unacceptable for the Soviet public. Nothing published outside the Soviet Union was allowed to appear in the country, either as a reprint or as an import, and in most cases even the names of their authors and the titles were unmentionable in print or in any public venue. As a result the overwhelming majority of Russians in the Soviet Union had never heard the name of Gaito Gazdanov (or of most other émigré authors, for that matter) until Gorbachev's perestroika finally loosened the restrictions and the first reprints of Gazdanov's works started appearing in the late 1980s.

The relative neglect of Russian émigré writers in the West between 1917 and the 1990s is harder to explain. It was most likely the result of a complex combination of factors. One such factor was the widespread misconception that most émigrés of the first wave (those who left roughly between 1917 and 1925) were reactionary, conservative members of the former repressive czarist establishment: aristocrats, White Army generals, officers, and the like. The ironic truth is that, at least among the more-educated members of the émigré community, a significant and influential segment came from liberal or even revolutionary backgrounds: socialist revolutionaries, Mensheviks, terrorists, and so on. Another factor was a general lack of knowledge and understanding of Russian affairs, as a result of which numerous misunderstandings and misconceptions prevailed and the general public was often puzzled by things Russian. A good recent example of this is the case of Alexander Solzhenitsyn, who was lionized in the West for his heroic anti-Soviet crusade only to be ridiculed later when, as an émigré in Vermont, he criticized the modern West in his famous Harvard speech.

A third factor was the rather common leftist or even pro-Soviet attitudes in the West, especially in Europe between the two wars, that predisposed many intellectuals to disregard or distrust these Russians. A remarkable and unique attempt to bring Russian and French intellectuals together, and to go beyond the Left-Right division, was the Studio franco-russe, a series of lectures and dialogues between some of the most famous French and Russian writers and philosophers that took place in Paris from 1929 to 1931. It did not, however, seem to leave a lasting impact on most of its participants (including the young Gazdanov). A fourth factor may have been the belief, indirectly promoted by Soviet propaganda, that émigré writers could not possibly be really good or significant because they are separated from their country, their people, and their language. It is hard, in retrospect, to see how anyone could have thought this way in the twentieth century, a century characterized so much by major political and ethnic migrations, exile, and dislocation, including, most important, the movement of writers, artists, musicians, and other creative people. Solzhenitsyn's case is again illustrative: he was widely published and admired while in the Soviet Union and widely ignored after becoming an émigré writer. This attitude seems to have prevailed even more so in the interwar and the postwar periods.

The next question to consider is: what kind of writer was Gazdanov? Gazdanov felt that the kind of prose he wrote, deeply emotional, relying on the subtlest psychological nuances, he could write only in the language that was in his blood, that was truly his native tongue, where he knew the exact weight and the exact connotation of every word and every phrase, and whose rhythm and inner melody he was intimately familiar with and possessed totally. For him, this meant that switching to another language, even if known in near perfection, was out of the question. So he never wrote anything in French, the language of the country he spent much of his life in, unlike Nabokov, for example, whose knowledge of English, as well as his method of writing, allowed him such a switch, with the result of becoming much better known in the Western world.

Another reason for Gazdanov's relative obscurity in the West may have much to do with his style and the fact that so much of his literary mastery is embedded in his language. In this respect he is much like Pushkin, whose language is the purest music (often compared to that of Mozart) to Russian ears, whereas, translated (usually poorly) into English, it falls flat and can make English-language readers wonder what it is about him Russian readers admire so much. The problem is perhaps exacerbated by the absence in the English-speaking world of a tradition, present in Russia, of major writers working as translators. It thus rarely happens that the English translator of a foreign work is as much a great writer and stylist in English as the foreign author is in, say, Russian. Consequently, most such translations are unequal to their corresponding originals, especially to works of fiction whose excellence comes largely from their stylistic and linguistic brilliance (as opposed to, say, clever plot, compositional inventiveness, deep psychological understanding of characters, or profound philosophical or religious insight) and are likely to cause an underappreciation among readers and critics of the true value of the original works and their authors.

This seems, by and large, to have been the case with Gazdanov. The translations of his first novels into English (*The Specter of Alexander Wolf* and *Buddha's Return*), published in England and America in 1950 and 1951 (as well as the translations of *The Specter of Alexander Wolf* into French, Spanish, and Italian in the early 1950s), were considered competent but unremarkable. They lacked, in other words, precisely that musical quality of the language that makes Gazdanov special and worthy in Russian. As a result Gazdanov was not "discovered" by the non-Russian-reading public, and none of his other, earlier and later, novels or any of his short stories were translated and published during the next three decades or so. Ardis, a small academic publishing house in

Ann Arbor, Michigan, specializing in modern Russian literature, brought out Gazdanov's successful first novel, *An Evening with Claire*, in 1988 in a translation by Jodi Daynard (after having reprinted the original Russian text a decade earlier, in 1979). None of his short stories were translated into any language, as far as I know, during the writer's lifetime. The first English translation of a Gazdanov short story was published, in 1981, in *A Russian Cultural Revival: A Critical Anthology of Émigré Literature Before 1939*, edited by Temira Pachmuss. Three more of his short stories were published in English, in the 1990s, in a journal of translations called *Metamorphoses*. In the late 1970s the writer's widow donated Gazdanov's papers to the Houghton Library, the rare books and manuscripts collection at Harvard University. For years the archive remained largely uncataloged and unused, and it was only well into the 1990s that Russian scholars finally could visit and start studying this material.

The situation began to change significantly around and after the time of the collapse of the Soviet Union, from the late 1980s on, clearly as a consequence of his posthumous revival in his homeland and his rediscovery and recognition there as a minor twentieth-century classic of Russian literature. It is no exaggeration to say that an avalanche of Gazdanov publications occurred in the 1990s, a phenomenon not too surprising and much like what happened to other resuscitated émigré writers, given their longtime status as "forbidden fruit." This flood of reprints was accompanied by a series of international scholarly conferences in the 1990s and early in the following decade in various locations—Moscow, Kaliningrad, and Vladikavkaz, the capital of Gazdanov's ethnic homeland, Ossetia. By 1996 scholars were ready to publish an authoritative annotated three-volume *Collected Works* of all Gazdanov's known fiction. A Society of Friends of Gazdanov was founded in Moscow in 1998 (its Web site is one of the best online resources on Gazdanov

in Russian: http://www.hrono.ru/proekty/gazdanov/index.html).
In 2001 a new memorial to Gazdanov was unveiled at his grave site
in the Russian cemetery in Sainte-Geneviève-des-Bois, near Paris,
with the participation of such luminaries as the well-known Russian
writer Andrey Bitov and the internationally recognized maestro
Valery Gergiev (also of Ossetian background), who was instrumen-
tal in bringing the project to fruition. In 2003 academic conferences
were held in Moscow and in Vladikavkaz marking the centennial of
Gazdanov's birth, and a book-length biography of Gazdanov was
published in Moscow as a part of the series Lives of Remarkable
Men. Perhaps to accompany that book, in 2005 a documentary film
was made on Gazdanov as a part of a film series of the same title.
The electronic catalog of the Russian Academy of Sciences lists a
total of almost one hundred fifty publications about Gazdanov that
have appeared since 1991 (http://www.slavistik-portal.de/en.html).
The bibliography in the forthcoming second and expanded edition
of his *Collected Works* lists thirteen book-form editions and ninety-
nine journal publications of his fiction in Russia between 1988 and
2004. The full text of a large number of Gazdanov's stories and
novels is available free at various Russian Web sites.

With the collapse of communism, there was a change in attitudes toward émigrés in the West as well. After the pioneering, rare
instances of early Western attention to Russian émigré literature
(see the 1977 Karlinsky volume listed in the following bibliography or the aforementioned Pachmuss anthology), major studies on
Russian emigration, by Marc Raeff and John Glad, came out in
America in the 1990s. Another sign of the changing times was the
special volume in 1991 of the British journal *Coexistence* dedicated
to Russian emigration. Closer to Gazdanov, 1992 saw the first-ever
publication of the full text of Gazdanov's 1939 novel *The Flight* in
a Dutch series of books dedicated to Russian émigré literature.
After the completion of the cataloging of the Gazdanov archive

and its publication, Harvard's Houghton Library held, in 1997–98, an exhibition of the material called *Gaito Gazdanov and Russian Literature in Exile*.

The publication history of *Night Roads* can serve as a good illustration of some of the other kinds of problems that plagued Gazdanov much of his life. The first sixty pages or so of the novel were first published in two installments in the last two issues, in 1939 and 1940, of the Russian-language monthly *Sovremennye Zapiski (Annales contemporaines)*, perhaps the most prestigious periodical of the Russian emigration in Paris, a literary journal that was home to almost all the great writers living in exile, from the Nobel Prize–winning Bunin to the young Nabokov. Both facts (the dates and publication in installments) suggest recurring problems in Gazdanov's life. *Sovremennye Zapiski* ceased publication in 1940, and *Night Road* (as it was first called) remained unpublished in Russian in its entirety until 1952 (likewise, another of his prewar novels, *The Flight*, had to wait until 1992 for its complete publication in Russian [in the Netherlands, of all places!] and until 1993 for publications in Russia). Another problem was a certain degree of carelessness on the part of the Russian publishers (and perhaps writers as well, Gazdanov included) when it came to bringing novels out in installments. *Sovremennye Zapiski* published both installments without any indication whether they were part of a novel or a short story, and certainly without making clear they were excerpts from the beginning of a novel. Similar situations arose with several other Gazdanov novels, so much so that up to this day there remains some textual detective work to be done to establish with final authority the actual full text, and its correct sequence, of some of his works.

Orion, a literary almanac published in Paris in 1947, included excerpts from *Night Roads* (now in the plural), but mostly from the latter parts of the novel, thus readers could not form a true impression of it. The 1952 edition was brought out by a New York Russian-language publishing house named after Chekhov. After World War II the flourishing literary life of the Russian emigration in Paris came to an end: many died, others were old, the political and economic situations changed, some emigrated farther, to America, and others changed languages. But cavalier attitudes toward authors' rights and the sanctity of the text did not change. The Chekhov Publishing House, for example, felt free to divide the text of *Night Roads* as it saw fit and even dropped the novel's epigraph, a quotation from fellow writer Isaac Babel. They also insisted that the French phrases in the novel be translated into Russian, even though, as he makes plain in a 1964 letter, Gazdanov felt they should remain as he originally wrote them, in French.

An early draft of a manuscript called "Notes of a Cabdriver," dated 1932, was found among Gazdanov's papers. It shows that Gazdanov was interested, as always, in real-life experiences and contradicts somewhat the claim of his widow, who, in the 1970s, told me that *Night Roads* was written at her suggestion (Gazdanov did not meet his future wife until 1936). It is more likely that Gazdanov was somewhat reluctant to write the book because of its documentary nature—not a genre he particularly liked or held in high esteem, being, perhaps, too close to journalism for him—and so he needed his wife's encouragement and support to go ahead with it. And this may also be reflected in the fact that this is the only book Gazdanov dedicated to his wife (and only in the 1952 edition). Gazdanov's lack of interest in the documentary genre is also clearly shown by his attitude toward his only other documentary work, a book he wrote about Soviet partisans fighting in the French Resistance during World War II. It was published in a French edition in Paris in 1946, and although he wrote it in Russian, he never bothered to have it published in that language (which he could easily have done), and, in fact, many of his closest friends did not even know of its existence. The book, which is definitely not a novel, unlike *Night Roads,* which, in spite of its documentary nature, is a novel, was first published in Russian half a century later, in 1995.

The manuscript of *Night Roads* is dated "August 11, 1941, Paris," revealing another habit of Gazdanov the writer: starting publication before the entire text is finished. Although the habit may seem strange, friends and colleagues all agreed in their reminiscences that Gazdanov wrote in his head, during his interminable walks (and rides?), first spending years digesting his material and then mentally composing the text, so completely that by the time he sat down to write he could produce the whole story or novel with few additions, corrections, or changes. Most of his manuscripts bear this out.

Although a great deal of Gazdanov's fiction is directly, and sometimes openly, inspired by his life experiences, *Night Roads* is special in that it appears wholly autobiographical, based entirely, as far as we know, on actual events and real people. Gazdanov did not at first want to change the names of the people in the work and did so only at the insistence of his wife. We know that Plato was the clochard Socrate, Raldy was a certain Jeanne Baldy, a former "queen" of the Parisian demimonde (a newspaper account of her life—a clipping from a French newspaper of 1935, extant among Gazdanov's papers—is entitled "Jeanne Baldy qui fut une des reines de Paris, est arrêtée pour trafic de stupéfiants"), and the café where some of the action takes place was the Café d'Alençon, near Gare Montparnasse.

Finally, the remaining questions are: what are Gazdanov's main themes, what are his works mostly concerned with, and, specifically, what is *Night Roads* about and how do its themes and messages, if any, differ, if they do at all, from those of his other works?

Gazdanov was often criticized for the episodic nature of his writing, for his seemingly unstructured narratives, for stories that do not appear to lead anywhere and contain many details that at first glance may seem unimportant, and for ideas that are scattered around in the text without cohering into a "message" or even a unified vision of life. While these initial impressions are common and understandable, they are wrong and reflect either a superficial reading or, more likely in the case of serious critics, an inability to think along the lines of Gazdanov's mind. The main issue here, briefly, is his conviction that the preferences of our intellect, our ideological, political positions, our social and moral choices, even our religious beliefs are ultimately determined by our biological (today we would perhaps say biochemical and genetic) makeup. This attitude toward life, people, society, history, characters, personality, moral choices, and so forth is, for many people, hard to accept and often leads to the charge that there are no ideas, no clear messages in Gazdanov. But this is not the case. A short list of some of the recurring themes from his earliest to last writings shows as much: life as a journey or pilgrimage; metamorphoses (of people, ideas, emotions); death; chance and fate; the difficulty of understanding the world, our existence and the concomitant metaphysical terror arising when our existence appears meaningless; the primacy of the emotional, visceral dimension of the human condition ("Feelings are the only subject you know something about," the narrator of *Night Roads* is told); art as the highest form of human activity; altruism (helping others even when all seems hopeless and pointless); and others. He is a psychologically oriented author in the best Russian tradition of Tolstoy and Dostoevsky whose main interest was always "the imperceptible psychological shell" or "the movements of the soul," as he put it, and he describes those subtle, delicate movements of the psyche ("the inner music of life") with tenderness and understanding and precision and in a language that on his best pages becomes the prose equivalent of powerful chamber music. This musical quality, coming from the rhythms of his soft, lyrical language, from his long, sometimes unwieldy but often hypnotic, sentences, combined with an intellectual precision probably learned from his French environment, makes him a truly unusual and remarkable writer. Years ago, I wrote that Gazdanov "enriched Russian fiction with a new *frisson:* with the welcome clarity of French meditative prose on the more emotional 'Slavic disorder' of Russian." Since his rediscovery in France, French critics have talked, paradoxically but pointedly, about his bizarre tour de force of becoming "un écrivain français de langue russe" and of being "le plus français des écrivains russes"!

Night Roads has many of these themes. Indeed, the title suggests two main ones: "roads," the theme of life as a way, a path, a journey with (or without?) a destination and hence meaning, and "night," the dark side of life, the underworld in every possible sense of the word: socially, economically, mentally, morally. It is about metamorphoses: consider the transformation of Fedorchenko, as well as the effects of the "social laboratory" on many of the other characters. It is also of course about exile, the émigré condition (Russian or otherwise), about dislocation physically, linguistically, culturally. In its dark vision of the debris of humankind, of this "living human carrion" (*zhivaia chelovecheskaia padal'*), with the portrayal of the "dark poetry of human perdition" without illusions and hope, the novel has been compared to Louis-Ferdinand Céline's *Voyage au bout de la nuit* and to Henry Miller's *Tropic of Cancer.* "*Night Roads* is a cruel, merciless book," I wrote in my book on Gazdanov in 1982, "by a man who is unable to deceive himself or his readers with conventional illusions about man or mankind. The 'somber poetry of human downfall' no longer appeals to him for he knows the reality behind its romanticized literary representation; and this reality, the reality of hopeless and incorrigible 'live human carrion' cannot, and does not, evoke in him any compassion, sympathy or love. Such an attitude is not . . . in the Russian tradition . . . There is no redemption, nor justification, for the scum of the earth. The consolations of Christianity are for Gazdanov just that; the only certainty is suffering, the inexplicable existence of evil and ignorance, and death. The rest is speculation."

Gazdanov is hard to translate. He "hides" his meanings in his seemingly simple, yet smooth and melodious Russian. His prose explores the minutiae of the human psyche in the only language it can be done in: the native tongue the heart and mind think and dream in, automatically, unconsciously, involuntarily. The challenge of translating such prose requires that it be recomposed into the chamber music of English. I hope this translation has successfully met that challenge.

Selected Bibliography

The reader will notice that Gazdanov's first name is spelled in various ways throughout the bibliography: Gaito, Gajto, Gayto, or even Gaïto (in French). The Russian version of his first name (Georgy) is sometimes used as well. Finally, following the Russian custom of the use of patronymics, he can also be referred to as Georgy Ivanovich Gazdanov, the patronymic Ivanovich coming from his father's first name, Ivan.

Editions of *Night Roads* in Russian

"Nochnaia doroga." *Sovremennye Zapiski* (Paris) 69–70 (1939–40) [first, incomplete, serialized publication in a journal].

Nochnye dorogi. New York: Chekhov Publishing House, 1952 [first complete edition in book form, the only one during the writer's lifetime].

Nochnye dorogi. In *Vecher u Kler, romany.* Moscow: Sovremennik, 1990 [first reprint of *Night Roads* in a one-volume collection of selected writings, in what was still the Soviet Union].

Nochnye dorogi. In *Sobranie sochinenii v trekh tomakh* [*Collected Works in Three Volumes*], vol. 1, edited by F. Khadonova, St. Nikonenko, and L. Dienes. Moscow: Soglasie, 1996 [first scholarly edition of nearly all Gazdanov's works].

Editions of *Night Roads* in Other Languages

Chemins nocturnes. Paris: Éditions Viviane Hamy, 1991 [in French, second edition in 2002, with a preface by the translator, Elena Balzamo].

Noćni putevi. Belgrade: Radio B92, 1995 [in Serbian].

Translations of Other Gazdanov Novels in English

Buddha's Return. New York: Dutton, 1951.

An Evening with Claire. Ann Arbor, Mich.: Ardis, 1988 [with an introduction by the translator, Jodi Daynard].

The Specter of Alexander Wolf. New York: Dutton, 1950.

The Spectre of Alexander Wolf. London: Cape, 1950.

Criticism on Gazdanov

No Russian-language sources are included here; for the reader or student who would like to explore the literature on Gazdanov in Russian, I recommend the following Web site as a good starting point: www.hrono .ru/proekty/gazdanov/index.html.

Dienes, L. *Bibliographie des oeuvres de Gaïto Gazdanov.* Paris: Institut d'études slaves, 1982.

―――. "Catalog of the Papers of Gaito Gazdanov." *Harvard Library Bulletin* 7, no. 4 (Winter 1996): 41–61 [also available online at http:// pds.lib.harvard.edu/pds/viewtext/2573358?n=19915&s=4].

————. "Gaito Gazdanov: Russian Émigré Literature at Harvard." *Harvard Library Bulletin* 7, no. 4 (Winter 1996): 21–40.

————. *Russian Literature in Exile: The Life and Work of Gajto Gazdanov.* Munich: Sagner, 1982 [in English; translated into Russian and published in Russia in 1995].

Göbler, Frank. "Zeit und Erinnerung in Gajto Gazdanovs Roman 'Vecher u Kler.'" *Zeitschrift für Slawistik* 44, no. 1 (1999): 79–87.

Hagglund, R. "*Numbers* and the Russian Émigrés in the 1930s." *The Slavic and East European Journal* 29, no. 1 (Spring 1985): 39–51.

Livak, Leonid. "A Journey to the South: The Art of Oblivion in Gaito Gazdanov's Novel *Vecher u Kler.*" *Wiener Slawistischer Almanach* 44 (1999): 49–66.

[Numerous publications in Japan by Yuichi Isahaya; see http://www .kinet-tv.ne.jp/~yisahaya/sub.e24.html#_jmpo_].

General Studies on Russian Émigré Literature

Andreyev, Catherine. *Russia Abroad: Prague and the Russian Diaspora, 1918–1938.* New Haven, Conn.: Yale University Press, 2004.

Dienes, L. "Studies on the Russian Emigration and Its Contribution to Modern Western Culture: Introductory Remarks." *Coexistence* (U.K.) 2, no. 28 (1991): 201–14.

————. "Studio franco-russe." In *Polyphonie pour Iván Fónagy,* edited by Jean Perrot, 103–13. Paris: L'Harmattan, 1997.

Glad, J. *Russia Abroad: Writers, History, Politics.* Tenafly, N.J.: Hermitage/Washington, D.C.: Birchbark Press, 1999.

Johnston, R. H. *New Mecca, New Babylon: Paris and the Russian Exiles, 1920–1945.* Montreal: McGill-Queen's University Press, 1988.

Karlinsky, S., and A. Appel Jr., eds. *The Bitter Air of Exile: Russian Writers in the West, 1922–1972.* Berkeley: University of California Press, 1977.

Livak, Leonid, ed. *From the Other Shore: Russian Writers Abroad, Past and Present.* Idyllwild, Calif.: Schlacks, 2001.

Livak, Leonid. *How It Was Done in Paris: Russian Émigré Literature and French Modernism.* Madison: University of Wisconsin Press, 2003.

Livak, Leonid, and G. Tassis, eds. *Le Studio franco-russe, 1929–1931.* Toronto: Toronto Slavic Quarterly, 2005.

Pachmuss, Temira, ed. *A Russian Cultural Revival: A Critical Anthology of Émigré Literature Before 1939*. Knoxville: University of Tennessee Press, 1981.

Raeff, M. *Russia Abroad: A Cultural History of the Russian Emigration 1919–1939*. New York: Oxford University Press, 1990.

Entries on Gazdanov and/or Russian Émigré Literature in Encyclopedias, Handbooks, and Reference Volumes

Beyssac, M. *La vie culturelle de l'émigration russe en France. Chronique 1920–1930*. Paris: Presses Universitaires de France, 1971.

Cornwell, Neil, ed. *Reference Guide to Russian Literature*. London: Fitzroy Dearborn, 1998.

———. *The Routledge Companion to Russian Literature*. London: Routledge, 2001.

Foster, Ludmila. *Bibliography of Russian Émigré Literature 1918–1968*. Boston: Hall, 1970.

L'émigration russe: Revues et recueils, 1920–1980. General index of articles published by the Turgenev Russian Library and the Library of Contemporary International Documentation. Paris: Institut d'études slaves, 1988.

Rubins, Maria. *Twentieth-Century Russian Émigré Writers*. Detroit: Thomson Gale, 2005.

Terras, Victor, ed. *A Handbook of Russian Literature*. New Haven, Conn.: Yale University Press, 1984.

Weber, Harry B., ed. *The Modern Encyclopedia of Russian and Soviet Literatures (Including Non-Russian and Émigré Literatures)*. Gulf Breeze, Fla.: Academic International Press, 1977–.

Night Roads

Dedicated to my wife

"And when I remember those years, I find in them the beginning of the ailments that have tormented me, and the cause of my premature and terrible withering away."

ISAAC BABEL

Several days ago, when I was working late at night on the Place Saint-Augustin, totally deserted at that hour, I saw a small carriage of the type used by invalids to get around. It was a three-wheeled carriage arranged like a mobile chair; at the front there was a sort of steering wheel that had to be turned in order to move a chain attached to the rear wheels. With astonishing, dreamlike slowness, the chair traveled around the circle of brightly shining polygons and began to ascend the Boulevard Haussmann. I drew closer to get a better look; sitting in it was a wrapped-up, tiny old lady; all I could see were her dark, desiccated face, looking almost no longer human, and a scrawny, equally dark hand, with which she struggled to turn the wheel. I had seen people like her often enough, but only ever during the daytime. Where could this old woman be going at night, why was she here, what could be the cause of this nocturnal excursion, who might be waiting for her, and where?

I watched her go, almost choking with pity, with a sense of complete hopelessness and a burning curiosity resembling physical thirst. I had learned absolutely nothing about her, of course. But the sight of this invalid carriage as it drew away from me and the slow squeak it gave out, clearly audible in the still, cold air of that night, suddenly caused me to feel that insatiable and immediate urge to know and try to understand the lives of all manner of strangers, a feeling that scarcely ever left me during the last few years. It was always futile, since I had no time to devote myself to it. But the feeling of regret that came from my awareness of this futility has been a constant throughout my whole life. Later on, when I thought about it, I began to feel that in essence my curiosity was an attraction that made no sense, since it was confronted by almost insuperable obstacles, obstacles which stemmed in equal measure from my material situation and from the natural limitations of my mind, and also from the fact that any remotely abstract insight I might have was undermined by my fierce, physical awareness of my own existence. Moreover, I was stubbornly resistant to understanding any passions or desires which lay outside my own experience; for example, it cost me an immense effort not to consider any person who, through weakness and blind passion, had gambled or drunk away all his or her money—simply a fool, undeserving of sympathy or pity—just because I happened to be unable to tolerate alcohol and found card games deadly boring. In the same way I could not understand Don Juans who spent their whole life going from one lover's embrace to the next—but this was for another reason, which for a long time I did not suspect, until I found the courage to think it through properly, and then I realized that the reason was jealousy, all the more surprising since in everything else I was entirely lacking in this feeling. It is quite possible, had things been different, had some subtle change occurred in me, that those passions which I could not understand might have become accessible to me, and I might have been subject to their destructive influence, and then other people, for whom these passions were foreign, would have looked upon me with that same pity and regret. And the fact that I did not experience them was, perhaps, simply a manifestation of my instinct for self-preservation, evidently stronger in me than in those acquaintances of mine who would lose their pitiful earnings at the races or drink them away in innumerable cafés.

But more than anything else, the chief obstacle to my disinterested curiosity toward everything around me, all of which I desired with a savage insistence to know more fully, was my lack of free time, which was caused by my having always lived in abject poverty, so that worries about earning a living consumed all of my attention. However, it was this same circumstance that provided me with a relatively rich source of superficial impressions, which I would not have had if my life had unfolded in different conditions. I approached what I saw without any particular prejudice and tried to avoid coming to generalizations or conclusions; but, in spite of my wishes, two feelings came to predominate in me, when I think about all this: contempt and pity. Now, when I look back on these sad experiences, I wonder if perhaps I was wrong and that such feelings were a mistake. But over many years I could find no way of suppressing their existence; these feelings are as inevitable today as death is inevitable, and I have never been able to escape them; it would amount to the same kind of spiritual cowardice if I were to deny the fact that deep within me there dwelt an obscure and insistent thirst for murder, complete contempt for the property of others, and a capacity for unfaithfulness and debauchery. And the habit of operating with imaginary things—things that had never happened, evidently as the result of a whole series of contingencies—this caused these possibilities to become more real than they would have been had they actually happened, and all of them came to possess an allure that was lacking in other things. Frequently, returning home after my night's work on the dead Parisian streets, I would imagine in detail a murder, everything that preceded it—all the conversations, nuances of intonation, the expression in people's eyes—and the characters in these imagined dialogues might be chance acquaintances of mine, or else passersby I had remembered for whatever reason, or, finally, I myself might be the murderer. At the end of reflections like these, I would generally arrive at the same conclusion, or rather feeling, a mixture of irritation and regret that such comfortless and pointless experiences should be my lot and that, because of absurd contingency, I had ended up being a taxi driver. Everything, or nearly everything good and fine in the world, had become as if hermetically closed off from me—and I was left alone, with a desperate desire not to be forever caught up in that endless and depressing human vileness with which my work brought me into daily contact. It was almost total; rarely was there room for anything positive. Even the Russian Civil War could not compare with this essentially peaceful existence for its repulsiveness and absence of anything good. Of course, this was explained by the fact that the inhabitants of nocturnal Paris differed sharply from its daytime population and consisted of several categories of people whose nature and profession more often than not rendered them doomed from the start. But more than that, to a taxi driver, in the attitude of such people there was always an absence of any restraining influences: what does it matter what this person thinks of me if I will never see him again and he has no way of telling my friends about it? In this way, I saw my chance clients as they were in reality and not as they wished to appear, and my contact with them showed them in a bad light on almost every occasion. Even while trying to remain entirely impartial toward everyone, I could not help noticing that differences between them were never very great, and in this none-too-flattering leveling process, a woman in a ball gown from the Avenue Henri-Martin differed little from her less successful sister who patrolled the sidewalk like a policeman, from one street corner to the other; and distinguished-looking people in Passy or Auteuil haggled with their driver just as degradingly as a drunken worker from the Rue de Belleville; and it was impossible to trust any of them, as I realized on more than one occasion.

I can remember how, when I first started work as a taxi driver, I stopped one day beside the sidewalk, drawn by the cries of a well-dressed lady of about thirty-five years, with a puffed-up face. She was standing, supporting herself on a sidewalk bollard, moaning and making signs to me; when I pulled up, she asked me in a faltering voice to take her to the hospital; she had broken her leg. I lifted her up and laid her in the car, but when we arrived there, she refused to pay me and told the man in a white coat who had come out that I had knocked her over in my car and that she had fallen and broken her leg. Not only did I not receive any money, I was also at risk of being accused of what is known as involuntary homicide. Fortunately, the man in the white coat reacted skeptically to her words, and I drove away as quickly as I could. And subsequently, whenever I was signaled by people standing over someone's body stretched out on the pavement, I merely pressed harder on the accelerator, without ever stopping. A man in a fine suit who had just come out of the Hotel Claridge, and whom I took to the Gare de Lyon, gave me one hundred francs, but I had no change; he said that he would go and get change inside, walked off, and never came back again; he was a distinguished, gray-haired man with a good cigar who looked like the director of a bank, and quite possibly that is exactly what he was.

One time, after dropping off a female passenger at two o'clock in the morning, I stopped the car and noticed, lying on the seat, a woman's comb inlaid with diamonds—in all probability fake, but in any case its general appearance was luxurious; I could not be bothered to get out of my seat, so I decided I would pick up the comb later. Right then I was stopped by a lady—this was on one of the avenues leading off the Champs-de-Mars—wearing a sable *sortie de bal;* she had me drive her to the Avenue Foch. After she had gone I remembered the comb and looked over my shoulder. The comb was no longer there; the lady in her *sortie de bal* had stolen it, just as a servant girl or prostitute would have done.

I would think about this and many other things almost always during the same hours before dawn. In winter it would still be dark, in summer it was light at that time, and there was no longer anyone on the streets; very occasionally I would see workers, silent figures who would pass by and disappear. I hardly looked at them, since I knew by heart their external appearance, just as I knew the *quartiers* where they lived, as well as those other areas where they would never venture. Paris is divided into several fixed zones; I remember how one elderly worker—I was working alongside him in a paper factory off the Boulevard de la Gare—told me that during the forty years he had lived in Paris he had never been to the

Champs-Élysées because, as he explained, he had never worked there. In this city there still survived—in the poor *quartiers*—a primitive psychology, dating almost from the fourteenth century, that existed alongside the contemporary world, which it remained separate from, indeed, had almost no contact with. And it would sometimes occur to me, as I drove around and chanced upon such places, that I was witnessing even now the slow extinction of the Middle Ages. But it was rare for me to be able to concentrate on one thought in particular for any decent length of time, and after the next turn of the wheel that narrow street would disappear and a broad avenue would commence, where the buildings had glass doors and elevators. The fleeting nature of such perceptions often exhausted my attention, and I preferred to shut them out and think about nothing at all. In this type of work no impression, no amount of charm, could last long—and it was only later that I tried to remember and to make sense of what I had managed to glimpse over the course of my latest nighttime excursion, out of the details of that extraordinary world that is typical of nocturnal Paris. Always, every single evening, I would encounter several lunatics; they were mostly people who were a step away from the asylum or hospital or were alcoholics or tramps. In Paris there were thousands of such people. I knew in advance that on this street I would find a particular lunatic wandering along, while in a different *quartier* there would be another. It was extraordinarily hard to find out anything about them, as what they said was usually completely incoherent. Occasionally, however, I did manage to find out something.

I remember how at one time I was particularly interested in a small, ugly man with a little mustache, quite decently dressed, similar to a workman in appearance, and whom I saw roughly once a week or fortnight around two o'clock in the morning, always in the same spot on the Avenue de Versailles, on the corner opposite the Pont de Grenelle. He was usually standing in the road, close to the

sidewalk, threatening someone with his fists and muttering barely
audible curses. All I could make out was a whispered, "You swine!
You swine!" I had known him for many years—always saw him at
the same time, always in the exact same place. Finally, I went up
and spoke to him, and after a lengthy series of questions, I learned
his story. By profession he was a carpenter; he lived somewhere
near to Versailles, about seven miles from Paris, and therefore
could come into Paris only once a week, on Saturdays. Six years
ago he had quarreled one evening with the proprietor of the café on
the other side of the road, who had slapped him across the face. He
had gone away and ever since had harbored a deadly hatred toward
him. Every Saturday evening the small man would travel into
Paris; and, since he was terribly afraid of the man who had hit him,
he would wait until the café had closed. He would drink to get up
his courage, one glass after another in the neighboring bistros, and
when, finally, his enemy had closed up his establishment, he would
come to this spot and threaten the unseen proprietor with his fist
and mutter curses in a whisper; but he was so frightened that he
never dared to utter a word out loud. He would spend all week, as
he worked in Versailles, eagerly awaiting the arrival of Saturday,
and then he would dress up in his best clothes and travel into Paris
to spend the night on a deserted street, uttering his barely audible
insults and issuing threats in the direction of the café. He would
remain on the Avenue de Versailles until dawn—and then head off
in the direction of the Porte de Saint-Cloud, stopping from time to
time to turn around and shake his little, dry fist. After hearing this,
I went into the café belonging to the man who had offended the
small man and found there behind the counter a magnificent, red-
headed woman who, as always, complained about business. When I
asked her if she had owned the café for long, it turned out that she
had been there for three years and had moved there after the death
of the café's previous owner, who had died of an apoplectic fit.

Around four o'clock in the morning I would generally go and drink a glass of milk in a café opposite one of the stations, a café where I knew absolutely everyone, from the owner, an old lady who had difficulty chewing her sandwich with her false teeth, to a little middle-aged woman in black who never could be parted from the large oilskin shopping bag that she constantly dragged around with her; she was about fifty years old. She was usually sitting quietly in a corner, and I could not understand what she was doing here at this hour; she was always alone. I asked the café owner about this; the owner replied that she was working, like the other women. In the beginning I was astonished by things like this, but later on I discovered that even quite elderly and slovenly women had their own clientele and often earned no less than the others. At that hour there would appear, dead drunk, a skinny, toothless old woman who would come into the café and yell, "Damn all!" When the time came for her to pay for the glass of white wine she had been drinking, she invariably reacted with astonishment and would say to the waiter, "No, you are pushing your luck!" I was left with the impression that she really did not know any other words; in any case, she never uttered any. As she walked up to the café, someone would turn around and say, "Here comes Damnall." But one day I came across her deep in conversation with some scruffy individual, dead drunk, who was holding on to the counter with both hands and swaying. The words she spoke to him—so unexpected coming from her mouth—were these: "I swear, Roger, it's true. You know it is, Roger. I did love you. But when you're in this state . . ." And then, breaking off from this monologue, she shouted out once again: "Damn all!" After this, one fine day, she simply vanished, having yelled out, "Damn all!" for the last time, never to appear again; several months later, when I inquired about her absence, I discovered that she had died.

Twice each week a man in a beret, smoking a pipe, would visit this café—he was known as Monsieur Martini, because he always ordered a martini—this was usually some time after eleven o'clock at night. But by two o'clock in the morning he was already completely drunk; he would buy drinks for all and sundry, and by three o'clock, after he had spent all of his money—usually around two hundred francs—he would start asking the owner to let him have one more martini on credit. At that point he was usually ushered out of the café. He would come back in then be ushered out once more, and after that the *garçons* just stopped letting him in. Indignant, he would shrug his sloping shoulders and say: "I find this amusing. Amusing. Amusing. That's all I have to say."

He was a teacher of Greek, Latin, German, Spanish, and English; he lived outside the city; and he had a wife and six children. At two o'clock in the morning he would be setting out philosophical theories to those who would listen to him, usually pimps and vagrants, arguing furiously with them; they laughed at him; I remember how they guffawed even more than usual when he recited Schiller's "The Glove" to them in German; of course, they were amused not by the content, of which they could have had no understanding, but by how funny the German language sounded. Several times I took him to one side and suggested he should go home, but he invariably refused, and all my arguments had no effect on him whatsoever; he was essentially rather self-satisfied and, to my astonishment, very proud of being the father of six children. One day, when he was still half sober, I had a conversation with him; he was reproaching me for my bourgeois morality, and, angry with him, I shouted, "For heaven's sake, don't you understand that you'll end up in a hospital bed with delirium tremens, and nothing's going to stop you now?"

"You don't understand the essence of Gallic philosophy," he replied.

"What?" I asked, astonished.

"Yes," he repeated, filling his pipe, "life is given to us for pleasure."

Only then did I notice that he was more drunk than I had initially thought; it transpired that he had appeared an hour earlier that day, which I had not accounted for.

As the years went by, his resistance to alcohol diminished, as did his financial resources, until he was refused permission to enter the café at all; and the last time I saw him, the *garçons* and pimps were egging him on, trying to provoke a fight between him and a tramp, then both of them were thrown out; they fell down, and Monsieur Martini tumbled along the sidewalk and out into the road, where he lay for some time—beneath the winter rain in the ice-cold, watery dirt.

"If I remember correctly, this is what you term Gallic philosophy," I said, as I lifted him up.

"Amusing. Amusing. Highly amusing. That's all I have to say," he repeated, parrotlike.

I sat him down at a café table.

"He's got no money," one of the waiters told me.

"If only that was all!" I replied.

Monsieur Martini suddenly sobered up.

"In every instance of alcoholism there is some root cause," he said unexpectedly.

"Perhaps, perhaps," I replied distractedly. "But you, for instance, why do you drink?"

"I am embittered," he said. "My wife despises me, she has taught my children to despise me, and for them the only meaning to my existence is that I give them money. I cannot bear this, and so in the evenings I go out of the house. I know that it's all hopeless."

I looked at his suit, which was now covered in dirt, at the scratches on his face, at his lost-looking little eyes beneath his beret.

"I don't think there's anything more we can do," I said.

In this café I was acquainted with all the women who spent long hours sitting there. Among them were a great variety of types, but they retained their individuality only at the beginning of their careers; then, after a few months, when they had mastered their profession, they came to completely resemble all the others. The majority of them had been maids, but there were exceptions: shop-girls, stenographers, in rare instances cooks, and even one former owner of a small grocer's shop, whose story everybody knew. She had insured the shop for a large sum then set fire to it, but so clumsily that the insurance company refused to pay her; the result was that the shop burned down without her receiving any money. And then she and her husband had decided that for the time being she would work in this particular manner, and then they would open a shop once again. She was a rather beautiful woman of around thirty years, but the profession took hold of her so much that, after a year, all talk of her opening another shop completely ceased, particularly as she had found herself a regular client, a distinguished and well-off gentleman who gave her presents and considered her his second wife; he would go out with her on Saturday and Wednesday evenings, two days a week, and so on these days she did not work. My regular neighbor at the bar was Suzanne, a small, heavily made-up blonde woman, very fond of particularly extravagant dresses, bracelets, and rings; she had had one of her upper front teeth replaced with a gold one, and she was so taken with it that she was constantly looking at herself in a little hand mirror, raising her upper lip like a dog.

"It really is beautiful," she said one day, turning toward me, "don't you think?"

"I can't think of anything more stupid," I said.

From that time on she began to treat me with a certain degree of hostility and occasional rudeness. She was particularly scornful of the fact that I always drank milk.

"You're always drinking milk," she said to me three days or so later. "Wouldn't you like some of mine?"

She very much loved change and would sometimes vanish for several nights—this meant that she was working in a different area—then one day she disappeared for a whole month, and when I asked a waiter if he knew what had become of her, he replied that she had found herself a permanent job. He put it differently, in fact, saying that she now had a permanent position—which turned out to be in the biggest brothel in Montparnasse. But she did not stay there: she was incapable of sitting still. At that time she was still very young, twenty-two or twenty-three years old.

At the register every night, from eight o'clock in the evening until six o'clock in the morning, sat the owner of the café herself— and the café was worth several million francs. For thirty years she had slept by day and worked at night; during the day she was replaced by her husband, a distinguished old man in a good suit. They had no children, they did not, apparently, have any close relatives, and they had dedicated their whole lives to this café, as others dedicate themselves to charitable works, serving God, or a career in government; they never went away, never took a holiday. However, at one time the wife did not work for around two months—she had a stomach ulcer and spent the whole of this time in bed. She had long since accumulated a substantial fortune, but she could not stop working. In external appearance she resembled a benign witch. I had chatted with her several times, and one day she became angry with me when I told her that, in essence, her life was just as pointless as Monsieur Martini's. "How can you compare me to that alcoholic?" she asked, and I remembered, rather too late, that people capable of understanding any kind of dispassionate judgment, particularly one that touches on them personally, exist in a tiny minority, perhaps one in one hundred. To Madame Duval herself, her life appeared complete and full of certain meaning, and to some extent this was true; she was indeed complete and even perfect in her total uselessness. For her to now undertake anything at all, it was too late. But she would never have agreed with this. "Well, madame, when you die . . ." I wanted to say, but I refrained from doing so, having decided that for the sake of what was essentially an abstract question it was not worth spoiling my relations with her. And I said that perhaps I was mistaken and that I thought this way because I would feel myself to be incapable of this thirty-year exploit. She relaxed and replied that, of course, it was by no means everybody who was capable of this, but for all that, she was now sure about one thing: she could live out the remainder of her life contentedly—as if her present age, her last sixty-three years, were not the end but the beginning of her life. There were many objections I could have made to this, too, but I kept silent.

Later on I came to understand that she was in no degree exceptional: her case was completely typical; I knew millionaires with dirty hands who labored for sixteen hours a day and old taxi drivers who owned apartment buildings and lands and who, in spite of their shortness of breath, heartburn, hemorrhoids, and generally disastrous state of health, carried on working for the sake of an extra thirty francs a day; and even if their profits went down to two francs, they would still work until one fine day they could not get out of bed, and this would be a brief respite for them before death. One of the *garçons* from this café was also remarkable: he was a happy man. I discovered this one day during a brief philosophical discussion initiated by an elderly man of unremarkable appearance who was, I think, a former driver. He had started speaking about the lottery and said that it was like the sun; as the sun revolves around the Earth, so the wheel of the lottery turns.

"The sun doesn't revolve around the Earth," I said to him. "That's not right, and the lottery's not like the sun."

"The sun doesn't revolve around the Earth?" he asked sarcastically. "And who told you that?"

He was entirely serious about this; I then asked him whether he could read and write at all, and he took offense and kept trying to discover where I could have obtained more reliable information about the mechanics of the heavens than he had. He would not recognize the authority of scientists and maintained that they knew no more than us. At this point the waiter joined in the conversation and said that none of this was important; what was important was for a person to be happy.

"I've never seen any such people," I said.

And then he, with a certain triumphant note in his voice, replied that this possibility was finally available to me because at that moment I saw before me a happy man.

"What?" I said in astonishment. "Do you consider yourself a completely happy man?"

He explained to me that this was indeed the case. It transpired that he had always had a dream of working and earning his living, and it had been realized, so he was completely happy. I looked at him closely: he stood there in his blue apron, with his sleeves rolled up, in front of the damp zinc counter; from one side could be heard the voice of Martini—"amusing, amusing, amusing"—from the right, someone was saying in a hoarse voice, "I tell you, he's my brother, understand?" Next to the man I was speaking with, who was convinced of the sun's movement around the Earth, a fat woman—the whites of her eyes were covered with a dense web of red veins—was explaining to her protector that she could not work

in this neighborhood. "I never find anyone. I never find anyone."
And in the center of all of this stood the waiter Michel, and his yel-
low face really was happy. "Well, my dear fellow, congratulations,"
I said to him.

And even as I was leaving, I kept remembering his words: "I
always had this one dream, always, of earning my living." This was
even more pathetic, perhaps, than Martini or Madame Duval or
fat Marcelle, who could not find any clients in Montparnasse; and
business really was bad for Marcelle until some shrewd person told
her that her beauty would definitely be appreciated more in another
neighborhood, with a less-refined clientele, that is to say, in Les
Halles; and she really did go and work there; six months later I saw
her in a café on the Boulevard Sébastopol, and she had put on even
more weight and was much better dressed. I spoke about the happy
waiter to one of my alcoholic friends, whose nickname was Plato
because of his fondness for philosophy; he was not all that old and
spent every night at the bar of this café, drinking one glass of white
wine after another. Like Martini, he had been to college, had lived
at one time in England, had been married to a beautiful woman,
was the father of a lovely boy, and had plenty of money; I do not
know how or why all of this had very quickly disappeared into the
past, but he had left his family, his relatives had disowned him,
and he was now on his own. He was a pleasant, polite man; he was
quite well educated, spoke two foreign languages, was well read,
and at one time had been writing a philosophical thesis, it could
even have been on Boehme; and it was only lately that his memory
had begun to fail and the destructive consequences of alcohol had
begun to show in him fairly clearly, which had not been the case
in the early years of our acquaintance. He lived on a very small
allowance his mother gave him in secret, and this was enough for
only one sandwich each day and his white wine.

"What about your apartment?" I asked him one time.

He shrugged his shoulders and replied that he did not pay anything at all and that, whenever the landlord threatened him with sanctions, Plato answered that if the landlord did anything to him he would light the fuse on a bomb filled with dynamite, which would, in a certain sense, satisfy the demands of the landlord—who lived in the same building—because after that he would no longer have any need to worry about any rent from any of his tenants whatsoever. Plato related this in a quiet voice and with complete calm, but with such unwavering sincerity and conviction that I did not for a moment doubt his readiness to do it. To me the strangest thing of all, however, was that Plato had very strong and quite archaic convictions about society; in his words, everything must be founded on three principles: religion, family, and king. "And what about alcohol?" I asked, unable to resist. He replied quite calmly that this was a secondary and indeed inessential detail. "You, for example, don't drink," he said, "but this does not prevent me regarding you as a normal person; of course, it's a shame you're not French, but that's not your fault." He was skeptical about the happy waiter and said that our conceptions of happiness were not applicable to primitive beings like him; although he allowed that the waiter might be happy in his own way—in the same way as a dog, or a bird, or a monkey, or a rhinoceros. As morning drew near Plato would begin to come out with absurdities; his ravings were astonishing for the unexpected serenity with which he uttered them, but his ideas would become muddled: he would compare Hamlet with Poincaré or Werther with the then minister of finance, who was a fat old man, about as far as possible from resembling Werther in any respect whatsoever. I knew what this minister looked like, because one time I had been with my car in a line of taxis outside the senate while a nighttime debate was in progress, and all my colleagues were hoping that they would get to drive the senators home; it was already past four o'clock in the morning. But at the

last minute several buses drove into the senate courtyard to collect the senators and take them home. When the last bus, with its
sign saying COST OF JOURNEY 3 FRANCS, was already driving away,
the minister of finance came out of the courtyard and, seeing the
departing bus, ran off after it as fast as he could; I could not help
laughing at him, although the other drivers cursed and swore at
him for his meanness. From that night on I remembered him very
well—I had seen him quite close up—his figure, his belly, his
breathlessness, the unbuttoned fur coat he was wearing that night,
and the agitated and stupid expression on his face.

I was speaking to Plato about the happy waiter on a Saturday
night. This was the most boisterous night of the week; the most
unexpected visitors would appear in the café, most of them drunk.
A sad old man with a gray mustache was singing Breton songs in
a cracked voice; two vagrants were arguing over some incident
that, as far as I could understand, had happened the year before;
one of the regular female customers, a woman of astonishing ugli-
ness with a squashed, froglike face but reckoned to be good at her
work, was pressed right up against a fifty-year-old man wearing
the Legion of Honor—someone had been buying her drinks that
evening—saying, "You must understand me, you must understand
me," while a complete stranger listening to her, a particular type of
vigorous drunk, could finally stand it no longer and said, "There's
nothing to understand; you're just a whore, and that's all there
is to it." Some scrawny middle-aged man with a look of genuine
terror in his eyes had forced his way through the crowd and was
asking Madame Duval to let him clamber up one of the columns
in the café—just up to the ceiling and back down: "As you can see,
madame, I am asking politely. Just once, madame, just once." And
the well-built maître d'hotel led him out of the café and, once they
were out on the street, suggested to him that he might like to climb
the pole of a streetlamp. Outside, beside the steamed-up windows

of the café, two policemen would pass from time to time—like the ghost of Hamlet's father, I said to Plato. Then in the cold and foggy dawn the Saturday night customers disappeared from the café; the streetlights glowed dimly above the sidewalks; occasionally one would hear the rush of car tires over the slippery roadway as they turned a corner.

"Every morning I give thanks to the Lord," said Plato, who had come out of the café with me, "for creating the world we live in."

"And are you sure that He really did the right thing?"

"I'm completely sure of it, however much of a sad drunkard I am," he said, as calmly as ever.

I walked with him as far as the corner of the Avenue du Maine, along the way he talked about Toulouse-Lautrec and Gérard de Nerval, and I immediately imagined to myself Nerval's awful death: the creepy little alleyway beside the Châtelet, his body hanging there, and, like something dreamed up in somebody's nightmarish fantasy, that black hat on the head of the hanged man.

On occasions I was able to spend several hours in that café because I had parked my car at the station, waiting for the first train to come in at half past five in the morning, and from two o'clock until the arrival of this train, while the other drivers would be playing cards or sleeping in their cars, I preferred to go off to a café or to take a walk, if the weather was fine. It was only this enforced idleness that made it possible for me to get to know the clientele of this café more closely. My idleness was almost always rewarded; each night I would leave there more and more corrupted, and it was several years before I began thinking of all of these nocturnal beings as living, human carrion—before then I had held a better opinion of people and undoubtedly would have preserved many idyllic notions which are now forever alien to me, as if a stinking poison had burned up that part of my soul where they were destined to dwell. And this dark poetry of human perdition, in which

I earlier had found a singular and tragic charm, ceased to exist for me, and I am now of a mind that its initial appearance was founded on ignorance and error, the same error that had proven to be so irrevocable for Gérard de Nerval, whom Plato had spoken about in our early morning conversation. And those people who created it, and those drawn to it as some are drawn to death, do not even have the consolation of knowing that when they die they have seen things as they really were and as they have described them; their delusion was as much beyond any doubt as it was beyond doubt that the distinguished gentleman in love with the former owner of the grocery store, who went out with him on Wednesdays and Saturdays, was wrong to consider her his second wife.

And perhaps it would have been right to envy those two clients of Suzanne whom I saw one day; both were well dressed and, evidently, of ample means, and both came into the café smiling the same smile and leaning on the same white sticks: both were blind. Suzanne sat down with them, and I watched all three of them from the side and tried to imagine how Suzanne's voice and laughter would sound to them coming out of the darkness. Then all three went off to the hotel directly opposite the café, and Suzanne carefully—because they were her clients—led them across the square. An hour later they returned; the blind men remained seated at a table, while Suzanne came up to the bar and stood beside me.

"Still on the milk?" she asked.

"They couldn't appreciate your beauty," I said, not bothering to reply, "and to think that they didn't even see your gold tooth."

"That's true," she replied, and suddenly, with unexpected childish curiosity in her voice, she said that of course they could not see her, but to make up for that they had explored all of her by touch, and it had tickled her. When I walked past them, I paused for a moment; they had that special innocent smile on their pink faces which is characteristic only of blind people.

As in earlier periods of my life, in Paris it was only rarely and for a brief while that I was able to see from the outside the reality I was obliged to live in, as if I were not taking part in these events myself. The ability was, like the recollection of certain landscapes, the result of some act of visual perception, and the reality then remained forever fixed in my memory; and like the memory of a smell, it was surrounded by a whole world of other things that accompanied its appearance. Usually it manifested itself without breaking the long chain of earlier visions but only adding to it, and from this emerged the possibility for me of comparing the various successive lives which I had been forced to live and which seemed to me remote and sad, regardless of whether it was something that had happened recently or many years ago. And it was then that the tragic absurdity of my existence was revealed to me with such clarity that only at these times did I clearly understand things which a person ought never to think, since after them come despair, the madhouse, and death. But strangely enough, these thoughts were never followed by the idea of suicide, which was completely alien to me, always, even in the most terrible moments of my life; and I knew that it should not be confused with that constant, burning desire felt each time that a Metro train came up to the platform from out of the tunnel—to step away for an instant from the firm stone edge of the platform and hurl myself under the train with the same movement as when I hurled myself into the water from a swimming-pool diving board. And now thousands of trains have gone by, and each time I go down to a Metro platform I feel a ridiculous desire to smile and say hello to myself, and in my intonation would be both mockery and the certainty that all the remaining Metro trains would pass by me like all those before. This feeling— the urge to perform one truly final action, once and for all—was an old and familiar one; it would take hold of me when I was driving in my car beside the fragile railings of a bridge over the Seine, and

I would think: just put my foot down a little harder on the accelerator, turn the wheel sharply, and it will all be over. And I would turn the wheel a few inches and immediately straighten it, and the car, after swerving toward the railings, would straighten up and continue on its harmless way. Whereas the one time—a sweltering, black night in Constantinople—when I really was in danger of falling from the fifth floor of a building, I did not have this feeling at all but rather an overwhelming desire to save myself at whatever cost. That time I was in a desperate situation. There was a big fire in the Asiatic part of the city, and from my window on the third floor I could see only a deep red glow; the building I lived in was in Pera, in the center of the European quarter. I decided to go up on to the roof and found it quite easy to clamber up there from a closed-off stone landing with head-high walls on all four sides. I climbed out from there onto the nearly flat tiled roof and set off across it, heading for where, according to my calculations, the fire should be visible. The glow had indeed grown somewhat brighter, and a dark background could be discerned through it, although so far there was not so much as a glimpse of the flames themselves. After standing there for some ten minutes, I set off back again. It was a very murky night, with neither moon nor stars. I moved by guesswork, and I did not imagine I could make a mistake. Finally I came to the edge of the landing and began to lower myself down, my back facing outward. When the edge of the roof was level with my eyes, I reached out with the soles of my feet, but there was no floor beneath them. I was surprised by this; I lowered myself farther, then finally hung with my arms fully stretched out, holding on to the tiles with my fingertips, but I still could not locate the floor. At that point, with some difficulty I turned my head to one side and looked down: very far below, at what seemed to me a terrifying distance, I could see the faint glow of a streetlamp above the road; I was hanging over the windowless, completely flat rear wall of the building, above an abyss six stories deep. With improbable swiftness my shirt became soaked. I was just clinging to the tiles—I immediately became convinced the tiles were slipping and sliding off—clinging with my fingers alone and could not count on anybody's help. For the first second I experienced the most amazing terror. Then I began to climb up again. Earlier, when I was in Greece, I had trained with one of my friends as an acrobat in order to work in a circus, and what would have been impossible for the average person was relatively easy for me. Hugging the wall with my face and chest, I hauled my body upward and was able to cling to the corner of a tile first with my right and then with my left wrist, and then slowly, without the rhythmic and almost unavoidable jolt that is used in gymnastic exercises, but which I did not dare risk here because a split-second loss of balance might cause me to fall, I pushed up my right elbow and immediately raised myself an inch—and the rest was now easy; but I still crawled a good distance up the roof in order to get away from the edge. Then I found the landing without difficulty and went back down to my bedroom. From the mirror my face looked out at me, contorted, smeared with lime, with the eyes of a total stranger. All of this happened many years ago, but I still remember that glimpse from a great height of the dim streetlight above the uneven stones of the roadway—one of those endless landscapes of a city drowning in the depths of night, which I was to see so many times later on in Paris. And in my rare and sudden moments of lucidity it would begin to seem to me completely inexplicable why I should be driving in a car at night through this huge and foreign city, which ought to have rushed by and disappeared like a train but which I was still never able to pass through—as when you are asleep and struggle, but cannot manage, to wake up. It was almost the same kind of painful sensation as the inability to shed the burden of memories; in contrast to most people I knew, I forgot almost nothing of what

I saw and felt, and a great many things, a great many people, several of whom had long since passed away, weighed down upon my thought processes. I would remember forever a woman's face seen once. I remembered my feelings and thoughts practically every single day over many years, and the only things I easily forgot were mathematical formulas and the contents of a few books and primers read many years before. But people I remembered always, every one of them, although the vast majority of them did not play an important role in my life.

And whenever I thought about how absurdly my life abroad had turned out, the first period of my life in Paris would immediately come to mind, when I had a job unloading barges at Saint-Denis and lived in a barrack with Polish workers; they were a collection of criminals who had been in numerous prisons and who finally had landed in Saint-Denis, where a person could be driven only by hunger and the complete impossibility of finding any other kind of work. Not one of them spoke French, nor did any of the others: two Russians who had come there from the German coal mines, one Spanish refugee, several Portuguese, and a little Italian with delicate features and white hands, whose reasons for coming from Milan to France no one knew—these were my fellow workers. When we lined up in the morning, the director would arrive, a fat man with bloated eyes behind a gold pince-nez; he would look us over and say to the foreman who accompanied him, "They're just runaway prisoners."

But none of them understood these words, and they would all smile ingratiatingly and expectantly. All of the Poles were passionate card players, and after work they would play late into the night until they had gambled away all their money; then it would invariably turn out that someone was found guilty of cheating, someone else of theft, and a furious fight would break out among them, and I would be woken up by someone's body landing on me;

as things came to a head I would always see the Spaniard get up from the end bunk; he would hurriedly dress and leave for an hour or two; he understood nothing of what was being said, but clearly long experience of life had taught him that in moments of crisis it was preferable to be as far away as possible. And when everything was quieting down, his narrow head would poke through the door; he would come back in and get back into bed again. I lasted two weeks at this life. Beside me in the barrack lived a Russian, a calm and athletic man who approached everything, even his own fate, with complete and deliberate indifference. He was so physically strong that carting 210-pound sacks around for eight hours did not tire him out, and when after my first day at work I had collapsed in a state of exhaustion on my bunk and was about to doze off, I heard him murmuring sympathetically, "The poor lad's whacked." Sometimes he would quietly sing songs of his own composition and with the most unexpected contents. His favorite song began like this: "I will tune my lyre to . . ."—there followed an obscene swear word.

It was the end of November, the mornings were already frosty; during work we would get hot, but then I would start to shiver; on top of that it often rained for lengthy spells, and one morning I did not get up for work, saying that I was ill. I slept until eleven o'clock and then left, taking with me the little suitcase that held all my worldly possessions. It was a warm and sunny day, and even the appalling poverty of squalid Saint-Denis seemed to me less severe on that occasion. Soon, however, I would find myself returning, on this occasion to the Chemins de Fer du Nord depot, where I was taken on to wash locomotives. When for the first time I heard the words *wash locomotives,* I was astonished; I had not known that they were washed; I then learned that this work consisted of cleaning out the pipes inside the engines, in which a deposit built up. This was easy but unpleasant work; it was done out in the open;

in the winter the water was icy cold, and after only the first hour I
was usually soaked from head to foot, as if I had been caught in a
heavy shower of rain; during January and February it was impossible not to become frozen through like this, and by the end of my
day at work my teeth would have started chattering. I would only
get warm again in the barracks, which this time were significantly
cleaner and always well heated. They were lived in exclusively by
Russians; among them I recognized one old acquaintance, whom
I had met in earlier times in Sebastopol; he was a partisan leader
or ataman, and someone quite out of the ordinary. A long time ago
in Russia he had been a skilled worker, in the Obukhov factory, I
think, then during the Civil War he had formed a partisan detachment in Siberia, where for some reason he had ended up. In one
particular clash his detachment was defeated by Red Army forces,
and Max—that was his name—was taken prisoner. He managed,
however, to escape, and he made his way on foot from Siberia to
the Crimea. Now I had met him in this depot; he was by this time
a tall old man with a shaven head and smiling black eyes. Despite
knowing barely a word of French, he earned roughly as much in
an hour as I earned in a day, and when I asked him the reason he
earned so much, he replied that the French had no clue about work
at all and that their skilled workers were useless, while he, Max, a
Russian and skilled worker, was more like one of their chief engi-
neers. He told me how when he first started he had been subjected
to various tests and that after that, without a quibble, they had put
him at the top of the pay scale; he did not have a specific job, and
he was called on anywhere that something was not working properly. He repaired electrical faults, fixed various broken machine
parts, made essential calculations, and generally worked at a steady
pace while spitting contemptuously at the floor. He was passionate
about poetry; I discovered this one evening when he spoke these
devastating words to me: "Well, I look at you, and it upsets me to

see what bastards young people are nowadays. I've been watching you for two weeks now. You haven't once so much as picked up a book. As soon as the evening comes you're off into the city, and then you come back at night; what kind of a life is that?"

And he began telling me that when he was young he had read a great deal and had been interested in everything. Then he asked me if I knew anything at all about literature and if I had ever read any poetry. When he heard my answer he was delighted; he even got up off his bunk and said that tomorrow evening, on Saturday, he would take me to a particular place and we would talk about poetry. The following evening we went to a small café; at the entrance he said to me, pointing to the owner, "Talk to her in French, order some red wine. Let her see that we can speak French, too."

I ordered a bottle of red wine; he shook his head and said, "I like it when one of us lot can speak French. Where did you learn it?"

Then he asked me if I knew these poets—he mentioned some ten or so names. I nodded. He recited several poems out loud, he had a good memory; when he recited, he closed his eyes and swayed from side to side, he spoke with extraordinary feeling, but in the way that actors usually read poetry—that is, forgetting about the rhythm and emphasizing only the flow of meaning. He then said that he would recite his favorite poem; he closed his eyes, his face turned pale, and in an altered voice he began:

"Condemned to shameful punishment,
the Hungarian count lies in chains . . ."

Like all simple and spiritually naive people, he was very fond of extravagant and superficial descriptions; the lot of the Russian peasant affected him less than the fate of a Hungarian count or an Austrian baron. I often had occasion to observe this astonishing attraction of people to a world which was completely foreign to them but whose luxury had an enduring impact on their imagination.

In those days I had only a very approximate understanding of Paris, and the look of this city at night always struck me as being like the set of a gigantic and near-silent theatrical spectacle: the long lines of street lamps along the endless boulevards, the lights' dull reflection in the still surface of the Canal Saint-Martin, the barely audible rustle of leaves in the chestnut trees, the blue sparks on the Metro lines where they pass over the streets and not underground. Now that I know the city better than any in my own country, it requires a considerable effort over myself for me to be able to see again this almost vanished, almost lost image of Paris. But at the same time the appearance of its suburbs has remained unchanged; and I know of nothing more dismal or piercingly depressing than the working-class Paris suburbs, where it seems as if even the air itself is filled with a centuries-old, desperate poverty, where entire generations of people have lived and died, whose lives in their daily misery were worse than anything imaginable—other than perhaps the area around the Boulevard Sébastopol, where for centuries the smell of putrefaction has lingered and every building is impregnated with the same unbearable stench. My constant curiosity kept drawing me to these places, and many times I would wander around all of the districts of Paris where this frightful poverty, this human carrion resides; I passed through a narrow medieval lane joining the Boulevard Sébastopol and the Rue Saint-Martin, where in the daytime beneath the glass canopy of a cheap hotel a light shone and there stood a prostitute with a violet-colored face and a tatty fur around her neck; I went to the Place Maubert, where the cigarette-butt collectors and tramps would congregate from all over the city, continually scratching at their unwashed bodies, which could be seen through their unbelievably filthy garments; I went around Ménilmontant, Belleville, and the Porte de Clignancourt, and my heart was filled with pity and revulsion. But I never would have known much of what I do know—and half of that would be enough to poison several human lives for good—if I had not had to become a taxi driver. Before that, however, I was a factory worker, then a student, then an office worker; I then taught French and Russian, and it was only after the total inadequacy of these occupations became clear to me that I took the exam testing my knowledge of Paris's streets, as well as my driving test, and obtained the necessary papers.

Factory work turned out to be impossible for me not because it was particularly exhausting—I was perfectly healthy and rarely became physically tired, especially after my time at Saint-Denis—but because I could not bear the constant confinement in the workshop; it felt as if I were in prison, and I genuinely wondered how people could live their whole lives, over many decades, in these conditions. It is true that more often than not their lives had been preceded by generations of their ancestors who had always done physical work—and I never came across a protest against this intolerable existence from any professional factory worker, not a single one; all of their agitation boiled down in the main to the fact that they considered themselves to be inadequately paid for their labor, but they did not rise up against the principle of this labor; this idea never entered their heads. I did not yet know at that time that different types of people whom I was to meet are separated from one another by almost insurmountable distances, and although living in the same city and the same country, speaking virtually the same language, they are as remote from one another as Eskimos and Australians. I remember that I never could get it across to my fellow workers that I was going to go to a university; they could not understand this.

"What are you going to study?" I replied by enumerating in detail the subjects which interested me. "You do know it's hard; you need to know a lot of special words," they would say. Then in the end one of them declared that it was impossible; to get in to university you had to complete your secondary education and study at a *lycée,* where only rich people could go. I said that I had passed the school examinations I needed. They shook their heads doubtfully, and one woman worker advised me to give up all of this completely useless stuff, that it was not for working people like us, and tried to persuade me not to take the risk but to stay there, where, in her words, in ten years' time I might become a foreman or the head of a team of workers. "Ten years!" I said. "I'll die ten times over in that time." "You'll come to a bad end," she said to me finally.

In spite of the fact, however, that I had absolutely nothing in common with my fellow factory workers—milling-machine operators, drill operators, metal workers—I got on with them extremely well, and in purely human terms they were no worse, and often better, than members of other professions whom I had occasion to come across and were, at any rate, more honest. I was struck by, and could not but be impressed by, the cheerful courageousness with which they lived. I knew that what for me seemed a prison-like deprivation of freedom was a normal state of being for them; the world seen through their eyes looked very different from the world I saw; their reactions to it were all correspondingly different, as happens with the third or fourth generation of trained animals—and as would have been the case, of course, with me if I had worked in a factory for fifteen or twenty years. But regardless of how their cheerfulness, mockery, and lightheartedness was to be accounted for, these qualities were so good in them that I could not help succumbing to their peculiar attractiveness. In order not to attract the constant attention of my neighbors, I attempted as best I could to smooth over the glaring differences that existed between them and me and which unwittingly pointed out the absurdity of my situation, and so after a little while I learned to understand and use French *argot* and started dressing the same as them. But the fact that in my external appearance I began to look exactly like a worker earned me the scornful displeasure of one of my neighbors, a tall, black-bearded man who would arrive on the shop floor in his blue suit and university badge. He was a Russian who had graduated from the law faculty in Prague. His suit was worn and shiny and was unbelievably disgusting, and he always had metal shavings lodged in his beard, as well as in his tousled hair. He had a thin face with prominent cheekbones and big eyes; on the whole he resembled one of the portraits of Dostoevsky, who was, incidentally, his favorite author. The workers, especially the women, used to ridicule him; they would mess around with the setup of his drill, stick paper tails onto his back, or tell him that he had been summoned by the foreman, who had done nothing of the sort. His French was poor, and he did not understand a lot of the mockery his work colleagues directed toward him. But he responded to all of this with completely stoic contempt, and only occasionally could one see from the look in his eyes how much it did upset him. I felt sorry for him; I intervened several times and tried to explain that it was shameful to ridicule a person who was not capable of answering back. But, with childish cruelty, after a certain time they would begin their persecution of him once again. During these disputes he would usually stand to one side, keeping silent, and only his eyes, always very expressive, would follow the rest of us. He never spoke to me. But then one day he came up to me and asked whether it was true that I was Russian, and when he found out I was, said, "And aren't you ashamed?"

"What am I supposed to be ashamed of?" I asked, puzzled.

And he explained to me that I was disgracing myself—these were his exact words, disgracing myself—because it was impossible to tell me apart from a factory worker.

"You dress the same way as them—you wear the same scarves, the same flat cap—in short, you look as much like a hooligan and proletarian as they do."

"You must excuse me," I said, "but I think it's better to wear workers' clothes and then get changed than to go around completely inappropriately dressed in a suit, which may have the virtue of immediately distinguishing you from the other workers, but it's the same suit that you've been wearing for the past six months, and, to put it mildly, it's pretty filthy at this stage. I fail to see the virtue in that."

"Your manner of speaking suggests you are an educated man," he said, "so how can you not understand that none of this matters, that what matters is maintaining one's essential humanity?"

"I don't see why a clean suit would be such an impediment to that."

But he went on to give a lengthy speech about how "existence determines consciousness" and that one needed to protest with all one's strength against this. He did not consider the workers to be people at all and held them in infinite contempt. Then he said that the Revolution had taken away everything he had but that he had held on to something of infinitely greater worth that was beyond the grasp of whomever was now sitting in his house in Petersburg, namely Blok, Annensky, Dostoevsky, *War and Peace*. He would not be swayed by any objection, so I did not insist on making any; I felt I understood that this was the only thing of value in his possession and that apart from it he had absolutely nothing in the whole world. And in spite of the fact that he had no comprehension of many very basic things, despite myself I could not help but feel respect for this man who was aware of only one side of the world; the things that he so loved were nevertheless worthy of both renunciation and sacrifice. On the other hand, he was indifferent to the universal complaints typical of previously well-off people like him, which I had heard and read thousands of times, and which more or less boiled down to sighing over lost material comforts of the most trivial kind.

On the same shop floor, not far from me, worked another Russian whom I had known before, since at one time we had studied together. He was several years older than I was. I never could establish either his origins or the circumstances in which he had grown up in Russia, since the stories he told about these were absolutely incredible and resembled the descriptions of upper-class luxury found in cheap novels. I remembered only that his parents possessed, according to his descriptions, some totally hideous chandeliers and a French chef. However, he spoke Russian with a Ukrainian accent, and abstract topics never figured in his conversation. Working in foreign factory conditions he was completely at home, and he never suffered there; rather, to have gone to a university would have been a tragedy for him. He made friends and got along better with the factory workers than anyone else, although he spoke hardly a word of French. He worked hard, was strong, and took a real interest in whatever he was doing in the factory. As well as this, he was amazingly thrifty and notoriously stingy; he lived on only broth, bread, and pork fat, of which he would buy a large quantity for next to nothing because, as he explained, on top it was a bit rotten; and the whole time he saved and saved. Then he bought himself a fine, expensive wrist watch, although all week long it did not work, since he wound it only on Saturday and Sunday, saying that otherwise the mechanism would wear out. His life was astonishingly simple: he worked all week long, and as soon as he returned from work he would go to bed; on Saturdays he went first to the public baths and then to a brothel. The culture he had encountered during his education had passed him by without leaving any trace, and no abstract question ever occupied his attention. And for a long time it seemed to me that his entire life, all his thoughts, impulses, and feelings, could be reduced, as in algebra, to two or three basic formulas—all the rest was a useless and extravagant luxury. I never could have foreseen the implacable revenge that this unnecessary culture and those abstract notions were preparing for him; I had always thought that he had a powerful natural immunity against them.

But he was one of the first people in my life about whose existence I was able to form a definitive judgment, because I met him periodically over a number of years and saw the changes which occurred in him and which were particularly surprising in the last two years; and the most important thing was that everything stopped at that moment when it had reached the point of maximum tension. He had all the qualities required for a happy life and, first and foremost, an instinctive and complete adaptability to those conditions in which he was obliged to live: he quite genuinely reckoned that his existence was not at all bad, that the paltry sum of money he had set aside and which each month increased in the same paltry proportion was a significant amount of capital, that his two suits—of a particularly exaggerated modish and tight-fitting cut typical of bad tailors from the poor districts of Paris—meant that he was well dressed, and that the periodic increases in his pay, by fifteen or twenty centimes an hour, increased his "economic potential." In short, in assessing his own situation, he applied the criteria of the working-class environment he lived in and had no idea that there existed other, broader criteria—however, I suspect that the word *criterion* did not figure among the words he actually knew. In the early days in Paris, it was still possible to imagine, when talking to him, that this man had studied something, but already, two years or so later, there was nothing left; it was as if he had forgotten it all so deeply and irremediably that it might never have existed at all. Like the majority of simple people who ended up living abroad, he avoided speaking Russian, and were it not for his accent and mistakes with his verbs, tenses, and gender, his speech might have been taken for that of a French peasant. Then he left the factory where we had worked together, and several months later I saw him in a Metro carriage; on his ruddy hands, which I knew well—with bulges at the end of his fingers and rounded fingernails—he wore gloves of a delicate yellow color, and on his head was a bowler hat. His name was Fedorchenko, and this caused him much distress since, according to him, it was very difficult for French people to pronounce, and so to all his new acquaintances he styled himself Monsieur Fédor. He possessed in a very highly developed form a characteristic that I observed frequently in many Russians: everything that had existed previously and that, ultimately, had determined the course of their life, had ceased to exist and was replaced by that miserable, foreign reality in which—usually as a result of their poor command of French and the absence of any critical sense with regard specifically to this reality—they now saw virtually their ideal mode of existence. It was, or so it seemed to me when I thought about all these people—among whom were public prosecutors, lawyers, and doctors—the expression in many different forms of an instinct for self-preservation that brought about the gradual atrophy of certain faculties that had become not only unnecessary but even harmful for the life these people now led—most of all the faculty of critical judgment, as well as that familiar indulgence in intellectual pursuits which they had been accustomed to in earlier times but which in present circumstances would have been inappropriate and impossible. I was discussing this one time with one of my friends, and he suddenly said, interrupting me, "Do you remember the book by Wells we read many years ago, *The Island of Doctor Moreau*? Do you remember how the animals that had turned into people, after Dr. Moreau had lost control over them because of some disaster or other, do you remember how quickly they forgot human words and reverted to their animal condition?"

"That's not a very flattering comparison," I said. "It's a monstrous exaggeration; I can't agree with you on that."

But later on, after I had had occasion to see numerous examples of this spiritual and intellectual impoverishment, I wondered whether my friend had been possibly more correct than I had initially thought. The transformations which occurred in people under the influence of their change in circumstances were so marked that, to begin with, I was unwilling to believe them. I had the impression that I was living in a gigantic laboratory, where experimentation was being conducted with forms of human existence, where fate mockingly transformed beautiful women into old hags, rich men into poor, distinguished people into professional scroungers—and did so with astonishing, incredible skill. I would remember and recognize these people as if in a dream: a drunken old man with a gray mustache and lifeless eyes, whom I met in a little café in one of the Parisian suburbs where I happened to be quite by chance—he slapped his neighbor on the back, an elderly French worker, who then made a particular facial expression characteristic of the French common people, where he screwed up his mouth with a short, soggy cigarette butt clinging to his lower lip, and said, with a heavy accent, "We really had them there!" His glazed-over eyes suddenly looked sad, and he said, "Another glass of white wine." And finally I understood from their conversation what the cause of their delight and their drinking was: their work gang had managed to pass off defective material and had been paid for it; and in this man I recognized a fierce, mustachioed general whom I remembered from Russia, an arrogant and cruel leader. His drinking colleague went off, he was left alone, and he ordered another drink with a sweeping gesture and in an uncertain voice and then stared at me, occasionally shuddering and jerking his head. "What are you looking at me for?" he shouted at me in irritation. "Fate hasn't been kind to you, has it?" I said in Russian. He grew angry, paid his bill, and in a silent, drunken rage, he walked out of the café without looking in my direction. Then I learned from my friends that, according to their information, this general was supposed to have obtained an excellent position either in Argentina or Brazil and had moved there some time ago; he was supposedly teaching ballistics or something of that kind in a local military academy. I was told that he had left about eight years ago but that he did not write letters from over there to anyone. However, he had marked his departure with astonishing extravagance: he had organized a banquet, and everyone had drunk champagne and had congratulated him on finally obtaining a position in keeping with his merits and that in the Russia of the future, of course . . . "It's his own funeral he organized," I said. "That's the reason for all this commemorative pomp." Brazil or Argentina! The reality was a dank workers' hotel four miles from Paris, the factory siren, red wine, the daily walk to the factory, pain in his rheumatic joints, degeneration of the liver—as medical science so aptly terms it— and no Brazil, no Argentina, and of course no Russia of the future, and not a single crumb of comfort since that same moment when on a smoky autumn evening a steamship filled to overflowing had set out across a stormy sea, leaving behind forever the shores of the conquered Crimea. And through an association that I could never understand, every time that I thought of this general I would remember an image that had stuck in my imagination of a penniless little old lady I had seen in Sebastopol who used to sing an inaudible tune in her feeble voice; she would always stand on the same street corner, and I knew her well and grew quite accustomed to her. I stopped one day to try to make out what she was singing. In her feeble, old voice she intoned liltingly:

"My darling, my beloved,
Tender shepherd boy . . ."

This was on Primorsky Boulevard; the weather was beautiful, it was nearly evening, the sun was setting over the sea, and off the shore lay the English cruiser *Marlborough*. For a second I closed my eyes and quickly walked on. Not a single book I had read, no fruits of lengthy study, could have possessed such terrible conviction as this mournful echo, dying away in sunlit and youthful magnificence, of an era that had fallen silent and vanished long ago. And my imagination conjured up pictures that took me back to the youth of this woman; it created around her a complete world, dim and unreal, yet full of infinite charm and of which nothing now remained but this naive melody, like soft music from a grave, in a churchyard, on a summer's day, in a silence broken only by the noisy buzz of insects.

At that time I was sixteen years old, even then I already knew a feeling that later would discomfit me very often—as if it was becoming difficult for me to breathe—a feeling of shame that I was young, healthy, and well fed while others were old, sick, and hungry; and in this involuntary juxtaposition there was something infinitely troubling. This same feeling would take hold of me when I saw cripples, hunchbacks, sick people, and beggars. But I felt genuine suffering when they grimaced and contorted themselves in order to amuse people and earn a few extra kopecks. And it was only in Paris, on its nocturnal streets, that I saw beggars who did not elicit any pity, and however hard I tried to convince myself that I could not simply let things go, that I could not descend to such a degree of callousness that the sight of them would elicit nothing in one but revulsion, I could do nothing with myself. I could never forget how once, late at night, a woman had approached me dressed in black rags, with dirty, gray, uncombed hair; she came up very close to me, so that I could smell the heavy, many-layered smell that issued from her, and muttered something that I could not make out; I took out a coin to give her, but she refused it and carried on mumbling. "What are you after?" I said. "Are you coming with me?" she asked, attempting to take me by the arm. "What?" I said in amazement. "Are you out of your mind?" She took a step back and replied more distinctly that she would find others, better than me, and vanished. It was foggy on that winter's night; I was walking past Les Halles, where trucks thundered by, horses whinnied, and where floating over everything was the smell of rotting vegetables and of that special variety of miasmic foulness that is characteristic of this district of Paris. Several times I was overcome by despondency: how, through what form of social injustice, could the existence of such people have become possible? But later on I became convinced that they were a whole social class, a class whose existence was just as legitimate as the class of business people, as the profession of lawyers, as the guild of civil servants. Their belonging to this world was not by any means determined only by their age—there were young people among them; here, too, there was a peculiar hierarchy and a differentiation between one degree of poverty and another; I witnessed, for example, how a not yet very old but extremely ugly woman who used to roam the deserted streets of nocturnal Passy was able to establish an unanticipated career for herself; this, however, resulted from a particular, unexpected event, which she was very happy to recount. Because of disease of the liver, the doctor had forbidden her to drink, and from that time on she had been sober; and in her sober state she had suddenly realized that, instead of begging, she could now turn to prostitution. Until then this thought would never have entered her head. But this was an unexpected moment of illumination, of enormous and unprecedented importance for her, something like the fortunate concatenation of circumstances and chance to which humanity is indebted, quite possibly, for the appearance of several religions and many philosophical systems and scientific discoveries. And I saw how she became better and better dressed, and on the day of her definitive apotheosis she drove off at night in a taxi in the tight embrace of some young man of remarkably decent appearance; and in that fragment of a second when their car was passing by a streetlight and its interior was illuminated, I was able to make out the bowler hat of the young man lying on the seat and a fox fur around the neck of this woman, and her powdered face with its expression—never changing, evidently, in any circumstances—of cold imbecility, which I knew only too well. I managed to see all of this because of my long years of nighttime taxi driving, which demanded constant visual concentration and a sharp eye, essential both to avoid running into another car and to spot a vehicle unexpectedly coming out of a side street. This sharpness of visual perception had evolved in me, just as it had in all of my fellow drivers, to a degree that was unusual for a normal person and typical of racers, boxers, skiers, acrobats, and sportsmen. This visual reflex functioned sometimes with mechanical and unfeeling precision and was completely unconscious: I might be driving along quite fast, thinking about something and not looking to the sides; then, without anything actually happening, I would press hard on the brakes, the car would stop, and then, cutting across my path, another car would rapidly drive past. I had apparently seen the other car, yet without realizing it, without thinking about it, and essentially without knowing that I had seen it. In exactly the same way, by turning my head to the right or to the left if I needed to cross a major street, I could see from the side what my clients were doing, and on one occasion I can remember feeling an unpleasant, cold sensation in my back because my passenger, a very drunk man, working class, in a badly ripped suit, was seated behind me and kept transferring two large-caliber revolvers from one hand to the other, although it subsequently became clear that these were not intended for me since he paid his bill in the most normal manner imaginable and walked off with an uncertain step. I was completely convinced that I had given a ride to a murderer, and the next day, with great curiosity, I searched the evening papers for information about a new crime but did not find any; evidently, he had thought better of it. But I am almost convinced that he did commit it; there are people whose fate is written on their faces, and his face was just such a one. In just the same way, there was something terrible on Fedorchenko's face, on that sleek, reddish physiognomy lacking any kind of spiritual quality, something that I could never quite grasp, but I always felt uncomfortable next to this man, although there was nothing about him that could have posed a threat to me in any degree. And all the same, every time that I saw him I felt uneasy; it was like the sensation I would have felt if I had seen someone slide off a roof and fly downward, or fall through the grille of an elevator.

After the period when he and I worked together in the factory, I lost track of him for a time. But one day, on a frosty February evening, after I had parked my car and was getting ready to climb out to go into a café—this happened on the Boulevard Pasteur—I saw him; he was walking along looking from side to side and carrying a small black suitcase. He was nattily dressed, with a bowler hat on his head, but he seemed preoccupied. When he saw me he cheered up for some reason and said that he had something he needed to ask me, but then he could not resist any longer and asked me how I liked his suit and overcoat.

"Very smart," I said. "Splendid. Only you shouldn't do your tie in such a small knot—that's how grannies in Russia tie knots in their handkerchiefs so as not to forget things, and then I don't think it's a good idea to wear shoes with lacquered toes. But overall, of course, you look magnificent. What's going on?"

He told me that he was on his way home from Montparnasse and was upset that things had not worked out for him. It turned out that some time ago he had seen there—always at the same time, in the evening—a lady in furs, who would come to the café with a magnificent Angora cat. Fedorchenko was indifferent to cats himself; but his fiancée, he told me, was very fond of this breed, and he had thought that it would give her pleasure if he gave her an Angora cat as a present. So he decided to steal it. To this end he set off for the café and took with him his small black suitcase, which he continued to hold in his hand as he told me all of this. At the café he waited for his opportunity: when the lady left for a moment, he put the cat in the suitcase and left. He had spent many days getting this plan ready; he had kept going to the café, had watched the clock, sat drinking beer, and waited for a time when the lady would leave her table and there were no other customers on the terrace. Luckily, the lady always preferred the terrace; and although there was a small stove outside the glass screens and it was warm there, most of the customers usually sat inside; even so, a few people always stayed on the terrace. This evening had been particularly opportune, since, apart from the lady and Fedorchenko, there was only one pair of lovers sitting out there; the lovers were kissing and paid no attention to what was going on around them. In this way the plan came off very well. But unfortunately, on the way back the suitcase fell open—as he described it—and the cat, who had been inside the suitcase all that time, jumped out and ran off with, in Fedorchenko's words, uncommon speed. Fedorchenko spent a long time looking for it but failed to find it. "It just ran off, the son of a bitch," he said with sudden anger. "What do you say to that?"

"It's a stupid cat, of course," I said. "But I'm not too sure if it was a good idea to steal it. It could get you into a nasty situation."

Fedorchenko waved away my concerns and then said with despair in his voice that he would do anything for the sake of his fiancée and that there was no other way of getting hold of a cat; the cat cost a fortune, and he, Fedorchenko, was no millionaire. The whole thing concluded in him asking me to drive him to the Rue de Rivoli, which was where his fiancée lived. We arrived there, and I stopped when he said to me, "Just here," at the corner of a narrow alleyway, no wider than a corridor, one end of which came out onto the quays, and the other onto the Rue de Rivoli, right in the middle of the St. Paul *quartier,* one of the poorest and filthiest in Paris. This alleyway was notorious because there was a huge and very cheap brothel on it, and now, late in the evening, there was a large amount of commotion there, with soldiers, Arabs, and workers going in and out.

"Just round the corner here; it's close by," said Fedorchenko. And he explained to me that this was where his fiancée worked.

"What does she do?" I asked. He replied that she had a special kind of job here. I nodded and said good-bye to him, and his bowler hat—the only one on this street, where flat caps predominated—disappeared around the corner. This business with his fiancée seemed odd to me and, to a certain degree, not unlike the business with the cat in Montparnasse. But every time I thought about Fedorchenko it was as if I came up against a wall: he seemed not to have a single fault. He was almost perfect in the sense that everything that can inhibit a person in his or her life was absent in an ideal degree—disappointments, sadness, doubts, moral prejudices—thoughts of all of this never entered his head. And I could not imagine what kind of woman, unless she was an unhappy and downtrodden, half-starved creature, could make up her mind to join her destiny to this dull and spiritually barren existence.

Late at night, after my evening's work itself was over, I would often drive to the districts near the Place de l'Étoile. I liked these *quartiers* more than any others for their nocturnal silence, for the strict regularity of their tall buildings, for the stone chasms between them which occasionally appeared along these streets and which I would see as I drove past. And the night of the day I had taken Fedorchenko back to his fiancée, as I drove along the Avenue de Wagram, I saw at some distance a tall female figure in a fur coat standing at the edge of the sidewalk. I slowed down, she made a sign to me, and I stopped the car. She came right up to the car and looked at me, and I was struck by the expression of surprise and astonishment on her face. Then she said to me, "Dédé, how did you come to be driving a taxi?"

I looked at her, not understanding. From her appearance she might have been around fifty years old, but her very large, black eyes, with a tender yet reserved expression, stood out on that faded, powdered face, and her figure still retained, by inertia, a sort of uniquely youthful panache, and I thought to myself that probably, many years ago, this woman had been very attractive. But I could not understand why she had turned to me, calling me by someone else's name. This could not have been yet another technique for attracting a clientele—both her voice and her expression were too natural for this.

"Madame," I said, "this is a mistake."

"Why don't you want to recognize me?" she continued, speaking slowly. "I never did anything bad to you."

"Undoubtedly," I said, "undoubtedly, if only for the reason that I've never had the pleasure of seeing you before."

"Aren't you ashamed of yourself, Dédé?"

"But I assure you . . ."

"Do you mean to say that you're not Dédé the roofer?"

"Dédé the roofer?" I said in astonishment. "No, not only am I not Dédé the roofer, I've never even heard that nickname before."

"Get out of the car," she said.

"Why?"

"Please get out of the car."

I shrugged my shoulders and got out. She stood opposite me and stared at me hard. I could not help but feel the total absurdity of the scene, but I stood patiently and waited.

"Yes," she said at last, "maybe he was a bit taller. But what an astonishing resemblance!"

"I tell you what, madame," I said, getting in behind the wheel once more, "so as to convince you once and for all, I must tell you that not only am I not Dédé, but I'm not French, I am Russian."

But she did not believe me. "I could tell you that I'm Japanese," she said. "That would be just as unconvincing. I know Russians pretty well, I've seen lots of them, and that's proper Russians—counts, barons, and princes—and not miserable taxi drivers; they all spoke good French, but they all had an accent or foreign intonation, which you don't have."

She addressed me with the familiar *tu,* and I continued to address her as *vous;* I could not bring myself to reply in kind—she was twice my age.

"That doesn't prove anything," I said. "But tell me, please, who was this Dédé?"

"He was one of my lovers," she said with a sigh. She said, "amant de coeur," which cannot be translated into Russian.

"I'm very flattered," I said, unable to contain a smile, "but it wasn't me."

There were tears in her eyes, and she was trembling from the cold. Then she turned to me with a proposal that I go off with her; I began to feel sorry for her, and I shook my head in refusal.

"I haven't had a single client today," she said. "I'm frozen. I couldn't even get a coffee."

I could see the lights of an isolated café on the corner. I offered to buy her something to eat and drink.

"And you won't demand anything from me?"

I hastened to say that no, I really didn't want anything from her.

"I'm beginning to think that you really are Russian," she said. "But don't you recognize me?"

"No," I said, "I've never seen you before."

"My name is Jeanne Raldy," she said. In vain I scoured my memory but came up with nothing.

"That name means nothing to me," I said.

She asked me how old I was, and I told her. "Yes," she said thoughtfully, "perhaps you're right, your generation no longer knew me. Did you never hear about me? I was the lover of the duc d'Orléans and the king of Greece; I went to Spain, America, England, and Russia; I had a chateau in Ville d'Avray, twenty million francs, and a house on the Rue Rennequin."

And it was only when she mentioned the Rue Rennequin that I immediately remembered it all. I knew the name of this street very well; I had first heard it while I was still in Russia, many years ago. I immediately saw before me a remote railway station, sidings, snow-covered rails, carcasses of horses, from which dogs would tear out the innards with a squealing sound, the meager light of the railway lamps, around which light snow whirled and scattered in the frosted air—unique in the whole world—in my home country. In those days—it was the last year of the Civil War—in the evenings an elderly civilian would come into our carriage, Prince Nerbatov, who was fond, as he put it, of young people and who would talk for hours about Paris. He was old, poor, and unhappy; his clothes were threadbare; and he always gave off a slight smell as if of carrion. I remembered his tiny eyes, tearful from the frost, his dense, gray stubble, and his ruddy hands, which trembled when he took a cigarette and raised the flame of a match to it, the match dancing in his fingers. We would feed him, give him money, and listen to his stories. This man had given up his whole life to women; he had lived for a long time in Paris, was interested in art, and had loved good books, good cigars, good dinners, theaters, the races, premières, boxes, flowers—these always featured in his recollections. In his own way he was not unintelligent, capable in particular of understanding what he himself called "feminine perspicacity," but he was marred by that variety of culture of whose value he had never been in any doubt. He adored *L'Aiglon* and *La Dame aux Camélias,* was not far away from comparing Offenbach with Schubert, and took great pleasure in reading badly written society novels; he was not bad in himself but was the victim of his wealth, and it was not his fault that he had never in his life come into contact with people for whom culture did not bear those operetta characteristics which he unwittingly bestowed upon it.

He had been a Russian boulevardier of the Paris of old, the Paris of the turn of the century, but the chief thing now was that by the time of the Civil War his days were numbered. He had tuberculosis; he coughed terribly, struggled to breathe, and turned purple; during these attacks he was incapable of speaking a single word, and there was utter despair in his tear-filled eyes at these moments. As well as the tuberculosis, he was ill with scurvy, so that he was literally dying before our eyes—not physically, as no dramatic deterioration of his health occurred, but in time; it was clear that if we could speak of what would happen in five years' time, in his mouth these words would be meaningless, and he knew this just as well as we did. He would liven up after drinking vodka, and it was usually then that he began telling his stories. But whatever he was speaking about, he would always return to his amorous recollections, and at the end of the evening he would always get sidetracked onto one particular theme which, clearly, had had a profound effect on him; and if it happened that he had drunk more than usual, he would begin to cry when he recalled it. It was a story about a woman whose name I did not remember and who lived in Paris on the Rue Rennequin. He had had a lengthy affair with her, and he would recount to us, without a trace of shame, the most obscene and detailed circumstances and would frequently cry bitterly when remembering these particular unprintable details. The woman he described might have seemed a perfect goddess were it not for these details, and she possessed, as he put it, both unusual, irresistible charm and exceptional intelligence and good taste and overall had every possible quality, with the exception of virtue. I remembered that he had told us about her career—and specifically about the duc d'Orléans, the king, bankers, ministers, these "fleeting caprices" of hers, as he called them; he was very fond of expressions like this, and it was astonishing how his own personal—and often genuine—misfortunes and sufferings were only ever articulated in inexpressive words like these which corresponded to nothing living; but he was full of this kind of linguistic inanity; it was the same when he spoke in French, in that outdated and idiotic language that was typical of the turn of the century. And in spite of the obvious partiality and exaggeration of his descriptions, at that time we were in no doubt that she really must have been a remarkable woman, and perhaps this impression was enhanced by the fact that it was a bitterly cold winter during the Civil War in the remote depths of icy Russia, and that distant life in Paris, brilliant in his naive notion of it, of which we as yet knew nothing, suddenly acquired for us, too, the allure of illusory and impossible splendor. We had to part from the prince when we were hurriedly transferred to another place, and I managed to call on him to say good-bye at the tiny and filthy house where he was living; he was lying on his bed, suffocating with his coughing. There was an oppressive smell in the house, the windows were shut, and the stove was stoked up until it glowed red. I had brought him a bag of coal, some vodka, and some jars of food as a farewell gift; I shook his trembling, burning hand—he was not at all well—and I wished him a speedy recovery; he replied hoarsely, "I am staying behind to die. Farewell," and I left with a heavy heart. After that I never went back to that part of Russia and never saw a single person who might have been able to tell me when and how the prince had died, because there could be no doubt that he had died soon after our departure. But for me the memory of him was always bound up with that worthless, operetta world that he so loved with his naive heart, and the story of which would have elicited nothing but automatic contempt and scorn were it not for the fact that all of it lay in the shadow of the tragic and indecent silhouette of this woman.

Standing beside her in the café—she was drinking her second cup of chocolate and eating a sandwich—I looked at her intently. She ate her sandwich by tearing off small pieces with her long and very clean fingers—I paid particular attention to this—and she had difficulty chewing these pieces since she did not have enough teeth left in her mouth. Now in the lamplight it was evident that she was much older than fifty; in fact, she was most likely older than sixty. I looked at her for a long time, and then suddenly I saw myself as a withered old man with wrinkly, yellow skin, with a flabby body and scant muscles which would be unfit for any kind of exertion. It was very late at night, and outside the window light flurries of snow occasionally fell. I felt a cold and very unpleasant sensation. But I made an effort to master myself and said, "Excuse me for asking an indelicate question. But how did it happen that, when you had a fortune like that, right now you, well, when you should be living peacefully in a warm and comfortable house and reading books, if that's what interests you, instead of this . . ."

She shrugged her shoulders and replied that it was a long story, that drugs had ruined her, that everyone had robbed her, and that she could not stop herself even though she knew how it would end. She spoke to me in such beautiful, pure French as I very rarely had occasion to hear and which gave a certain conviction to her tales of her earlier magnificence. Now she lived in severe poverty in a cold room in an old building on the same street where she had once owned a mansion. She told me that for many years—in the second, less brilliant half of her life—she had owned one of the best *maisons de passe* in Paris.

"Yes, yes," I said distractedly. "It's always the same old story."

The café was already closing. I paid the bill, and we went out onto the street. The whole time she was trembling with cold, and tears once again briefly appeared in her eyes.

"Go on home," I said. "You'll catch cold, then things will be even worse."

She shook her head and refused, saying that she had not earned a single franc. I felt very sorry for her; I gave her a little money and drove her home.

"Thank you, darling," she said, already standing on the sidewalk before the door to her house. "I don't think you're quite normal, and I believe now that you are Russian. If you're ever in this area, you'll always find me here. I'll be glad to see you; we can have a talk."

I went back there after a few days at the same late hour and saw her figure from some distance away. This time she and I spoke for a long time, and after that on several occasions I spent long hours in conversation with her. She really was genuinely intelligent, with a particular, tolerant, and indolent mind in which there was a complete absence of resentment or harsh judgment, and in the beginning this seemed astonishing. She had an excellent memory.

One day I asked her whether she remembered Prince Nerbatov. She suddenly burst out laughing in a very particular way, so that, if I had only heard this laughter and not seen her, I would have thought that it was a young woman laughing. She said, "A little Russian prince with a lorgnette, who lived on the Avenue Victor-Hugo? Did you know him? Where? In Russia?"

I nodded. She thought for a moment, obviously recalling that long-distant time.

"He wasn't a bad man; he offered to take me to Russia with him and was always talking about his estates. But he wasn't very intelligent and was very sentimental."

"Like all boulevardiers, I think."

"Most of them," she said with a smile. "Not absolutely all of them, but most of them. They were a special breed of people."

"Yes, yes, I know," I said, "bad taste and the sentimentality that goes with bad taste, and adulterous sighs, and now foul-smelling old age after a long life resembling an idiotic melodrama without even the excuse of a tragic dénouement."

"It's strange," she said, not replying, "what a surprising mixture you are: you have a good heart and yet such obvious spiritual baseness. No, your generation is no better. You talk of bad taste. But bad taste is down to the age, and what is bad taste now wasn't that before. You ought to know that, darling."

After I saw Raldy for the first time and she mistook me for Dédé the roofer—in spite of her mentioning the Rue Rennequin—her story had seemed to me improbable, and I asked the older taxi drivers about her, and one of them in particular, who had been working nights for thirty years. It turned out that she really was known to everyone.

"She wasn't a bad girl," he told me, "and she didn't get above herself at all. And there were so many of those aristocratic bastards who kept her! How could I not know her? Just you ask her if she remembers René the driver; she'll tell you herself. Why are you asking me about her? She came up to you on the street? That's so sad! You feel miserable just thinking about it. That's how they all end up; they're no-hopers."

I felt sorry for Raldy. I lacked the cruelty to speak with her as I would have wished, that is, with complete frankness. But even so I did question her, and she recounted her life to me, which consisted of nothing but the grossest mistakes and incomprehensible passions, which seemed astonishing given her exceptional mind, especially for a woman of her circle. I said this to her, and she replied that passion is more powerful than anything else. I could not help myself and once again looked at her intently, at this old and wrinkled face with its astonishing and tender eyes.

"Are you surprised to hear me talk about passion?" she said, guessing my thoughts. "A quarter of a century ago, when I uttered this word it produced a different impression from what it does now."

She had her own philosophy: tolerant and accepting; she did not value people very highly but considered their shortcomings to be natural. When she said this to me, I observed that the whole of her considerable experience related essentially to only one category of people: a truly worthless one, of those people who frequent the *demimonde*—the pretentious stupidity of this expression always irritated me—the *maisons de passe,* the special nighttime cabarets, who keep actresses and ballerinas and whose sole attribute is spiritual and physical decrepitude and that self-same, all-conquering bad taste. She listened to everything I said, watching me with her mocking yet tender eyes.

"So would you like to destroy all of that? Blow it all up?"

"No, but if it disappeared it wouldn't be worth worrying about it."

She shook her head and said, smiling the whole time, that they were not actually a special category of people.

"What, then?"

"It's down to a particular degree of affluence, and if you attained it yourself, you would probably be just the same as them."

"Never," I said.

"I should hope not," she replied, "but I wouldn't vouch for it."

One day she said to me, "Doesn't it seem ridiculous to you that you're a taxi driver? Don't you think that the work perhaps doesn't suit you?"

I replied that I had no choice. And then she offered to help me, so as to thank me, as she put it, for my humane disposition toward her. "I'll arrange it so you can have a different life; you're still very young and, as far as I can see, healthy." I stared at her, bewildered. She explained to me that she had a large number of acquaintances, that there were women who were not really that old, forty-two or forty-three, French or English . . . I sat with her in the café and guffawed like a lunatic, unable to stop myself. Then, with tears of laughter in my eyes, I thanked her.

"What? You would find that impossible? But surely it's better than sitting behind the wheel of your car. Do you have such strong prejudices?"

The evening that this conversation took place, I was not working; I had been to the cinema on one of the boulevards, then, strolling around Paris, I had walked as far as the Place de l'Étoile and, remembering about Raldy, I set off down the Avenue de Wagram and met her. It was a light, clear spring night. We sat on a terrace; occasionally, people would walk past us on the sidewalk. From the depths of the café came the quiet tinkling of a gramophone record; a chanteuse with a voice perfectly devoid of melodic qualities, so that it was astonishing that she produced a tune at all, was singing a song that was already dated, "Avant je me moquais de l'amour." And through this melody I suddenly sensed the unexpected presence of someone close by me. I turned my head and, two steps away from me on the sidewalk, saw Plato, my constant café companion, who had turned up in this district far from his own *quartier,* God only knows why. But I was even more astonished by his appearance than by his presence there. He was wearing a dinner jacket, and his permanently neglected face was closely shaven, which totally altered it, giving it a sad solemnity, and it struck me that what could now be clearly seen were obviously his normal traits, but they were usually concealed by his heavy stubble. He greeted me and bowed low to Raldy, taking off his hat with a hand grown unaccustomed to this action. I invited him to sit down at our table and was about to order him, as always, a glass of white wine, but he stopped me and asked for beer instead.

"My dear friend, you are positively determined to subject me to every possible degree of astonishment," I said. "How did you end up in these parts, and how do you account for your dinner jacket, which, to the best of my knowledge, you were not given to abusing before? Madame Raldy, permit me to introduce my friend Plato."

Plato was just as mournful and courteous as ever. He asked Raldy whether she was bothered by smoke, lit up a cigar, and explained that he had been at the première of a certain play, had decided to walk home on foot, and then, strolling through this district of Paris, had chanced to see me and had stopped. Raldy asked him whether he liked this area of Paris; he replied that he was indifferent to it, that he preferred the Left Bank, the narrow streets that lead down to the Quai de Conti, the Isle Saint-Louis, the Boulevard Saint-Germain, the Rue Mazarine—generally speaking, *quartiers* that had preserved the kind of archaic charm that was absent in the large, central *quartiers* on the Right Bank. Raldy began to speak about other cities, and here also their difference in taste was revealed in their views on London, Madrid, or Rome.

"A man," said Plato, "who asserted that the external aspect of any city is a living illustration of its cultural history would, in essence, be correct, although this theory suffers from difficulty in its application, from a certain opacity; these changes can be discerned only through painstaking observation and comparison; at first glance they are imperceptible."

Raldy did not fully agree with him; Plato began to speak about individual perceptions, and then the conversation turned to the theater, of which he was very fond. When I said that I preferred the cinema, both Plato and Raldy looked at me with disapproval.

"How can you even compare these things?" asked Raldy.

"Does it not seem to you, my friend," said Plato, "that a certain fondness for paradox, which I have noticed in you on previous occasions, might on this one be leading you down a dangerous path?"

It was now late; there were fewer and fewer passersby, and on the brightly lit terrace of the café, surrounded by the light of streetlamps which was now growing dim—fading away into the distance, blending in with the rays of the moon—we remained alone; everyone else had already left; and I thought of the astonishing improbability of this conversation, the participants in which were a prostitute, an alcoholic, and a nighttime taxi driver. But Raldy and Plato continued talking with their previous lack of constraint, and that final stage of social degradation we had all now reached had long since become habitual and natural for both of them, and perhaps in this contemptuous acceptance of their fall, or more properly their willingness to accept it, could be seen one of the chief causes of their present condition. We bade farewell to Raldy—Plato once more bowed and removed his hat—and set off on foot along the deserted streets toward Montparnasse, which was close to where we both lived.

"Had you heard of Raldy before?" I asked Plato.

"Yes, of course," he said.

"And were you not struck by seeing her in that condition?"

A smile appeared on his normally immobile face. He was completely sober, and his conversation gained considerably from sobriety in coherence and logic, although that abstract and bookish quality it possessed, and which took so much getting used to, was even more pronounced than ever. To the uninitiated he gave the impression of reading passages out loud from some unwritten treatise—it was precisely this abstract quality in his speech that had earned him in the café, where his companions were mostly simple people, the reputation of being a lunatic.

"The comparative method," he said, "when we examine the various states of being of one and the same individual at different periods of his life, is one of the most important elements, an almost-infallible criterion for practical judgment. If we can manage to refrain from invariably tempting but trivial effects, which have an undoubted value in literature but which are absolutely inadmissible in the elaboration of an impartial judgment, then the results of such an investigation are nearly always fruitful."

"The trivial effects in this instance, of course, being her 'splendor and decline.'"

"Trivial—and incorrect. Because in the present state of Raldy, who is certainly to be considered a remarkable woman, we see the conjunction of those very elements which have conditioned both the splendor and what is, from a practical point of view, the senseless nature of her existence."

We were walking down the Avenue Marceau, and I found it a joy to stride out into this limpid, silent, and bright night. Paris was fast asleep at this hour; and passing by the slightly open shutters of one ground-floor apartment, we clearly heard someone snoring, with sighs interspersed with very brief pauses. "I suppose that's the concierge," said Plato. On the other side of the street, coming toward us, walked a poorly dressed and extremely drunk man, staggering along uncertainly. His appearance immediately aroused in me such a clear, such an irresistible association, that I was unable to control myself in time and asked, though I understood that I should not have done so, "Plato, why do you drink?"

He took several paces without replying and then said, "Here again, in this instance, the majority of people deal with the problem incorrectly. The truth, the sad nature of which I am not about to try to refute, consists in the following: we are alcoholics not because we drink, no—we drink because we are alcoholics."

But I was already stricken with remorse, and I had no wish to continue this conversation, though subsequently I realized that I was wrong; it was awkward for me, but Plato himself had long since moved on from that world of powerful and instantaneous sympathies that had suffocated me throughout my life.

"We were talking about Raldy," he said. "How are we to account for her astonishing career? How could a simple French girl from Toulon who spoke with a strong southern accent, the traces of which you would seek in vain in her present manner of speaking, become for a time one of the most brilliant women in Paris, and why were her favors sought after by very rich and titled people who were prepared to fight duels because of her?"

"I have a very low opinion of those people's taste, Plato," I said. "The fact that she was first chosen by a duke, then a king, and then a hemorrhoidal senator does not seem at all persuasive to me. You know as well as I do that they could have been people whose aesthetic sensibility was no more refined than the aesthetic sensibility of a peasant or an artisan."

"I do not refute this a priori. But the quantity of people who strove to possess this woman, regardless of whether they were titled or not, their readiness to risk their lives or even a temporary loss of their health for the sake of her calculating and, in essence, dubious and illusory love—this alone suggests that she was unlike other women of the *demimonde*. And so, what was the secret of her astonishing and undoubted charm?"

"I think that this is something we will never know, Plato. Those people who—I make a flattering and most probably incorrect assumption about them—might have been able to tell us about this have either died or fallen into senile imbecility. We did not know it; I acknowledge the analytical agility of your mind and its impartiality, but I consider that the solution to this problem was lost some thirty years ago and now no longer exists."

"I am very far from Cartesian ideas," said Plato. "I consider that they have caused great harm to our thinking. The possibility of a full and clear answer to a complex question seems attainable only to a limited imagination: this was Descartes' fundamental flaw. But in certain cases one highly significant and definitive aspect of a question seems to me irrefutable. It is precisely thus with the question of Raldy. She always knew that she was doomed—she could see the inevitable approach of that state in which we saw her when we left her an hour ago. She always knew this, and it is this same tragic understanding of certain final truths, an understanding that could not but be reflected in the whole of her life, in every expression in her eyes, in every intonation of her astonishing voice, and, probably, in her every embrace; it is essentially this that was the foundation of her incomparable charm."

"Yes, I think I understand," I said. And I reflected that now, at this very minute, Raldy would probably be asleep in her tiny room on sheets warm and damp from her body; I imagined the quiet, dry rustling of her hair on the pillow when she turned her head in her sleep, the muscles of her face disfigured by age—that face grown mortally weary over the years, her pitifully drooping lower lip over her scarce yellow and black teeth. And I immediately remembered once again the poor prince and his drunken babble: "She lay in the bed in a delicate, pale-blue nightgown. I knelt before her, and she stroked my head like this"—he moved his scented hand over his perspiring bald head, which was traversed by gray-blue veins.

"Plato, this is impossible," I said, almost in a frenzy. "Circumstances are conspiring to make me see death and destruction everywhere I go, all the time, and because I can't just forget about it, my whole life is poisoned by it."

This was the first time I had spoken to Plato about these things, which I normally did not divulge to anyone; I perhaps would not have said this had Plato—and indeed Raldy—not attained that state of nonbeing which yet retained a spectral and illusory resemblance to real life and where there was no longer any sense in keeping silence or making calculations. But my long-standing habit of lying—the lies which had dominated the whole of my life, the lie that my existence was essentially a happy one, and that I never viewed things in a tragic light—in the end prevailed, and I changed the subject of the conversation without allowing Plato time to reply. I was desperately keen to know the explanation for this unexpected and brief—this I did not doubt—return of Plato to that rapidly disappearing Paris to which he had once belonged, the evening-time Paris of dinner jackets, premières, and so-called decent people. As I might have expected, it was a chance occurrence: one of Plato's friends, who had burgled a villa in Neuilly and bundled up suits, silver, a fur coat, and several other miscellaneous items in what Plato described as a very fine tablecloth—the friend was under strong police suspicion and restricted in his movements—had given out all these things to anyone he happened to meet, and it had fallen to Plato to receive the dinner jacket and a razor with a large supply of blades. I asked whether the friend was a professional thief. Plato shrugged his shoulders and replied that he was an entirely decent person from a good family who had only recently commenced this career—as a result of the unfortunate way his life had turned out.

"What does it matter, essentially, whether he's a professional thief or not?" asked Plato. "I didn't quite understand the reason for your question; what I mean is, what induced you to ask it?"

I explained to him that the behavior of this man contained two unusual elements: the absence of any personal, irresistible greed, first of all, and, second, a certain flexibility of forethought. If he had sold the stuff off cheaply to a fence there would have been evidence against him; the supposition that he had simply given away the things had a good chance of simply not occurring to those to whom the investigation had been entrusted. Therefore I had thought that Plato's friend did not belong to the category of professional thieves—his actions were at the same time too intelligent and too unselfish for that. I had come across professional thieves on many occasions; some of them were fairly decent people and true friends, but the defining characteristic that they all shared, almost without exception, was an inflexible and limited mind or, more accurately, a very one-dimensional one; they were capable of showing a certain degree of inventiveness at the start of a job, but afterward they acted with a complete lack of imagination in the way they disposed of the stolen goods or spent the money, as if they were all characters in the same stupid, badly written play.

"Even," I said, "in a case where their use of the stolen goods bears entirely unexpected characteristics, the absence of basic flexibility of imagination is the undoing of these people."

And I reminded him of the story of a young married couple, apparently of peasant origin, who murdered a rich old man, made off with his money—around one hundred fifty thousand francs—and three days after this bought themselves a grocers' shop, in which they intended to set themselves up as honest shopkeepers; and when the police went in there, they found him in a white apron behind the counter and her, just back from the hairdresser's with a new hairstyle, sitting on a high stool at the shop's cash register.

"I don't doubt that they would have been excellent shopkeepers," said Plato.

"That's very possible."

We came to Montparnasse and drew level with the café where Plato usually spent his nights. He stopped and invited me to have a drink with him.

"No thank you, my dear friend, I'll go home," I said. "Perhaps I, too, am a secret lover of theatrical effects: I wouldn't like the memory of this evening and our walk together to be combined with certain other moments which would destroy the integrity of the impression it has left. If I were an author I would not allow them, but since I am merely the person who has been walking and talking with you, I would prefer to leave you now. Good night."

I always remembered this clear spring night: the dawn about to break, that uncertain and somehow magnanimous gesture of Plato's when he doffed his black hat, and his clean-shaven, mournful face above the white shirt and dinner jacket, which I saw him in for the first and last time because later on, when I saw him again a few days later, neither the dinner jacket, nor the hat, nor the starched shirt existed any longer because, of course, they had been sold to pay for the very next evening.

I was working at that time in a small garage on a cul-de-sac not far from the Boulevard de la Gare, along which on one side stretched the windowless, dark gray wall of a sugar factory, while on the other were miserable single-story houses where people lived in seventeenth-century conditions. More than once I saw the yellow light of paraffin lamps through the dim glass of their windows; in the summer, wet washing hung from the balustrades with large patches on it, visible dozens of yards away; in the mornings, poorly dressed urchins played around the doorways in unusually large numbers; and when they ran, one could hear the rapid clatter of their hobnailed boots. I set out in my car at eight or nine o'clock in the evening and carried random passengers about the city until midnight, and it was only at midnight that Paris grew completely quiet, with only a few animated crossroads left in the city like oases in a stone-clad nocturnal desert: Montparnasse, Montmartre, certain spots on the Grands Boulevards—what was known as nighttime Paris.

One time, some time after nine o'clock, I was stopped by a neat, gray-haired little old man, who turned out, as I later discovered, to be a lawyer from a small town about twenty miles from Paris, and with an affectionate, old man's smile, he said that it was his intention to hire me for several hours, since today he had traveled up to Paris and was planning to carry out what he called the *Tournée des Grands Ducs*. Immediately he took out his wallet and began to count his money: he had eleven one-thousand-franc notes, several hundred-franc bills, and an amount of change as well.

"Well, let's go then," he said. And we set off. He knew by heart the addresses of all the most expensive brothels and cabarets; I drove him to these places, and each time he came out of the latest establishment less and less steady on his feet, and his speech gradually lost any coherence. I was witness to everybody mercilessly fleecing him, starting with the people who opened the door of the car for him—whom he was careless enough to give large-denomination banknotes to; tediously and at great length they would count out his change for him; he would stand there patiently, looking at the money with glazed-over eyes, and as a result they would give him back some twenty francs in loose change—and ending with the chambermaids and other characters he met by chance and who became his companions and go-betweens, who slapped him on the back and spent the whole time laughing loudly, along with the naked women, inside these establishments. This was a rule of *le bon ton,* which I was long familiar with and the origins of which I believe should be sought in the advertising literature that served this branch of industry and where it is customary to view visits to brothels and other establishments of a similar type as an expression of joie de vivre, merriment, and that same famous *gaité galloise,* which accorded least of all with this abysmally dreary pornography. At all events, the girls themselves and their heterogeneous fellow workers in this business invariably followed this peculiar etiquette and guffawed at every reply; and at times, through the gray fog of tobacco smoke, I began to imagine that the little old man was sitting surrounded by male and female ventriloquists. He himself, however, evidently found all of this quite natural—at least at the beginning, before he had become completely drunk. Yet he retained to the end a sufficient degree of spasmodic will power to be able to continue this excursion, which had long since lost all meaning; although the initial old man's affection had disappeared from his eyes, to be replaced by a particular expression of impotent terror, he kept coming out, squeezing himself into the car, collapsing onto the seat, and, gathering all his strength, he would utter yet another street name and house number. His tie was long since, and irrevocably, skewed to one side, his shirt was unbuttoned, his hat he had forgotten somewhere, and his gray head twitched rhythmically, helplessly, against the back of the seat. It all ended some time after five o'clock in the morning, when he was no longer capable of saying anything other than an interrupted "ah-ah" sound; I understood that he still wanted to go to Les Halles in spite of his utter exhaustion and total incomprehension of what was happening to him. I asked him where he lived, and he looked at me with hostile, drunken, and melancholy eyes and was unable to say anything in reply. I did not want to take him off to the *commissariat de police,* so I drove up to the first policeman I saw and, after explaining to him what the problem was, said that we ought to find out where the old man lived and get him home. The policeman and I together lifted up his light body, took his wallet from his pocket, and found there his business card and the address of the Paris hotel where he was staying. He had very little money left: around two hundred francs; I reckon that he spent around seven thousand and that the rest was stolen from him. We brought him to the hotel, carried him out of the car, and handed him over to the hotel staff at the entrance; the policeman paid me with the little old man's money, and I drove off. Just as I was going the old man had opened his uncomprehending eyes and once again said, "ah-ah," but now in a barely audible voice.

"What's he on about?" asked the policeman.

"Strange as it may seem, he wants to go to Les Halles," I said.

"He'd be better off going to Père Lachaise cemetery," said the policeman angrily, and we parted; the sun was shining, and it was around seven o'clock in the morning.

As I walked home, I kept wondering why this old man, who probably had grown-up grandchildren by now, felt the need to spend all that money so pointlessly and to drag himself with such incomprehensible, desperate insistence from one brothel to the next, even though after the first two visits the mistress of one such residence which we came to, after showing him in ahead of her, said to me regretfully, "Well, that one won't take a woman. He'll just have a drink, nothing more than that."

"How do you know?" I asked.

"I don't need to know; I can see," she said. "He looks exhausted as it is. Besides which, at his age, my friend . . . You'd better believe me; I've seen all sorts."

I was able to appreciate the accuracy of her assessment; the old man did indeed limit himself to two glasses of champagne—one of the chambermaids told me this—although, when he was sitting in the car again, he said to me, "You know, the women here aren't bad. Especially the one I chose for myself."

And I thought that he must have lived for years in that same little town of his, writing up legal documents—the same things over and over again: "at the attorney's office," "legal signatory," "nineteen hundred and . . ."—while secretly, unknown to his family and close friends, he nurtured the pitiful and naive illusion that he was, deep down, a fabulous playboy and lover of women, and so because of this illusion, which gave his whole life a secret significance, he would travel to Paris, "on business," and here he felt obliged to follow in every way that mode of conduct that would have been characteristic of that same fanciful playboy and debauchee who existed only in his imagination. And for this he paid such a high price.

Subsequently I saw on many occasions people who after a night of debauchery were in more or less the same condition, women just as often as men. But amidst the infinite variety of people with whom I had dealings, there would always be unexpected and unforeseen nuances of behavior, although the purpose of their trips and entertainment was always one and the same. I had one client, an Englishman, a man of very businesslike and anxious appearance, who stopped me on the Champs-Élysées and asked in English—he evidently did not think that he might not be understood—whether I knew a place where there were beautiful women, and who, after my affirmative reply, got into the car and said, "Let's go." We arrived there, he asked me to wait, and literally ten minutes later he came out again, and we drove to a hotel that was two steps away. The whole of this together took no more than twenty-five minutes. Then he settled up with me and walked away, smiling just as he was leaving with a peculiar, fixed grin, and saying to me "*Merci*," which was evidently the only word of French he knew. There was a Dutchman whose train was due to leave the station at ten minutes to ten and who arrived at a brothel shortly after nine o'clock and asked me to summon him if he had not returned by twenty to ten since, he said, he might get carried away and miss his train. At twenty to ten he had not appeared, so I went to look for him. In the bluish haze of tobacco smoke, illuminated by myriad bright lights, naked women and a variety of visitors were moving around and sitting; a large and very heavily made-up woman in a glossy black dress came over toward me, and as she walked, little tremors ran over her enormous fat body. She was about to start saying how delighted she was to see me, but I cut her short and explained why I had come, after which her face changed instantaneously and clouded over and she replied, "What am I supposed to do? I have thirty-two rooms, twenty-eight of them are occupied. How can I go around looking for your client? And if it comes to that, if he misses his train, what does it matter to you?"

But when I went downstairs again, the Dutchman was already waiting for me; he had arrived only seconds before my return.

Every night I would come across prostitutes and their clients, and I could never get used to this. I found it all to be beyond my understanding, although I understood perfectly well that my ideas about women of this type were substantially different from their clients' ideas; the difference lay in the fact that I really knew them, since they spoke with me as with one of their own, and they were especially fond of comparing their work with mine. "We do the same kind of work"—this was their favorite phrase. As morning drew on, on my way to the garage after finishing work, I frequently gave these women lifts home, after they too had finished their night's work, and without fail they would offer the same payment for this. I usually had them sit in the back of the car and not beside me, as they were all drenched in strong cheap perfume, something like a caustic solution of poor-quality soap, and their proximity gave me a nauseating taste in my mouth.

I would generally return home after five or six o'clock in the morning, through unrecognizable empty and sleepy streets. Sometimes I would drive through Les Halles, and I remember how I was particularly struck when I first saw people harnessed to small carts on which they transported goods; I looked at their weather-beaten faces and their strange eyes, as though covered with a transparent and impenetrable film, which is typical of people unused to thinking—most prostitutes had the same sort of eyes—and thought about how Chinese coolies probably had the same kind of eternally veiled look in their eyes, how Roman slaves had the same kind of faces and essentially the very same conditions of existence. The entire history of human culture had never existed for them, just as history in general had never existed, or changing political regimes, the bloody competition between ideas, the growth of Christianity, or the spread of literacy. Thousands of years ago their benighted ancestors had existed almost exactly as they did now, had done the same work, and had been equally ignorant of the history of people who had lived before them—and everything had always been more or less the same. And all these people were still more or less the same: Arab workers, peasants from Poznan who had come to France on contracts, and these slaves working in Les Halles; all the splendor of culture, the treasures of museums, libraries, and conservatories, that artificial and solemn world which unites people involved in it and living tens of thousands of miles apart from one another, all of those names—Giordano Bruno, Galileo, Leonardo da Vinci, Michelangelo, Mozart, Tolstoy, Bach, Balzac—all this was merely the futile endeavor of human genius; and hundreds and thousands of years of human civilization have gone by, and once again, at the dawn of winter or a summer's day, harnessed by a system of straps, that same old slave hauls his cart. After I had lived for several years amid various categories of such people, and especially after my terrible time doing factory work, later on, at the university, when I attended the lectures given by my professors and read the books that were essential for the sociology course I was taking, I was astonished by the most profound, improbable discrepancy between their content and what they were discussing. Without exception, all theoreticians of social and economic systems—this seemed obvious to me—had a very particular understanding of the so-called proletariat, which was the subject of their study; all of them reasoned as though they—accustomed as they were to a life of culture, to the demands of an intellectual life—placed themselves in the worker's situation; and the development of the proletariat was envisaged by them as something like the opposite of their own self-development. But my conversations on this subject usually went nowhere and convinced me yet again that the majority of people are not capable of that titanic overcoming of the self which is essential in any effort to understand a person from a different background, with different origins, and whose brain is organized differently from how they are used to envisaging it. Indeed, I noticed that people from very narrowly defined professions, and in particular scholars and professors, who had grown accustomed over decades to operating with the same theoretical concepts, and which often existed only in their imaginations, would only admit to any changes within the limits of this same set of concepts, and they were organically incapable of tolerating the idea that something could be added to it—and alter everything—which was new, which they had not predicted, had not noticed. I knew one old economist, a proponent of classical and archaic conceptions; he was a nice fellow, spent hours playing with his little grandchildren, got on very well with younger people, but was completely intransigent in his understanding of the economic structure of society, which, he thought, was governed by the same set of fundamental laws and which, in his account of it, resembled the grammar of some nonexistent language. One of these laws was, in his opinion, the unfortunate law of supply and demand; and no matter how many examples I gave him of the countless violations of this law, the old man would never admit that it might be subjected to doubt and finally said, close to tears and with utter despair in his voice, "You must understand, my young friend, that I cannot agree with this. It would mean canceling out forty years of my scholarly work."

In other cases, stubbornness in the defense and propagation of clearly dubious ideas could be best explained by more complex considerations, although here, too, I suggest, they were mostly considerations of personal pride and infallibility; although to an impartial person it became obvious from the very beginning that it was merely a matter of an unfortunate misunderstanding: the works of such-and-such would still go on being considered worthy of attention and helpful in understanding something in some scholarly field or other in spite of their evident absurdity and artificiality or even signs of incipient madness, as in the books of Auguste Comte or Stirner and several others—writers, thinkers, poets. And almost always in these flashes of madness there was something resembling other forms of human understanding, which probably corresponded to some actual reality whose existence we simply did not suspect.

I came across other instances, partly similar to these only rather less tragic, though almost as exasperating in their patent absurdity. In the winter months, usually in late autumn, on a Saturday, when I stopped on the Avenue de Versailles opposite the Pont de Grenelle, in the quiet of these silent hours I could hear from afar hurried footsteps and the tapping of a cane against the pavement; and when the man who was producing these sounds passed beneath a nearby streetlamp, I immediately recognized him. He was on his way home—he lived several buildings farther on—after a round of bridge. If he had won, he would sing an old Russian song in a quiet, tuneless voice, always the same song, and his hat would be pushed back a little on the back of his head; if he had lost, then he would walk in silence, and his hat would sit squarely on his head. This was a man known many years ago throughout Russia, whose fate had lain formally in his hands, and everywhere I had seen innumerable portraits of him; tens of thousands of people listened to his speeches, and his every word was repeated, as if proclaiming some new gospel truth. Now he was living, like many others, in emigration, in Paris. I had met him on several occasions; he was almost a cultured person, not without a sense of humor, but was blessed with an abnormal inability to comprehend the most elementary political truths; in this respect he resembled those particularly unsuccessful pupils who are to be found in any class in any educational establishment, and for whom the simplest algebraic problem seems like something impossible to solve because of their innate uselessness at mathematics. I found it impossible to understand, however, why he had, with such grim determination and often putting his own life at risk, involved himself in an activity to which he was so unsuited, just as a person with absolutely no ear for music is unsuited to be a violinist or composer. But he had dedicated his whole existence to this; and although his past political career contained nothing but monstrously irreparable mistakes, which were, moreover, as obvious as they could possibly have been, nothing could make him depart from this path; and now, deprived of any possibility of action, he nevertheless involved himself in something like a spasmodic surrogate of politics and edited a small journal, for which his former associates from their long-defunct political party also wrote, and they were equally staunch proponents of archaic theories which corresponded to no reality whatsoever.

And nevertheless this man was more fortunate than others; in that vast and joyless world formed by his fellow countrymen, who over long years had dragged around an identical and irremediable sadness everywhere that their difficult and tragic fate had cast them—on the streets of Paris or London, in provincial towns in Bulgaria or Serbia, on the quaysides of San Francisco or Melbourne, in India, China, or Norway—he, one of the few, lived in blissful ignorance of the fact that everything for the sake of which he had led a selfless existence, almost denying himself any personal life, and which he had misunderstood just as much before, many years ago, had long since ceased to exist, like the popular anger after Peter's reforms or the stubborn insanity of the Russian schismatics. And he continued to remain true to those same imaginary and worthless ideas whose adherents numbered several hundred people out of the earth's two billion inhabitants. I had heard his speeches several times; I was struck by the combination in them of naive political poetry and very solemn, archaic language, which was not without a certain purely phonetic effectiveness.

As a result of an astonishing concatenation of various circumstances, I was forced to lead several different lives and at the same time to meet with people who differed markedly from one another in every way, beginning with the language they spoke and ending with a complete disparity in what constituted the meaning of their existence; on the one hand, there were my nighttime clients, both male and female, while on the other, there were those whom Plato would undoubtedly have classified as respectable people. Sometimes—this happened most often after I had been listening to music—as before, in my distant Russian days, everything would merge together in my mind and in the soundless space that filled my imagination, through the silent melodies and the lengthy gallery of human faces, which resembled the moving and disappearing faces of an endlessly streaming screen on which there appeared and then vanished now the shriveled and wrinkled countenance of the old woman in her invalid carriage, now Raldy's half-dead face with its tender eyes, now Plato's calmly mournful expression, now the drunken ghastliness of a café clientele on a Saturday, now that impenetrable film beneath the heavy, long brown eyelashes of the prostitutes, and then, at the end, Fedorchenko's ruddy, shiny complexion, this man whom fate brought me close to more often than I would have wished and caused me to be witness to the entire history of his life, which was a brief and, in essence, cruel one.

After I had taken him home to his fiancée, I met him again a month later. Because he had never had any friends and since he felt the need to tell someone about his feelings and thoughts, he invited me to a café, ordered me coffee, and without me asking him any questions, began telling me about his love life. At this time he was experiencing the most turbulent period of his affair. He was incapable of talking about his feelings, and, in spite of the evident sincerity in all that he said, it did not quite ring true. It struck me that this happened because all the time he would use the same pathetically solemn expressions: "I am in love, and loved by her," "My heart beats in my breast like a bird," and so on. Moreover, he pronounced all of these phrases with his usual Ukrainian accent and from time to time would switch into bad French, especially if he was recounting his conversations with his fiancée. But nevertheless, there was in what he said a certain innocent quality that was not at all funny. It was obvious that if this woman, whom he was describing in very exaggerated tones, wished to deceive him, she would have no difficulty in doing so. The degree to which he had fallen in love was already evident when he decided to steal the cat for her, but now it had become completely obvious. There was nothing lofty about this, with the exception of the expressions he used, but it was beyond doubt that this passion had taken him over more than one might have expected. I had considered him incapable of this; this was the first mistake I made about him; my second mistake I did not realize until much later, several years afterward, on the day when I became a witness to his unexpected and unusual end.

He had met his fiancée two months earlier, in a café; she had made such a powerful impression on him that he had felt unwell for the whole of the evening, which seemed especially surprising given his robust good health, and it was as if all around him he could hear a distant ringing sound, as he described it, and everything swam before him as in a fog. He had talked a great deal—he himself did not understand exactly what about—then seen her home and arranged to meet her three days later. The next morning, after starting work at his machine in the workshop where he was employed, he suddenly saw her black eyes in front of him, became transfixed by them, and badly injured his hand. Their meeting was to take place in the Bois de Boulogne. It was December, and a cold wind was blowing; he walked around with her for two hours, along the firm, frost-hardened sand of the deserted pathways, amid the denuded and black trees, along the freezing banks of the lakes, until, eventually, she complained that she was cold, and then he took her to a cinema on the Champs-Élysées, where they saw a film he could only dimly remember, as he spent the whole time holding her hand. When they came out of there, they went first to a café and then to a hotel. He did not see clearly what was going on; he merely said that during these moments her eyes were even more black and unusual than ever.

I listened to his story, and from time to time I glanced at him. Sometimes, when he paused briefly—all the time he felt hot; he was drinking his third or fourth glass of beer—in his own small and always, it seemed, slightly puffy eyes there was a particular troubled and clouded expression which I had never noticed before then, as if something had happened to him for which he was completely unprepared and against which he had no means of defending himself. Then he suddenly said, with innocent candor, that this woman lived on the money she received from two or three rather rich and elderly benefactors but that now, after she had become his fiancée, this was over, and indeed, very recently, she had started work as a chambermaid; in the very near future, immediately after their wedding, they would settle down together; he had a little money, she had a little money, he would go out to work, she would do the housework, and then a new life would begin. He said that he was ready to sacrifice, as he put it, for the sake of this love everything which until then had seemed important to him in his life: his friends, his family, his homeland. The strangest thing of all, however, was that there could be no question of any sacrifice, because he had no friends, he had long since forgotten about his family, and the word *homeland* I was hearing from him for the first time only now; he had never spoken of it and, I suppose, never thought about it. But even he, as it transpired, needed this futile notion of sacrifice, evidently, in order to underline subconsciously the great importance of what was now happening.

All the time I felt uncomfortable as I listened to his story, in which it was as if there were not enough air; I felt embarrassment on Fedorchenko's behalf, as if I were in some way responsible for him, for this physical torment of his, which I could not think about without an involuntary sense of disgust. Round white lightbulbs blazed above our heads, and pale-gray smoke streamed from people's cigarettes. I closed my eyes for a second and suddenly saw the seaside on a summer's day, the trembling, burning air above the pebbles and a huge sun in the pale-blue sky.

Fedorchenko held my hand for a long time. His perspiring face shone with pleasure; with sincerity he thanked me—he himself scarcely knew what for. He said, "Because you understand everything so well," although I had not uttered a word the whole time. He protested vigorously when I tried to pay the bill, called the waiter, joked with him, gave him an uncommonly generous tip, and moved away with a particularly light tread, which was unusual for him, and after making several fluttering movements to me with his hand, which was completely out of keeping with his usual cumbersome peasant's sluggishness, he walked out of the café as he had never walked out before—with a ballet dancer's step, with an operatic and unnatural lightness, which I could not help my attention being drawn to.

And two hours after this encounter, after dining at home and having regretfully left behind my room, my table, and couch, I was again seated behind the wheel of my car and slowly driving about the city, abandoning for several hours of the evening and night what I usually lived by: memories, thoughts, dreams, my favorite books, the last impressions of the day before, the last conversation about what at that time of my life seemed most important. From long experience I knew that I could only work with any kind of effectiveness once I had forgotten about all of this and transformed myself into a professional driver. I had long since grown used to this daily actor's exertion, and I believe that it was thanks to this that, in spite of my many years of working as a taxi driver, I still retained some kind of interest, waning almost imperceptibly, in what was in essence an illicit and abnormal violation of my strictly professional interests. In the early days I would still take books with me to read, but later I made a decisive break with this; they disturbed me too much, creating an intolerable sense of my existence being split in two, which was unbearable in these conditions. I forgot about this enforced transformation only when I lost my self-control, but this happened extremely rarely. Sometimes, if I was in a good mood, I even began to feel that fundamentally things were not so dismal and that a few hours of nighttime work, which made it possible for me to exist in some fashion, took less time away from me than any conventional work would have done. Then I was ready to forgive my passengers everything that ordinarily caused me to feel disgust or contempt.

That evening, as I recall, my first client was an elderly abbé with a very lined face and tiny little eyes. I saw him from some distance away and initially took him for a midwife because he was holding in his hands a small case that looked exactly like those that midwives carry; the wind blew out his voluminous cassock, and he held it down with one hand, as a woman would have done. Only after driving up closer did I realize my mistake. He was going to the Gare d'Orsay. There he got out, paid his bill, and gave me a fifty centimes tip. I could not help smiling and said, "So, Father, has the church wasted its time trying to teach you charity? Imagine that St. Francis, for example, was in your place. Do you think that he would have given me only fifty centimes?"

The old man smiled and shook his head but replied immediately, as if his reply was one he had prepared long ago: "No, my son, no. If St. Francis had needed to get to the station, he wouldn't have taken a taxi—he would have walked on foot."

"You're right, Father," I said, trying not to laugh. "All I can do is wish you a safe journey."

Later on I often remembered this old abbé not because his reply was an indication of his ready wit but because he was so completely typical, with his tiny little eyes and his fine old woman's wrinkles: he looked as if he had just stepped out of an engraving, keeping by some kind of miracle both its stillness and its particular wooden gentleness, which is so rare in ordinary, living people. He appeared for a very short time and then disappeared, but his appearance immediately called forth in me a multitude of almost-forgotten ideas about times long ago; those same ideas I had loved so much and to which nothing, or almost nothing, had corresponded in the multitude of harsh and tragic things among which my life had passed. I retained another uncomfortable and disgustingly comic memory of a different abbé, who, by a strange coincidence, came my way a few days later. He could have been forty or forty-five years old; he got into the car and said, "Go straight on," then turned to me and asked in his professionally intimate manner whether I knew any streets in Paris where he might have a rendezvous.

"A rendezvous?" I asked. "What kind of rendezvous, Father?" He was clearly disconcerted by my involuntarily drawing attention to his status by calling him Father, and then, visibly making an effort, he explained that he had in mind a rendezvous with a woman. I continued to pretend that I did not understand.

"Please explain yourself, Father," I said. "I'm afraid I may not have understood you correctly."

He preserved an embarrassed silence; he felt hot, so he took off his black hat and mopped his perspiring brow.

"A woman," he muttered in complete embarrassment. "You know, one of those who walk the streets." I drove him to the street that encircles the Place de l'Étoile, and I stopped the car opposite a female silhouette at the edge of the sidewalk.

"Might you be so good, if you consider it possible, to ask mademoiselle whether she is agreeable?"

Even before I got out of the car I recognized her. People called her Foul-Mouthed Renée; I had known her a long time. Several days before this she had told me she had lost an umbrella that was worth four hundred francs; I was in a bad mood at the time and told her that I didn't think she was worth that herself, even with the umbrella.

"You have the opportunity to earn the money to buy an umbrella," I said to her. "My client would like to talk to you; he's a very nice abbé."

"Are you joking?" she asked, unconvinced, but even so she got into the car; we drove off to the Bois de Boulogne, along the avenues of which we cruised around for about forty minutes; afterward the abbé drove to the Gare de Lyon and left Paris, bearing away with him the memory of this encounter; I do not know whether he had occasion to remember it in less fortunate circumstances, as this woman had long before contracted syphilis, like the majority of her fellow workers. I learned of this by chance, because she became quite candid on her way home after leaving a nighttime café on the Place des Ternes, where she went at the end of her evening's work; she was always quite tipsy at this time and never stopped talking. When she was sober she was distinguished by her uncommonly nasty personality, and she was always involved in all sorts of unpleasant episodes, fights with other women, and scandals with her clients; one time she complained to the police that she had been the victim of a rape and thrust at the indifferent red-headed giant in uniform somebody's crumpled visiting card, insisting that it was this same person who had practically tortured her; another time I saw her noisy journey to the police station accompanied by two policemen and a thin little old man who had just spent several hours with her in a hotel room, who hurried after them with tiny steps and said in a high, quavering voice that this same creature had robbed him.

"Four thousand francs," he shouted, turning to either side and addressing the crowd of spectators that was following them at a certain distance. "I am not a rich man, messieurs; I have children to feed!"

Of course, the money was not found, because she had managed to pass it on to someone by then.

And so this same woman told me one day that five minutes ago a foreigner had been arrested right beside her who spoke no French and merely repeated the whole time, addressing the police, some word, something like *opoda*. I repeated this word to myself two or three times and suddenly understood that it was probably the Russian word *gospoda* and that it was a fellow countryman of mine who had landed in the police station. I drove off there in order to offer my assistance as a translator and, if possible, to sort out this misunderstanding. But when I drove up to the police station, this person, whose papers turned out to be in order and who had been mistaken for someone else, was already on his way out. I jumped down from my car, walked up to him, and recognized him at once, even though I had not seen him for some ten years. I had known him during the Civil War in Russia; he had served in the same army unit as I had. His name was Aristarkh Aleksandrovich Kulikov. In those years he had been a military administrator, then he had gone abroad, and I had not seen him again. I was told that he had been a coal miner in Bulgaria, then worked in a metallurgical factory, but I had heard nothing more about him for a long time. He also recognized me and was delighted to see me. In a nearby café he told me about everything that he had done in these years, and during our conversation it transpired that his true calling was to be the owner of a restaurant; and as it happened he was, as he told me, just about to open a restaurant in Billancourt, a working-class suburb of Paris, in very close proximity to the Renault factory. He insisted that I come to see him there. I promised I would but somehow was not able to until one day I met him again, on the metro, and was astonished by his formal dress, his bowler hat of unusual roundness and good quality, his splendid black overcoat, and the white silk scarf around his neck.

"Why haven't you come yet?" he said to me in a loud voice, without even troubling to greet me. "If you want, we can go right now to the restaurant and have dinner."

I agreed; on the way there he forewarned me that he and I would dine together at a separate table, as the whole restaurant had been taken by a group of Cossacks, whether they were from the Urals or the Terek or the Don, I never found out. It was an autumn evening with drizzle falling; Aristarkh Aleksandrovich and I spent a long time stepping over puddles of various sizes until we came to a large area of waste ground where there stood a building, half made of brick and half wood, which resembled a barracks and which turned out to be his restaurant. It was quiet inside; it was quiet all around; the workers were already asleep at that time, and one could hear the drops of rain striking the wooden boards. We went in; inside the restaurant only one very large, long table was occupied, laid out with a great number of bottles, and sitting at this table were some thirty Cossacks, all with closely cropped hair, all wearing the same dark blue suits that evidently had been made by the same tailor, and all in starched white collars that stood out sharply against their firm, ruddy cheeks. They were drinking red wine and all singing songs together, of which I remember one particularly mournful one:

> And we will never see each other more,
> And never we will meet again.

"They're putting it away all right," Aristarkh Aleksandrovich said to me, almost in a whisper. "Do you see? They no longer look human. But on the other hand, can you blame Russian people for that?"

He shook his head and then suddenly asked me, "Do you still not drink, the same as in Russia?"

"I'm still the same."

"That's good," he said to me with sudden approval and slapped me on the shoulder. "It's remarkable that you don't drink. God forbid, if you start drinking, that'll be the end of you."

He and I sat together talking for a long time after that. The Cossacks went away, and we were left on our own. In the middle of the huge room a stove quietly hummed, the rain continued to fall against the wooden boards, and listening to its monotonous pattering and to the forgotten sound of drops of water against wood, I remembered with unusual clarity rainy autumn evenings in Russia, damp fields drowning in the drizzly darkness, trains, the distant lantern of the coupler swaying in the black air, the protracted nocturnal hooting of the locomotive. It was very late when I left.

"Do you need any money?" Aristarkh Aleksandrovich asked. "You tell me, my dear fellow, don't be shy. Take a taxi home; you don't want to be walking about in this weather. There's a driver waiting at our taxi stand, a Russian; he used to be a deacon in the Vladimir district. I always use him."

But when one day, almost half a year later, I happened to be in Billancourt and wanted to call in to Aristarkh Aleksandrovich's restaurant, I was met by incomprehensible failure: I could not find it. And although I had the impression that I recognized the way there and even found my way to the area of waste ground on which it had stood, there was no restaurant there. And since the loss without trace of an entire large building seemed to me impossible, I decided that I had simply made a mistake and forgotten the place. I did not have time to devote to a lengthy search for Aristarkh Aleksandrovich, and I drove back to Paris, hoping that the next time I would be more successful. However, the feeling did not leave me that the restaurant had been on that very same waste ground which was now, early in the spring, turning pathetically green with its already-wizened grass and where were strewn here and there shapeless pieces of rubble. Several days later I saw Aristarkh Aleksandrovich on a metro train going in the opposite direction; it lasted two or three seconds, but I was astonished to see that he was wearing a shabby old jacket, a ragged cap, and a green scarf around his neck. Aristarkh Aleksandrovich did not see me. But I could not have been mistaken; it was definitely him. Another two months later I received a postcard from him, saying that he was coming into town and at such-and-such a time, would be in such-and-such a café, and would be glad to see me. I found him there in a fine gray suit, a straw hat, and gleaming yellow shoes; he was happy and said that as far as business went, he had no complaints.

I told him about the miraculous disappearance of his restaurant; he joked about how I always lost my way and reminded me that back in Russia I was never sent out on a scouting mission alone since it was feared that I would get lost. I nevertheless thought that he was a little embarrassed, albeit for a very short while. And it was only somewhat later that I found out the explanation both for the fantastic disappearance of the restaurant and for the unexpected changes in Aristarkh Aleksandrovich's dress. I was told about it by people who were old and close acquaintances of his.

He was a fine manager and a very good organizer. While working in a factory or down the mines, over long months he saved up his money. Then, having at his disposal a certain sum of money of his own, having borrowed from his friends whatever they could give him, and putting his capacity for obtaining credit to work, he would open a restaurant and immediately begin to make money. He paid back his debts, immediately began to grow rich, bought expensive suits, lived in a nice flat, and everything would go swimmingly for several months, sometimes almost a year, right up until the day when, after drinking too much, he would suddenly descend into a frenzy of charitableness. Standing in the middle of his restaurant, with disheveled hair and his tie pushed to one side, he would shout, "Drink, lads; eat, drink, it's all on me. We're Russians, fellows; if we don't help each other, who will help us? It's all free, lads, remember Aristarkh Aleksandrovich Kulikov; if anything happens, spare a thought for me!"

Crowds of his friends would arrive, along with half acquaintances and even people who didn't know him at all, and for two weeks there would be noise and shouting in his restaurant from morning till night. While this was happening his friends would try to take away everything they could—money, suits, and even crockery—knowing that the end was near and in the hope of saving even one thing. But if any of them ran into Aristarkh Aleksandrovich, he would fly into a rage, shout that he was being robbed, and take back the item that was being removed. Then, one fine day, everything would fall quiet, the restaurant would close, the suppliers would not be paid, and an emaciated, altered, and now very quiet Aristarkh Aleksandrovich would disappear. He would go to work in a factory again, would doggedly work long hours, pay his debts once more, humbly thank those who had taken away and hung on to his things, and after a certain time would once again open a restaurant. And the fact that I had found that waste ground empty of any building was explained not by my inability to find my way around but by the restaurant, which had genuinely been located there and had belonged to Aristarkh Aleksandrovich, having been pulled down and sold off down to the last sodden board to pay off debts.

The cold Parisian winter months went by and spring arrived; the nights were cool, but during the daytime and the evenings it was sometimes warm. On one of these evenings I met Raldy once again. She was sitting on the terrace of her café and seemed to have grown even more old and frail. But she was not alone. Beside her, with one impeccably formed leg crossed over the other—her skirt did not cover her knees—sat a young woman of around twenty or twenty-two years old. She was so good-looking that, when I saw her, for a second I found it hard to breathe; particularly striking were her red, unusually full-seeming lips, her elongated blue eyes, and fine teeth; she was smiling as she spoke with Raldy at the moment I saw her.

"This is my friend," said Raldy, greeting me. "Tell me, what do you think of her?"

And it was only then, after I had taken a close look at this beautiful woman, that I noticed in her eyes that same semitransparent film, that same patina of animal stupidity that I knew so well and which was typical of almost all women of her profession. But she was so beautiful, literally beautiful, that it required all my lengthy experience and all those reserves of melancholy which made me ready for any disappointment to be able to see this solitary, almost invisible detail in her expression, this solitary, half-physical, half-spiritual blemish.

"She's very pretty," I said to Raldy.

She looked hard at me and said, "You have never wanted to sleep with me; in the end that's understandable. But I hope that you won't refuse to spend some time with my friend. You know that it won't cost you anything."

I shook my head in refusal. "The more I get to know you, the more I become convinced that you're simply abnormal," Raldy said to me with a sigh. "Tell me how you're getting on; I haven't seen you for a long time."

But I could not take my eyes off Alice—for Alice was her name. A quarter of an hour later in Raldy's room I saw her completely naked—she got changed in front of me. I could never have imagined such astonishing perfection. She had firm breasts that stood well apart from one another, a belly that narrowed and then with magical imperceptibility filled out again, dazzling skin, and long, ideally shaped legs; after a few seconds it began to seem as if this beautiful body was starting to dissolve and float before my eyes.

"Don't move," said Raldy, "I want him to get a proper look at you naked."

When I left, it was some time before I returned to my normal state; I stood beside my car, getting ready to climb in behind the wheel but still not getting in: before me I saw that body and face, that dazzling, inscrutable beauty. And for a long time after, each time I remembered this it would take my breath away for a second.

"She is so good-looking," I said to Raldy when I was talking to her a few days afterward, "that it's worth spending a fortune just to look at her."

Raldy smiled, as always, half tenderly, half mockingly, and then said that without her—Raldy's—help, Alice would have remained a streetwalker forever, but that she was turning her into a *demimondaine*. She added that she lacked much that was required for this career, most of all intelligence and comprehension.

"Do you think so?" I said. "I would have thought that her looks alone . . ."

"There are a great many beautiful women," Raldy replied, "but only one in a thousand ever achieves something, have you never thought about that? Beauty alone is not enough. Don't you agree with me?"

"Yes, of course," I said. "It's just that I feel a little sorry for Alice. Are you suggesting that it is worthwhile devoting all your experience and all your understanding so that you can make out of this beautiful woman what you call a *demimondaine*? Do you think that she deserves no better than that?"

"I have no doubt about that," replied Raldy. "Only I am not sure whether she actually deserves this. But if I am successful, she will not forget me; I'll have a warm room and a little money so that I can live without having to work until the end of my days. Because she will be indebted to me for everything she has."

And herein lay Raldy's mistake. She worked hard on her protégée, taught her English, explained to her how she must hold a knife and fork, what she must say, how she ought to reply, and how to carry herself. She even summoned me several times so that I could be present at these lessons and asked me to explain to Alice certain things that she was unsure about herself. At her request I procured the books that Alice had to read: *Dangerous Liaisons*, Bocaccio, and Flaubert. I shrugged my shoulders and obediently agreed—there was scarcely anything I could refuse to do for this extraordinary old woman, even though all of this seemed to me excessive and in some degree indecent on my part.

"You oblige me to play a role that is quite out of character for me," I said to Raldy. "I really don't know why I am doing all this."

"You are doing it," she calmly said to me, "because you feel pity for me; it's very simple, my dear fellow."

"You give her Flaubert, yet she is barely able to read, so what will she understand of it?"

"She won't understand, but she'll know that it's very beneficial."

I put forward the hypothesis that, as soon as Alice had achieved any kind of material success, she would ditch Raldy, and Raldy would once again be left on her own.

"That's possible," said the old woman, "and of course that would be sad. That would mean that she had failed to understand the most important thing, because without my advice she will never make a career for herself. She must know that."

Alice continued working, but not very much, just enough so as to have enough to pay for a room and sustenance for herself and Raldy. In my presence Raldy explained to her how she would have to behave later on, when she would be dealing not with ordinary clients picked up on the street, but with those with whom her career as a lady of the *demimonde* would begin. "Never go to a hotel on the very first day of your acquaintance," said Raldy. "Never say no. Say, 'Yes, darling,' and then behave after that as you see fit. But make a point of saying, 'Yes, darling.'"

We sat with Alice and listened to her lessons; she would have some book on her lap, with her glasses on her nose, and resembled a nice old teacher from a small provincial town: a population of three thousand, a church, a curé, a *mairie,* a forest one mile away, squat oak trees with truffles beneath them, mushrooms and rain in the autumn, and a photographer's shop window in the center of the town, where naked little children are exhibited on velvet couches along with frozen, wooden newlyweds in unfamiliar formal attire. "Never undress yourself." After this there followed the most detailed explanations, so shameless that I began to feel uncomfortable; but Alice would listen to Raldy, looking straight at her with her beautiful, calm eyes through the half-transparent film over her pupils.

And then one fine day she disappeared; she left and did not return. I learned of this only a month later since, for some reason, I had no cause to go to their district. I can remember the summer evening with fine rain falling and the hunched figure of Raldy, who was standing beneath the awning of a café. She smiled sadly when she saw me. We drank coffee together; she was cold and wrapped herself up in a shabby man's overcoat. She told me that Alice had left exactly four weeks ago. I did not know what I could say to her to comfort her and remained silent for a while; it was getting quite cold out on the terrace; the drizzle fell, dancing before my eyes.

Finally I said, "There have been so many vicissitudes in your life. One more or one less . . ."

"No, no," she answered me. "This is the last one. There is nothing else left for me."

And once more tears appeared in her eyes. All of this was so irremediable, like much that I had seen in my life, like the leaden opacity in the eyes of dying people, like my final meeting with Prince Nerbatov, who had borne through his whole life his mournful, unquenchable love for this same Raldy, for this old woman in a worn-out man's overcoat, who was seated before me in front of her cold coffee.

"You can put up with anything," she said, not looking at me and with her head lowered, "but then, when you've no strength left, you can't put up with things anymore. Then all that's left is to die. When all's said and done, what she did is only natural." I asked Raldy whether among all her innumerable former admirers there wasn't anyone still living who could have paid her some trivial sum of money that would have allowed her to carry on living. She shook her head and immediately named several very well-known political figures. "They're all like Alice," she said. I remembered these names and that the career of each of these people had consisted of innumerable political betrayals, defections, of groveling and plagiarizing, and I understood why Raldy had nobody she could turn to. And I remembered how she had said to me, "If one day I wrote my memoirs, people would discover many interesting things and would understand how much of what people thought was completely wrong."

But she was unable to write; her rheumatic fingers would not obey her.

I knew that sooner or later I would come across Alice; nighttime Paris, the Paris of cabarets, cafés, and *maisons de passe* is not as big as people usually think, and every night I spent in this miserable space I drove around sixty miles, going from one place to another. But it was quite by chance that I saw her on one of the evenings when I was not working, through the window of a big café on the Grands Boulevards; she was wearing a fine outfit and hat with a heavy, sparkling necklace around her neck; a dark brown fox fur hung over her shoulder. It seemed to me that everyone in the café was looking at her: the women with hatred, the men with sympathy and envy. I asked if I could join her at her table.

"Hello," she said, holding out her gloved hand to me. "Have a drink with me." And a second later, lowering her voice, she asked, "Do you like me like this?"

"I prefer you naked," I said loudly. Two or three people turned to look at us.

"Are you out of your mind?" she whispered.

But I was in a fit of rage such as I had only experienced two or three times in my whole life. And, listening to myself from one side, I noticed that I was speaking to her in the sort of street French for which I would normally feel nothing but derision.

"A beer," I said to the waiter. "You're just a piece of shit, Alice, do you understand, a piece of shit, do you hear, a piece of shit."

Momentary fear flashed in her eyes. I was leaning over the table as I spoke to her, right up close to her beautiful, unforgettable face.

"If you've come here to heap abuse on me . . ."

The band in the café—a violin, cello, and grand piano—was playing a long, familiar, tender motif, the name of which I did not know but which I had heard many times in different countries, in different circumstances, and in different arrangements. And always when these sounds once again reached my ears, on each occasion during the interval of time that had passed there had been many events and misfortunes, and every time it was like a musical juxtaposition the results of which I already knew—and their meaning was in sharp contradiction to this flawless, immaculately tender melody. There have been a few rare seconds in my life when I have felt an almost physical sensation which I could not compare or confuse with any other and which I could only describe as a sensation of time passing—passing then, that very minute. Thus it was on the evening of my encounter with Alice; I listened to this melody and looked into her face, unable to tear my eyes away, and felt, as it seemed to me, coming through this melody a distant noise, and everything crowded in and swam before my eyes. It required an effort for me to return to my normal state, and then I had a sudden feeling of weariness. I raised my head, and said, "Did you expect me to be paying you compliments?"

Alice immediately sensed from the tone of my voice that the danger that she had evidently feared had now passed. She placed her hand on mine and began to speak in her usual voice, in which I always felt there to be something soft and sticky. She attempted to justify herself; she said that she wanted to live her own life, that she did not wish to be reliant on Raldy, that she had fed the old woman for many months and was really not indebted to her in any way.

"I told you that you are a shit," I said to her, my feeling of irritation now almost gone. "But aside from everything else, what you're doing is simply stupid. Do you think you'll get anywhere without Raldy's help?"

"Don't you worry about me."

"Your fate doesn't really concern me. But you'll never stop being what you are now, that's to say no more than—" and I said the word that precisely expressed what I thought of her. "What kind of clients can you expect to find? Petty businessmen with paunches who'll be counting up every last hundred francs?"

"You don't know who might come into this café."

"Yes, but if it's some exceptional person, you'll be able to seduce him, but you won't be able to hang on to him. Do you know the story of Raldy's life?"

"Yes. She was probably more beautiful than I am."

"No, it's not possible to be more beautiful than you," I said, unable to stop myself.

"Ah, you do understand, then?"

I shrugged my shoulders. It turned out that my refusal, when Raldy had offered her to me, had troubled Alice, and she had not been able to forget it. She even considered it a bad omen for her nascent career: if I had not wanted her, then perhaps neither would others.

I spoke with her for a long time after that, but I was unable to convince her of the necessity for her to go back to Raldy or at least to help her. It was a quarter past eleven o'clock when I parted from her; I did not want to miss the night showing at a cinema which began in fifteen minutes' time.

"Good-bye," I said to her. "Call me when you're lying on your death bed in the hospital. I'll come and tell you one last time that you've behaved like a fool and a piece of shit."

And, as I left, I imagined to myself Plato's unshaven face and his sullen eyes and how he might say to me, "One aspect of this wider ethical problem . . ."

But I did not speak to him about Alice, and when I met him next, our talk was of quite different and for me altogether unexpected matters.

In this nocturnal Paris I felt myself to be like a traveler who finds himself in an alien environment; and in the whole of this immense city there were two or three places that were like islands illuminated in that dark space, to which I came every night, generally at the same times; and, as I walked into my café, I seemed to myself like the oarsman of a small boat, which, after being tossed for a long time on the waves, has finally landed at a small quay, and upon getting out of it, instead of the sea and a harbor inn, I see a lighted sidewalk and the steamed-up windows of a café opposite a somnolent railway station and the wheels of my car, held fast by its brakes.

"Hello, m'sieur," the *patronne* said to me. "Milk?"

And always in the same place, in his pale-gray, very grimy raincoat—winter and summer—at the right-hand end of the bar near the register, Plato would be standing, in front of the inevitable glass of white wine. He would greet me always with unfailing friendliness, yet without the slightest hint of effusiveness, which was generally alien to his melancholy and gentle character; only he did not always recognize me, though we had seen one another every night over the course of several years; for this depended on how much he had drunk. Recently he had spoken altogether very little and with reluctance, and, standing in this busy café, with his glass in front of him, he would notice nothing of the world around him, lost in his profound, drunken oblivion. The *patronne* related to me with astonishment how when one day in the café the sensational arrest had taken place of a certain pimp and murderer—who had escaped from prison and returned here to the very place where everybody knew him and he should never on any account have come back, but a peculiar sort of vanity and provincial stupidity characteristic of people of his sort had led him to perform this senseless action, so as to appear in all his pimp's glory (a pale-gray cap, two-tone boots with high heels) in front of a handful of terrified prostitutes and deferential colleagues, that evening there had been gunfire and fighting, and then the police had hauled off this man with ferocious swiftness, his face bloodied, his cap lost, his suit covered with blood—Plato, who had been there the whole time, watched all of this in silence with a steady gaze and did not even move.

I preferred the days when he had very little money, enough for two or three glasses of wine; then he was almost entirely sober and able to talk to me. What I loved in him was the completely disinterested nature of his reasoning, as well as the fact that his own fate and, more generally, anything tangential left him completely indifferent. He came to life only when the conversation turned either to new and to him completely insignificant people, or else to abstract questions. However, he was by no means always of the same opinion about one and the same thing; he accounted for this by saying that a person's judgments on a particular subject are closely tied to a multitude of physiological and psychological factors, the totality of which it is extremely difficult to account for and indeed completely impossible to predict—with the exception of those cases when the question under discussion, in its primitive quality, could be compared with a question of a purely material nature, but even here there predominated what he called the law of relativity. However, he was just as damning in his judgments of all people as was Raldy, and of absolutely everyone, regardless of the rank, status, or profession of a person, which in his eyes counted for nothing; and I was delighted to hear from him one day that in his understanding, the average criminal who had in the past committed two or three major crimes differed very little from the average *député* or minister, and in the sphere of impartial judgment, as he would say, they stood on the same level as each other; and I was delighted to hear this, as I completely shared this view.

I saw Plato the night after my encounter with Alice and, upon entering the café, immediately noticed that he was short of money, since he was almost completely sober. I offered him a glass of white wine, and judging by the speed with which he accepted, I could tell that he had been there in the café a long time, unable to pay another one and a half francs, which he did not have. He drank a little of his wine and then said, apropos of nothing, "Do you know that we have some news? Suzanne's getting married."

"Suzanne with the gold tooth?"

"Suzanne with the gold tooth."

And he repeated it several more times, staring straight ahead into smoke-filled space: "Suzanne with the gold tooth. Suzanne with the gold tooth. Suzanne with the gold tooth's getting married, with the gold tooth, Suzanne."

He then repeated the same phrase in English, rapidly again, and then fell silent for a while. I expressed my astonishment that a woman like Suzanne, for whom legal formalities in this type of thing had always seemed entirely superfluous, should now consider it necessary to get married.

"Can you imagine," I said to Plato, "the white veil around that virginal face with the gold front tooth showing?"

Plato was looking at his glass of wine just then with his eyes screwed up. Then he replied shortly, "I can imagine it. Don't forget that people like her are deeply bourgeois by nature. They've failed to make it into the bourgeoisie, I grant you that, but they're extraordinarily bourgeois. Remember your murderers who opened the grocery store practically the day after their crime. People can commit murder not only out of jealousy or to destroy a tyrant and thus to help—by paying with their own life—in the achievement of a common human ideal or of a more rational system for the sharing of wealth. They can kill for the sake of a different ideal—a grocery store, or a butcher's, or a café."

"And it's on this basis that Suzanne, who has spent many hours in hotel rooms and had several thousand men, this same Suzanne is now getting married. You must agree, my dear friend, that if it is so, then all of our ethical notions, which you so much love to speak about . . ."

But at that moment we heard Suzanne's voice, as she had just walked into the café. She was very tipsy and replied loudly to the man who had followed her in, "I told you that I'm not working today!"

Plato was still looking straight ahead, screwing up his eyes.

"There's our bride in all her glory," he said. Between Suzanne and the thin, quite poorly dressed man of around thirty years who had followed her into the café, something resembling a battle now ensued. Suzanne tore herself away from him, while the flow of oaths from her never ceased; he, on the other hand, quietly attempted to persuade her of something, clinging to the sleeve of her coat the whole time.

"I said no," she said, finally, glaring at his face with her immobile, drunken eyes. And it was evidently only at that moment that he understood that her refusal was categorical. Then suddenly, unexpectedly, he shouted at her in a high voice, "You piece of shit!" and hurriedly walked out of the café.

"I ask you," said Suzanne, breathing heavily and stopping beside the counter. "I ask you! If a woman doesn't want to work for whatever bloody reason, she gets called a piece of shit! That can't be right, can it?" she said with drunken menace in her voice. Her eyes sought out faces that she might settle on. She looked first of all at Plato, but his expression was so lifelessly indifferent and remote that her eyes only skimmed over him—and then settled on me.

"Ah, it's you, is it?" she said in her drawling, drunken voice. "How's the milk today?"

I did not reply, and she turned away. Her coat was unbuttoned; a tight dress clasped her short figure, and for the first time ever, I noticed, with a shudder of involuntary revulsion, that there was in fact a certain animal feminine charm about her.

"You're all . . ." said Suzanne. "I'm not a wh—— anymore; I'm getting married. Maybe I've had a glass or two . . ."

"You can't count properly," said a man's voice from the other end of the bar. "Maybe you've had a few more than two."

"Do you remember, Plato," I said, "the words ascribed to Socrates by your illustrious predecessor? 'A philosopher's whole life is nothing more than a lengthy preparation for death.' . . . I can't get rid of the same constant thought the whole time: of a bed, sheets, someone dying, the foul smell of this person in his death throes, and the complete impossibility of doing anything to change things."

"That's not what Socrates was talking about," said Plato. "If you've not forgotten the *Phaedon* . . ."

"And I'm going to have a shop," came the drunken voice of Suzanne. "And I love this man as well; I can't live without him."

She was addressing herself to no one in particular and was speaking into smoke-filled space, in which her words about love dissolved and died away. I thought of Raldy, who had told me that women of Suzanne's type don't love in the same way as others, but I had only ever understood this degrading formula theoretically; I had never been able to feel and to believe conclusively that this was so.

Plato changed the subject of conversation, as if he found it unpleasant to think about Suzanne at that moment. It was several hours later when I stopped at that café again on my way home; it was already morning, everybody had left, and he alone was still standing motionless at the counter, alongside the *patronne* who, from time to time, would let her head drop onto her breast and doze off for a minute with an old person's light sleep and then, after slowly coming round, would yawn and then hurriedly mumble, "Oh my God, he told me that Suzanne's getting married to a foreigner, a Russian Cossack." A few days later Suzanne informed me of this herself as day was breaking after a cold autumn night, some time after five o'clock in the morning when I saw her on her own at a café table. Her face showed exhaustion, and there were dark blue circles beneath her eyes. "You look tired," I said, as I walked past her. "You ought to get some rest." She nodded and began to talk to me; I stood beside her table, not sitting down. "Is it true that you're getting married?" "Yes, it's true." She said she was twenty-three years old and that at that age her mother already had four children, that she wanted to live like everyone else, but she was working more than usual just then since the wedding was in two weeks' time. Her fiancé did not know she was working; she was governed by the desire to bring home, as she put it, as much money as possible and therefore she did not spare herself; and on the days when she was not seeing her fiancé she would go out onto the street at four o'clock in the afternoon and get home after four in the morning—this explained the extremely tired look about her which had so struck me. Then she described her fiancé to me and showed me his photograph, which she carried around in her handbag, and this handbag went everywhere with her, into all the rooms she went up to with her clients; and from the contact with the banknotes with which she was paid, the photograph had gradually faded and turned gray. It showed a beaming young man, and the expression on his face, thanks to some particular trick of retouching, revealed both cheerfulness and a wooden sort of dignity.

"What do you know!" I said, unable to restrain myself, for I had recognized Fedorchenko.

"Do you know him?" asked Suzanne. "You won't tell him anything about me? Because he doesn't know, do you understand?"

"Does he think you're a virgin?"

"No, but you understand, you mustn't tell him."

"All right, I promise. And if I meet you together, I don't know you, that's agreed," I said.

The wedding was preceded by intensive medical treatment—since not long before this Suzanne had been infected by some bastard, as she put it—along with preparations and letters to relatives, and so, on the day of the ceremony, at a long table in a rented hall in the poor *quartier* where she had rented a flat, there sat her relatives, who had traveled hundreds of miles from the country and brought with them their Sunday suits and their wind-blown, immobile peasant faces. Fedorchenko had neither relatives nor close friends, but he had invited one elderly and very dignified-looking Russian whose name was Vasiliev. After several glasses of wine, without any loss of decorum and only occasionally shuddering jerkily with a peculiar, soundless form of hiccups, Vasiliev began to relate in a quiet, confidential voice that some time ago the Bolsheviks had sent emissaries to him—that was his exact word—so that one had the impression that from time to time he was visited by a delegation of people in uniforms, of a special design peculiar to emissaries, but that he was unwavering. He explained all this with equal facility in Russian and in French; he sniffed the cheap wine with the air of a connoisseur and retained, whatever the circumstances, a noble and modestly important appearance. This foolish man, in whom even at that time the first signs of degenerative madness were already evident, was to play a very important role in the life of Fedorchenko.

Apart from Vasiliev, there was no one on the groom's side at the wedding; Suzanne had immediately explained to her relatives that her husband was a foreigner, that his family had remained in their own country, and that he had decided to start a new family here, in Paris. However, all of these details lost all meaning after a great deal of wine was drunk and Fedorchenko began to exchange kisses with the wedding guests. An hour later singing began, Fedorchenko climbed up onto a stool and began conducting, and Suzanne cried out in a piercing voice—and amidst all of this noise Vasiliev alone, though dead drunk, retained his appearance of formality and decorum; but he, too, had reached the state where he could not utter a single coherent sentence, although he kept trying to tell, in a very quiet voice, of those same emissaries. I was unwittingly present at this banquet because, as I was driving down that street at night, I had noticed several taxis waiting at the brightly lit entrance for the guests to come out. I joined the queue without knowing who these guests were; my colleagues told me that it was a wedding and, along with one of them, I went up to see if there were many people there. Stopping outside the entrance door, I saw Suzanne, with a real veil floating on both sides at once, Fedorchenko in a dinner jacket hired from a Jewish tailor on the Rue du Temple—the sleeves of the dinner jacket were too short, and the lapels astonishingly narrow—and Suzanne's relatives, who looked like peasants carved out of wood wearing city clothes who had suddenly come to life as a result of alcoholic miracle working. Fedorchenko was so far gone that he was yelling to Vasiliev in Russian, "Hold on, sailor, hold on!" And the pale and drunken Vasiliev nodded his head with great dignity. Suzanne never stopped laughing and screeching; she and Fedorchenko kissed many times, so that his face was covered with the rouge with which her lips had been heavily smeared at the start of the evening. "Now there's a wedding!" said the driver with whom I was watching the banquet, with approval. It was getting on toward morning when the banquet ended, the guests were taken home, and from the next day a new life began for Fedorchenko.

He and Suzanne moved into one of the new apartment blocks in a recently built district of Paris; the building was constructed of resonant reinforced concrete, which transmitted every sound on every side; it had an elevator, which jolted determinedly upward, glass lampshades in the form of tulips, and bathrooms of risibly small dimensions. With the money that Fedorchenko and Suzanne had, they opened a small workshop for the dying and cleaning of all kinds of fabrics. On the sign was written in gold-molded lettering of uniform size SUZY, with a flourish that traveled from the end of the word to the beginning of the even wooden edge. Suzanne took in orders, while Fedorchenko distributed the dresses and other articles to their clients. He spoke now of the high cost of cloth, of the price of dye, of the difficulties in this work, and about how he, as a tradesman in this *quartier*, had to keep his prices at a certain level. He also spoke of how difficult it was for him to make a living for himself; and the watch that he had bought his very first year in France that he used to wind only on Sundays he now began to wind every day. He entered into his new role with the same astonishing adaptability that he had shown when, while working up to ten hours a day in a factory, he had reckoned that it was really not a bad life at all; he got himself fishing gear and went down to the Seine with it; every Sunday he would make a trip outside of Paris with Suzanne, who had rapidly put on weight; and he would have turned imperceptibly and irreparably into a typical French *commerçant* had he not been prevented from doing so by unexpected causes which had first revealed themselves many years before, had since then been long forgotten, and, it would seem, had lost whatever power they may have had.

I saw Fedorchenko quite often in this period of his life; I met him once on a Saturday toward evening beside the Porte d'Auteuil; he was walking along with Suzanne, and each of them carried a chair on one shoulder. Accompanied by the astonished looks of passersby, they strode on in silence, apparently oblivious to all around them; it was a still and rather hot summer evening, and the sun was already beginning to set. After greeting them, I asked Fedorchenko why he was carrying a chair; was he perhaps moving to another apartment? He replied that he was not; he was simply going to get some fresh air in the Bois de Boulogne. "What are the chairs for, then?" He slapped me on the shoulder and explained to me indulgently—after telling me in as many words that I must be some kind of simpleton—that the chairs were for sitting on in the Bois since if you wished to sit on the chairs that were available there, you had to pay thirty-five centimes. Suzanne, who after her marriage had begun to address me using *vous* and talk to me as if I were someone she barely knew, but nevertheless quite politely, smiling and flashing her gold tooth, made it clear that this was her husband's idea and that she thought it a very good one. After saying good-bye to them, I watched for some time as they walked away down a straight street, getting farther and farther away from me, the dark outline of the slightly curved legs of their chairs sticking up in the air above their heads, and from a good distance away one might have mistaken them for two small horned animals of an unknown breed.

Once she was married, Suzanne had to turn her back on everyone she had known before; Fedorchenko had never really had any friends, and therefore for a period of time they saw no one else until they began to be visited by Vasiliev, whom Fedorchenko invited for some reason and who, after this first visit, proceeded to make himself completely at home in their apartment. He took a small room in a hotel quite close to them and came to see Fedorchenko every day; he invariably arrived with two bottles of wine, which they drank over supper between the three of them, and he spent long evenings setting out before Fedorchenko and Suzanne his complex political and philosophical theories. His whole life possessed a meaning only inasmuch as it bore the character of an unceasing daily struggle with dark forces, among which he considered Bolshevism to be the foremost. He would relate confused legends to Fedorchenko and Suzanne which, as he said, he had got from the Talmud, and he knew by heart a fantastical system of fearsomely strict rules which governed the lives of world Jewry—and since he was a naive person, he firmly believed any nonsense he had ever heard or read. His limited mental faculties were further impeded, apart from everything else, by his phenomenal memory, which overloaded his head with its infinite store of information. He knew the story of every political assassination, about which he would speak with particular pleasure, along with the reasons behind these assassinations, the biographies of the criminals, the names of the coroners and their family lives, the nicknames of the prison guards, the staging posts on the way to Siberia, and the love affairs of the counsel for the defense—in short, in his head was an entire fixed and murderous world awash with terror and blood. At the same time, he had never in his whole life taken an active part in any political activity and had never caused anyone any harm, but over the years the work of his imagination and memory had incorporated into itself, like an anatomy theater or a museum of horrors, an infinite series of crimes, cruelties, and murders. At that time his slow, infectious madness started to become noticeable. Instinctively and subconsciously Suzanne was fearful of this innocuous man, as dogs fear a thunderstorm; she felt uncomfortable in his presence, but she did not dare say anything because of her husband, who listened avidly to Vasiliev's stories, his face turning crimson and flushed. At that time Vasiliev was already showing the first signs of persecution mania; he knew, so he said, that he was being followed, and sometimes he would appear in a cap and a gray overcoat instead of the hat and blue overcoat he usually wore, fearing that he might be recognized; he went to every political meeting and sat in the corner, never making an intervention since he was present there, as he said, incognito. "There are people who would pay a high price to find out who I am," he used to say to Fedorchenko. In short, he had now reached that stage in his life when the entire sequence of murders which for years he had carried in him, all of the silent horror of his imagination, must instantly well up and appear before him in all its irresistible variety, and there was only one thing to which this could lead—the alpha and omega of this entire tragic series—to death. But as yet he was only half of the way there.

Fedorchenko did not exactly believe everything his new friend told him—not because he could oppose it with any different set of facts, but because his innate peasant's mistrust did not allow him to. He generally found it hard to imagine any human act which was not motivated by the lure of personal gain; in any disinterested action he invariably looked for the simplest motivational causes, and when he failed to find any he found himself in a mental cul-de-sac. Until then he had generally never thought about things which did not concern him directly, and it was for this reason that his life was so easy, so lacking in any kind of complications. The one thing that might have made him unhappy would have been if Suzanne had refused to live with him. But then, by pure good fortune, it turned out that out of the thousands of men who had passed through Suzanne's life and her five or six real lovers, Fedorchenko was the very one whom she needed. She deferred to him so much that in his presence she would begin making mistakes in her French and speaking with the particular un-French intonation patterns which were typical of him, and it was only when she was apart from him again that she went back to the street-Parisian flavor that characterized her normal way of speaking, the flavor of the Boulevard Ménilmontant, and Belleville, and the Rue de la Gaité, and the working-class suburbs of Paris, which blended in with her own ponderous Auvergne accent. And so, Fedorchenko was unlikely to be disappointed in his marriage. And his life had turned out even better in the material sense.

I met him one night in a café; he seemed to be completely drunk, with a particular, aggressive kind of intoxication. He invited me to join him at the bar and immediately began talking, mixing up Russian and French words, about how difficult it was for him to live in this world, *dans cette monde;* he had never properly learned to distinguish masculine from feminine words in the French language.

"You're drinking a lot, you know," I said to him in reply.

"You don't understand me either. Understand," he said, raising his voice and banging his fist down on the bar, "everything

I love in this world is up there," and he stared up at the ceiling. Involuntarily I lifted my head up and saw the slightly dirty lime wash, molded vases, and round electric lightbulbs.

"The serenity of the night sky up there," said Fedorchenko, "that's what my soul yearns for. But as for people! I despise them."

He carried on speaking, jumping chaotically from one subject to another; for some reason he remembered that at his secondary school everyone had made fun of him; he even remembered the nickname Count Fedorchenko that someone had given him, and said, "But I have no desire for revenge against them. I don't need anything, only serenity." He then began to insist that I drive him home, and when we stopped outside his doorway, he invited me to come up for some tea.

"What the hell would I want tea for," I said. "It's past four o'clock in the morning. Go to bed."

"Come on, come on," he mumbled with drunken delight, holding on to my sleeve. "Go to bed," I repeated.

He suddenly lost interest and slumped against the wall. I took two steps in the direction of my car and then stopped. In the brightening silence of the early dawn I could hear him whimpering and mumbling words I could not make out; the only thing I understood was the word *why,* which he pronounced several times. I shrugged my shoulders and drove off.

Several months after this, as I was walking along the street, I suddenly felt someone's heavy hand upon my shoulder. I turned around and saw Fedorchenko. He was alone, was very neatly dressed, and was completely sober, but what struck me was the expression in his eyes, in which some remote terror or something very like it seemed to have been fixed.

"I've been wanting to talk to you for a long time," he said, without greeting me. "We can go into a café, if you like."

This was on the Champs-Élysées, toward evening. A crowd of people out strolling swept past us in a dense wave. We sat down on a terrace.

"Now tell me, please," Fedorchenko began, "there's one question I want to ask you. Are you able to explain what we live for?"

I looked at him in astonishment. On his face there was a thoughtful expression, which was extremely unnatural for him and so unexpected and preposterous that it seemed to me just as peculiar as if I had suddenly seen a mustache on a woman's face. And yet it was without even the remotest element of the comic— it was not funny at all—and I began to feel ill at ease. I thought that I did not want to remain alone with this man and involuntarily looked around me; all the tables around us were occupied; beside us a very well-dressed elderly man, whose wig had slipped slightly to one side, was relating to two ladies who looked as if they had been taken out of the shop window of a fashion store and who were even sitting in the artificial poses of mannequins, how he had been telling someone, "'Imagine,' I say to him, 'my poor friend . . .' He says to me, 'But excuse me . . .' I reply, 'Listen . . .'"

"I don't know," I said. "Some people for one reason, others for another, but on the whole I don't think anyone knows why."

"You mean you don't want to tell me?"

"My dear fellow, I don't know any more about it than you do."

He sat opposite me with an angry, strained expression on his face.

"So, people have their lives," he said with insistence, "and you, for example, have your life. Well, tell me please, what goal are you heading toward? Or what goal am I heading toward? Or maybe we're going backward and just don't realize it?"

"That's very possible," I replied, just to say something. "But as a general rule I don't think you need to get so worked up over it."

"But what can I do, then? I can't just leave it like that."

"Listen," I said impatiently, "before this you lived a normal life, for God's sake; you worked, ate, slept, and now you've got married. What else do you want? Forget about philosophy; you're not up to it, do you understand?"

"Vasiliev says," said Fedorchenko and looked around him, "that . . ."

"It won't be long before Vasiliev has delirium tremens," I said. "You can't take his words seriously."

"But once he thinks something, doesn't that mean that what he's thinking of is real?"

I shrugged my shoulders. Fedorchenko fell silent; he slumped forward and stared fixedly at the floor. I paid the waiter and said good-bye to Fedorchenko.

"Oh? What?" he said, raising his head. "Yes, yes, good-bye. I'm sorry if I bothered you."

I walked along and thought about how Fedorchenko's present condition was plainly the result first and foremost of the daily influence of Vasiliev. This was, at all events, the external cause of the unexpected awakening in him of this interest in abstract questions, which up to that point had been completely alien to him. He was unable to accept what Vasiliev said, and everything this drunken and insane person told him about the struggle of the forces of light with darkness and about his beloved assassinations had a peculiar effect on Fedorchenko; he suddenly experienced doubts about the rightness of that unconscious comprehension of the world within which he had lived up until then. He could find no explanation for this; his lack of familiarity with and inability to grapple with abstract concepts would not have allowed him to relate what had happened to him. "Like a tumor in my soul," he would later say. But as it became clear just how impossible it was for him to find any answer to these doubts, the compulsion to find this answer became all the more urgent. He was incapable of any kind of compromise or of creating some illusory and comforting theory that might have allowed him to feel that this answer had been found; this was something he could not do. At the same time it was as essential to him as the very air, and he dimly understood that, from the moment when his first doubts had arisen, a threat to his personal safety had appeared before him. He was like a person who has been blindfolded and walks along a narrow plank without handrails between the roofs of two tall buildings, walking calmly, not thinking about anything in particular, and suddenly the blindfold falls from his eyes and he sees beside him the slightly bluish, unstable empty space and the scarcely perceptible downward movement—to the right and to the left, like two rivers of air on either side.

A few days later I received a written invitation from him to come and have dinner, and while I understood the futility of this visit, I went along all the same, submitting to my habitual curiosity about anything which did not concern me. They were sitting at the table—Vasiliev and Fedorchenko. Suzanne opened the door for me and greeted me with such unexpected delight that I could not help but ask her when we were in the hall, "What's the matter with you? Have you got me mixed up with a client?"

"Someone who I know," she mumbled, without listening to me, "and who's not insane, what joy!"

Above the mantelpiece in the dining room there stood a clock set in marble, and it showed half past nine o'clock although it was eight; next to the clock was a marble panther of a deep green color; above it, on the wall, in a gilded frame, was a large photograph showing Fedorchenko and Suzanne on their wedding day; they stood in the center of the photo, surrounded by whirling, air-brushed contours, which resembled the borders of photographic clouds. The large table rested on a single leg in the form of an inverted and truncated cone, which greatly discomfited Vasiliev, who had hidden his long legs beneath his chair. On the walls there were also several oleo-graphs of naked beauties of a pinky-white color.

Vasiliev greeted me, looking as self-important as ever. My arrival had interrupted the flow of his speech for a moment, but he immediately recommenced. He would occasionally throw his head back, and then one could see the yellowish whites of his eyes, which rolled around like those of a corpse. He was speaking about the latest plot against some government in Siberia, dur-ing the Revolution, and giving as he always did the most precise details—a captain from the Riazan regiment, a tall, fair-haired, handsome man with an impeccable service record; his father, who came from a priest's family in the Orlov district, initially a teacher of mathematics in the higher classes of such-and-such secondary school, then . . . and so on. After recounting this in Russian, he immediately translated everything into French for Suzanne, who had never in her life heard of the Riazan regiment, or the teacher of mathematics, or the Orlov district, or of any Russian govern-ment in Siberia. Vasiliev spoke as if reading from a book and even retained the narrative style typical of popular historical novels: "The plotters gathered at an agreed location. At exactly a quarter to eleven there was a knock at the door and Captain R. entered the room with hurried steps. 'Gentlemen,' he said, 'the time for action has come. Our people are ready.'"

And he immediately translated this for Suzanne's benefit.

"There was a noise of chairs being pushed back . . ."

I looked closely at this insane man. Sometimes with his eyes closed and sometimes with them open, he spoke in a monotone, only changing in those places where there was a parenthetic clause. His French was very clear and precise, with just a slight accent and a certain excessive slowness of intonation, and he generally nar-rated his story in the past historic tense. Fedorchenko listened to him intently. Suzanne shuffled about on her chair and looked at

me with despair in her eyes. Taking advantage of a moment when
Vasiliev had turned toward her husband, she whispered to me: "I
can't stand it any more! I can't stand it!"

But it was impossible to stop Vasiliev. Several times I interrupted him and began speaking about something different; he
would fall silent but then profit from the first pause in order to
return to his interminable narrative, which would only conclude
with his death. I left late in the evening. I went out at the same time
as Vasiliev, who turned up the collar of his coat and pulled his hat
down over his forehead. I could not help smiling.

"You look just like the hero from some cloak-and-dagger novel,"
I said to him.

"You wouldn't be joking," he replied, "if you knew what danger
I face every single day."

I knew this phrase. I knew that no amount of persuasion would
have any effect on this man, but all the same I said that, as far as I
could see, his fears were groundless, that since he did no harm to
anyone, took no part in any political activity, and was not a prominent revolutionary or counterrevolutionary, he was hardly at any
greater risk than any other mortal. He listened to me patiently. We
had already reached the hotel where he was living. A light rain was
starting to fall.

"The emissaries," he said, "who . . ."

And I felt an irresistible melancholy come over me. I stood not
far from the illuminated entrance to his hotel and looked at the rain
which was now falling steadily, while he held on to my sleeve and
carried on talking about emissaries, about counterespionage, about
the death of some grand duke in Moscow, about one of Savinkov's
assistants, about a Lebanese who was pursuing him, Vasiliev, a
swarthy man with a black beard, whom he had seen successively in
Moscow, Orel, Rostov, Sebastopol, Constantinople, Athens, Vienna,
Basel, Geneva, and Paris. Finally I was able to grab his hand, moist

from its constant inner trembling, to press it and then, making my excuses, to leave—and I swore to myself that in future I would steer clear of meeting either him or Fedorchenko and, if possible, forget about their existence.

But two weeks later, one morning when I was still in bed, there was a loud ring at the door. I put on my bathrobe and slippers and went to open the door. I thought that it would be one of the usual scroungers who come asking for money, claiming to be unemployed and in poor health, and go away after being given two francs; I knew that my name and address figured right at the end of the mysterious list of people who never refuse to give money and which was passed around among most of the scroungers. It existed in many variants; certain addresses, principally of rich and generous people, cost a good deal; others were cheaper, and some were simply passed on as a friendly favor. That I occupied one of the places at the very end I learned from a kindly old drunkard who became talkative after the first glass of wine.

"It doesn't cost much to buy you," he said to me with a touch of condescension in his voice, "well, for five francs or so, or if there's been drink taken for just three. My dear man, we know that you've no money yourself. So why do you give to those scum?" I said to him in reply, with a shrug of my shoulders, that the two francs I usually gave would not break the bank and that if a man goes asking for charity then one must assume that he is not doing so for fun. "Fun indeed, you're right there," he said, "but all the same, to give to everyone, whoever they are, that's the wrong way to go about it. You're too young, my dear man, that's what it is." And he left, after taking my two francs.

Still sleepy and bumping into the wall—I had gone to bed, as always, after six o'clock in the morning, and it was now no later than nine—I went over to the door, got a coin ready, opened the door, and saw Suzanne.

"Are you alone?" she asked, without greeting me. "I want to talk to you."

She walked into the room, looked all around it, then sat down in an armchair and lit a cigarette.

"Whose portrait is that?" she asked. "Is she your lover? She's beautiful."

I needed to sleep.

"Have you come to ask me about that portrait?" I said.

"No, no," she replied, and her voice suddenly altered. "I've come to ask your advice. I can't bear it any more."

"That's nothing to do with me," I said. "It doesn't concern me, and besides, I want to get some sleep. Come in the evening."

"No, no," she said, frightened. "You've known me so long, you've got to hear me out."

"I have known you a long time, of course," I said. "And I respect you in particular for your virtue."

"Listen to what I have to say," repeated Suzanne, and for the first time I heard something like a human note in her voice. "You know I was happy."

"Don't bother telling me your life story; I can manage without that."

"Listen, you know I'm just a poor woman with no education, not like that old lunatic, who I'm going to end up killing and who's ruined my happiness."

"If you're bothered by him being educated, there's not a lot you can do about it."

"No, listen, I'll tell you about it." And she began to tell me exactly how everything had happened. I interrupted her several times at those points when she spoke in a tender and slightly trembling voice about her happiness—they were happy, well set up, with their own flat and furniture. I remembered the green marble panther and the pink beauties on the walls. Everything was going perfectly, Suzanne said, nor did they have any complaint about the material side of things, particularly since, unbeknownst to her husband, she worked two evenings a week, but naturally far away from her own district and from those places where people had known her before. Her husband adored her, she adored her husband. "All right, all right," I said. That was what it was like until Vasiliev appeared. He had come to visit one evening, had dinner, and started off on his usual monologue, which continued late into the night. After that he had started coming every day. Initially this had annoyed Suzanne only because it meant that there was an extra person at the table.

"Take one extra client," I said, with a shrug of my shoulders, "and you'll make up the extra expense."

Suzanne understood nothing in his stories, which he inevitably translated into French for her. "Endless murders," she said in despair, "then names I don't know, and all sorts of ideas."

From her story it was evident that the innumerable murders Vasiliev always talked about were not the sole theme of his speeches; he included all manner of judgments and quotations from Nietzsche, whose name Suzanne even remembered; she asked me whether I had heard of a man called "Niche," apparently some German. I nodded. She put up with it all for a long time, and in particular the fact that her husband's attention was now entirely absorbed in Vasiliev and his stories, so that he had completely ceased to think about her, Suzanne. "He doesn't even sleep with me any more," she said. When she finally attempted to talk to him about this, he flew into an extraordinary rage and started to shout that she understood nothing, that for him there were more important things than her love and personal happiness. It was then that she became scared.

This had already been going on for several months and had recently become completely intolerable, ever since—Suzanne grew agitated as she spoke about this, her eyes wide with terror—some Russian general had been kidnapped. "Did you read about this? Why was he kidnapped?" I replied that I did not know. It transpired that after this Fedorchenko and Vasiliev had both bought themselves revolvers—"You understand," said Suzanne, "that of course it was me who paid for the shooters"—hardly went out of the house, and spent the whole time drinking red wine and talking. Sometimes they would both disappear somewhere in the dead of night, and Fedorchenko would return late the next morning, his eyes dulled and his face jaundiced. But the most important part Suzanne was unable to speak of with any kind of coherence. From her words and from the way that she kept turning to one side or the other when talking about this—sitting in my room where there were just the two of us and no one could have heard us—it was obvious that she had been living in a state of inexplicable, animal fear throughout the last few days. Though understanding nothing of the sinister metaphysics of terror and death about which Vasiliev held forth, she had an instinctive sense of imminent catastrophe, and a feeling akin to a deathly weariness never left her.

"It's choking me to death," she said. "I'm going out of my mind."

She sat in the armchair, her lip trembled above her gold tooth, her eyes filled with tears—she wiped the corners of her eyes, opening her mouth and drawing in her lower jaw. I thought about how her existence was now unfolding in this truly unbearable atmosphere, in this philosophy of murder and terror with quotations from Nietzsche and history of terrorist plots; I looked at her smooth, youthful, unwrinkled brow and her eyes full of tears and suddenly felt an unexpected pity for her.

"Maybe it would have been better for you not to have left your café and to have known nothing about either the Russian general or 'Niche' as you call him, though his name isn't pronounced like that. But what do you want me to do now?"

She started asking me to try to exert some influence over Fedorchenko, to tell him that he could not go on living like that, and to explain that she, Suzanne, had no education and could not answer all the questions he was constantly asking her: What are we living for? What is tomorrow? Why do people devote themselves to art? What is music? This last question was the only one she had given some sort of answer to—music is when someone plays something—and after this he had been angry and had not spoken to her for two days and went to have his dinner in a Russian restaurant, where she had also been several times and where no one spoke French. The fact that some people spoke other languages was for Suzanne not so much incomprehensible as unnatural to such a degree that she was wholly unable to accustom herself to this idea; for her it was almost as if the entire thing was no more than a pretense. She quite seriously doubted the possibility that one really could express everything properly in other languages: "Well, what can you say to each other in Russian?" How could anyone be so stupid? It was even more complicated than generals being abducted.

This all took place a few weeks after the disappearance in Paris of a well-known Russian general, who had held a prominent position in the White Army during the Civil War, and who was now the leader of those people, now scattered all around the world, who constituted the miscellaneous remnants of that army. The majority of them earned their living through hard physical labor; they had all formed a union together, the head of which was the general who had disappeared. The newspapers presented the most improbable and contradictory accounts of how the abduction had actually occurred; the left-wing press expounded a version according to which the general had been snatched and taken away by members of a right-wing terrorist organization; the right-wing press implicated the communists; one semipornographic magazine even suggested that the unexpected disappearance could be put down to causes of a sentimental kind; the police published highly significant accounts of everything, and from their large quantity and their diversity it was not difficult to arrive at the conclusion that they would be unsuccessful in their attempts to locate the general's abductors. As usually happens, in connection with this sensational story there followed a mass of exposures and accusations, denunciations and letters to the editor began to appear, various people expounded their personal theories about the general on the pages of newspapers and magazines, some took advantage of the unexpected possibility of expressing themselves in print by incorporating autobiographical confessions, often of a memoiristic character, so that it was entirely impossible to make sense of any of it.

According to what Suzanne told me, Vasiliev was unusually fascinated by everything to do with the general's disappearance; he would spend hours sitting at the window of her flat, writing down the numbers of passing cars in a tiny notebook; he read a huge number of newspapers, where articles about the general were circled in red pencil, while in the margins and in the text itself there were question marks and exclamation points; after each article the word *lies* had been inserted, and the name of each author was prefaced by two or three handwritten stars. Finally, one evening he had told Suzanne, after shutting the door and coming right up close to her, that he knew the secret of the general's disappearance but that this secret would go to the grave with him and that if Suzanne was careless enough to blurt this out to anyone, then he, Vasiliev, could not vouch for her safety.

"But we live in a republic after all," Suzanne had said, because she had often heard this phrase being used when people were talking about politics. But Vasiliev had replied that he was serious and had offered the example of the general. "He also thought he lived in a republic."

Terrified, she had related this to her husband, and he confirmed that this was indeed true and that he accepted it all.

The general who had disappeared and everything associated with him—the suspicions, the denunciations, the newspaper articles, the police inquiry, and the ever-clearer presence of someone's unseen death, here, among this furniture, beside the marble panther and naked beauties—all this bordered on the beginning of a common madness, and the ghost of the general began to pursue Suzanne.

"Murders, murders, murders, that's all I hear, do you understand?" she kept saying. And at the same time she was unable to and did not want to go away from there, give up her business, and leave her husband. "What should I do, what should I do?" she kept repeating.

"Say you're ill and go away to the country for a month."

"I can't leave the business."

"Then don't ask me questions, and don't ask me what to do."

She carried on sitting in my armchair and cracked her fingers.

"If you go away," I said, "then you've a chance of living on into old age and dying of the arteriosclerosis you're susceptible to."

"Don't talk to me about dying!" she shrieked. Her shriek turned into a howl, and I forced her mouth shut. She sank her teeth into her own hand, quickly slid off the armchair—as she did so her skirt rode up almost to her waist—and began to roll around on the floor, shrieking all the time; and her shrieks were interrupted by sniveling. I lifted her up and lay her on the sofa; she lost consciousness; I had to splash a whole glass of cold water over her face. Then she came to and looked at me with wild eyes.

"Will you forgive me?" she asked in a timid voice. "I'll try to follow your advice. But before that are you able to come to see us and talk to my husband?"

I categorically refused. I felt something close to an acute and incomprehensible curiosity about this whole absurd and tragic misunderstanding, but at the same time as this curiosity welled up inside me there was an equally incomprehensible and equally unfounded revulsion, as if I must enter a room in which the air had been poisoned by the unbearable stench of decay. Finally Suzanne left, saying that she would try to go to the country but that she did not know if she would manage to.

"Don't count on my help," I told her as she left.

But for some time I was unable to get rid of her. She kept coming to me at the most unexpected hours and stayed in my room for a long time, sometimes not even speaking, simply so as to spend some time with a normal person. I could never get her to explain why she had chosen me in particular. One day she came and related to me a long conversation she had had with Vasiliev. He had told her that he had already learned many weeks ago that he was being followed. He made reference to newspaper articles that left no room for any doubt and to several signs which only his acute powers of observation could have noticed: the behavior of the policeman on the street corner, the inexplicable daily absences of the *boulangère* who was in constant telephone contact with certain individuals whom he could not name, and so on. He added that the organization involved was a very powerful one with considerable financial resources that had all this time been feeling out his presence, as large numbers of searchlights would feel out a hidden enemy position. In his words, this secret organization spared neither effort nor gold—he knew for a fact that its agents were paid specifically in gold for their work—and it had now finally succeeded in surrounding him, it would seem, on all sides. There was one thing, however, that these people did not know: to wit, that he, Vasiliev, was aware of their every step.

"You understand," he said to Suzanne, who listened to his calm ravings in anguish and alarm, "they have everything: motorcars, detectives, innumerable agents, guaranteed safety for which the police have been bribed, all the money they need, radios, the tele-graph, all the limitless resources a modern state organization could enjoy. I have nothing: I'm a penniless Russian émigré. But I have something that they won't have counted on and which they cannot resist: my intuition and the implacable logic of my deductions."

Suzanne had an excellent memory and was able to repeat what Vasiliev had said to her almost verbatim, and it was strange to hear her talk of the implacable logic of his deductions and intuition. She closed her eyes as she uttered these words, like a person putting all her effort into abstract thought. This conversation took place at four o'clock in the afternoon; the sun was shining through the window, and on Suzanne's pale face, beneath her eyes, one could see the small, blackish fans of her eyelashes.

"Don't you find all of this truly absurd?" I said, more think-ing aloud than addressing Suzanne. "What need could there be for three people—one an old alcoholic, a second whom nature had not intended for thinking, and you, a poor girl who walked the streets—for all of you now to be destroyed by the flawless memory and madness of Vasiliev and the ghost of Nietzsche, whom you call Niche?"

Vasiliev had told Suzanne that the organization that was pur-suing him had calculated even the remotest possibilities, the most unlikely contingencies, and they had decided that Vasiliev could not get away from them. But, while giving them credit for their skill, he was still entitled to consider himself superior to them since, in his words, he possessed that instantaneous imaginative flexibil-ity which can topple the very best calculations and which carries within it the beginnings, as he put it, of a sort of fateful genius. In his reasoning there was nevertheless a certain ominous conviction, and if one were to suppose that this mythical organization, which occupied the last available space in this mind overloaded with murders, had actually existed, then—as the facts were to prove—it really would have been unable to lay a hand on him. Late in the evening on that same day when he had spoken to Suzanne about his pursuers' miscalculation, he went out of the building where Fedorchenko lived, turned the corner, and disappeared. It was a foggy March night. Suzanne saw Vasiliev walk away and noticed to her horror that he transferred from the back pocket of his trousers into the side pocket of his jacket his large revolver, which lately he had never been without. As on every other evening, he was prepared for anything. He walked along with his usual steady gait which, in Suzanne's words, recalled the movements of a robot, smoking a cigar, with his left hand thrust into the pocket of his coat, and his right in the side pocket of his jacket where his gun lay. That was how Suzanne saw him for the last time.

The following evening he did not show up either at Fedorchenko's or his own place. Another day went by, and there was still no sign of him. I carefully read the news items in the papers, hoping to find something about Vasiliev, but over the course of those two days there occurred nothing unusual except for the fact that the night before a French businessman named Dubois, who was returning to his home in Auteuil after a dinner with friends, was fatally wounded by three revolver shots on one of the bridges over the Seine; he died several hours later in a hospital, leaving a wife and two children. The murderer managed to get away, but the police did happen upon his trail, as was officially announced in the papers. I did not see how this chance murder could be significant. The only thing that seemed suspicious to me was that there had been no robbery and that the police investigation had been unable to discover any motive for the crime, in spite of the large number of interrogations of everyone or almost everyone who had known the victim. The dead businessman had been a family man, evidently of a mild character; he had had no love intrigues, nor political views, nor even any enemies. In short, his murder seemed beyond comprehension. However, as was demonstrated more than once in the crime reports, it was sufficient to suppose that, in the first place, the murderer was altogether unknown to the police, that is to say that he was not a professional criminal; second, to note the absence of any obvious visible reason for the murder; and third, to ascertain that close friends and acquaintances of the victim had no personal knowledge of this murderer, in order to arrive at the inevitable conclusion that in these conditions any police investigation was bound to lead to a dead end and would have no, or almost no, chance of finding the criminal. And I was inclined to think that this was one of a multitude of tragedies about which we can discover nothing, save that there was a businessman named Dubois who lived in such-and-such a place and who was no more since he had been killed by an unknown person for unknown reasons. His death held only passing interest for me since it seemed not to be connected with any direct gain or revenge, but with other reasons of some kind, of a more elevated, or less base, or at any rate of a not-quite-ordinary character. But the next day I bought another paper which carried a photograph of the victim, and I sat and looked almost in horror at that face, because then I pretty well knew how it had all come about: the victim was a thick-set man with a large black beard. Suzanne had told me that Vasiliev left at twelve o'clock at night, while the crime had been committed at around two o'clock, that is to say, half an hour after his departure; Suzanne's marble clock was exactly an hour and a half slow. Dubois—his biography had been printed in the newspapers—had never been outside of France. Reflecting on what had befallen him, I kept returning to this absurd and fortuitous coincidence: if he had not worn a beard he would still be alive, since it seemed to me beyond doubt that Vasiliev had mistaken him for his imaginary and constant pursuer, the unfortunate Levantine, that same swarthy man with a beard about whom he had told me the evening when he and I were leaving Fedorchenko's together. But Vasiliev himself had disappeared without trace. It was obvious, however, that he was not afraid of the French police, who scarcely knew of his existence and certainly could not have suspected him of anything. A few days later his fate became known: his body was hauled out of the Seine, and the investigation, having found no signs of any violence on the body, persuaded the authorities it could only have been a suicide. Vasiliev had found a way of outwitting his enemies who were as numerous as they were imaginary; it was indeed—the three revolver shots at the Levantine to begin with, then the leap from the bridge into the icy waters of the Seine—that fateful manifestation of genius that he had spoken about, that final flash of intuition that led him so unerringly from the stories of terrorist plots and arguments about Nietzsche to the bridge over the Seine in Paris on that chilly, foggy night in March.

The day I read the report about Vasiliev's death I was in a hurry to get dressed so as to get out of the house as early as possible, but even so, Suzanne managed to run over to me first. Without greeting me, without asking me about anything, and holding a newspaper in her hands, she shouted, "He's dead! He's dead!" Then, when she had got her breath back, she asked me, "Do you already know?"

"Yes, yes," I said. "Now I'm thinking about what's going to happen next."

"Fédor says that he was murdered, that things can't be left like this. He's beside himself; he hasn't slept for two nights. I implore you, go and talk to him."

"Leave me be," I said. "I've no intention of doing that. I couldn't care less about all that, the whole business. I'm not involved in it. If I take to heart every misfortune I see, there'll be no end to it at all."

"You're the only one who can save me."

"You're exaggerating. There's nothing I can do here."

"I'll do anything you want," said Suzanne. "Anything, do you understand? Do you want money? I'll give you money. Do you want the other? I'll give you that."

"There's only one thing I want," I said, annoyed. "I want you to leave me be. I've had it up to here with your lunatics and generals being kidnapped. It's nothing to do with me. Why are you clinging to me like this?"

She sat down in an armchair. I looked at her; she was paler than usual. She threw her head back and closed her eyes; her arms hung over the sides of the chair.

"I know all about that fainting trick of yours, Suzanne, do you realize that?" I said.

"No, no, it's not that," she mumbled barely audibly. "No, it's something more important."

"What else, then?"

"I think," she whispered and sighed, "that I'm expecting a baby."

It was not without some difficulty that I managed to avoid having to visit Fedorchenko; as before, I advised Suzanne to go away to the country. And when she had finally left, I breathed a sigh of relief and, after waiting a little while, went outside. It was a glorious spring day; there was a trembling coldness in the clear air, and I thought with delight that I could forget about the whole of that unremitting tragedy and remember about other things that were so distant from me and so beautiful, more beautiful the more distant they were, and more distant the more beautiful.

The following day I told Plato the story of Vasiliev. He listened with his usual condescending and unconcerned air, with that "defensive" facial expression of his, which was becoming more and more constant and characteristic the more hopeless his social and financial position became. While for the majority of people who had the misfortune to find themselves in a prolonged impecunious situation their faces acquired an unpleasant familiarity that often turned to obsequiousness, Plato's face followed the completely opposite principle. But he remained just as courteous as before. He was one of the five or six people I had known—over my whole life—with whom I could talk at length and, at all events, the sole Frenchman who did not seem to me in conversation a model of remoteness and detachment. I do not know if this would have been so had I got to know him at the time when he led a comfortable existence. But now, having lived through a multitude of failures and having attained profound misfortune and impoverishment, he had attained the kind of inner flexibility and understanding which can, perhaps, be compared with some kind of special individual giftedness, like the talent of an artist or the gift of a composer. Like the majority of genuine thinking people, his strength lay in making negative rather than positive judgments. As long as it was not his political program which was under discussion, he was inclined to doubt—as he told me many times—the genuine existence of any kind of schemes or constructs which aspired to a certain elegance and completeness, the artificiality of which nearly always seemed to him obvious. And yet as far as politics were concerned, his principles—religion, home and family, the king—were so hopelessly naive that it seemed astonishing that Plato should assert them. He, however, never tried to defend his views on this matter and spoke about it in an apologetic tone, as if he felt himself that he had committed some faux pas. When I told him how Vasiliev had lived and died and expressed my conviction that it was precisely he who was the murderer of the French businessman, Plato shook his head doubtfully.

"Your theory about the path he followed to his death," he said, "possibly has some foundation, that, ultimately, is fairly likely. But as for the murder, then your supposition seems to me more questionable."

"But what about the circumstances, or rather the coincidences . . ."

"I am not asserting categorically that things happened differently," said Plato. "But can one be sure of it? Vasiliev could have gone across a different bridge; it need not necessarily have been a bridge that Vasiliev jumped off into the water; and judging by the way you have described him, he was a somewhat sluggish person for whom leaping, generally speaking, would be uncharacteristic and slipping or climbing down would be more characteristic."

"You speak about this as if it were a question of a figure in a ballet."

"Yes," Plato replied calmly. "The plastic arts are not the prerogative of the theater or stage. Break down the life of a given subject into a series of consecutive actions; you will see that it is characterized by one set of dance figures, rather than another. You, for example, drag your feet when you walk—this happens because you are thinking as you walk along. Your movements will become lighter only when you run or do gymnastics. If you were to try to engage in reflection at those moments, you would be a very poor sportsman. It is easier for me to imagine Vasiliev slowly lowering himself down the bank and getting into the water."

"Who killed Dubois, then?"

"What do we know of Dubois' life?" asked Plato, with a shrug of his shoulders. "Nothing, apart from the most ordinary of facts in their most ordinary sequence. He could have known people whom no one had suspected; there could have been some drama no one will ever know about; and finally—though this seems the least likely, but it is not absolutely inadmissible—another lunatic could have walked across the bridge that night. Being a nighttime taxi driver, you ought to know that there are an extraordinary number of them in Paris."

What particularly struck me was the complete absurdity of this tragedy, of which Suzanne was the chief victim, but here, too, Plato failed to agree with me. In his opinion, the simple fact that Suzanne was a prostitute allowed for a wide range of the most varied and tragic suppositions about her fate.

"At the point of departure we can already observe an anomaly," he said. "Why do you expect the rest to follow naturally?"

"Yes, of course. But all the same—Suzanne, the Russian general's disappearance, and Nietzsche? What could be more absurd?"

"If we were not the daily witnesses of the most illogical and unexpected combinations of things, life would be reduced to algebra. Nietzsche?" he said suddenly, as if putting a question to himself. "He was a poor philosopher, of course, and as a person he was primitive to the point of naivety. But you are right about one thing: he was less primitive than Suzanne."

"What about Fedorchenko and his question about why we live and what tomorrow is?"

"These are signs of the death pangs of the soul," said Plato. "A glass of white wine, please. Yes, the same kind of signs as weakening activity of the heart or a sharp drop in temperature."

Just then someone touched me on the shoulder. I turned around and saw a man I did not know, who asked whether I was the driver of the taxi parked in front of the café.

"I wish you good night, my dear friend," I said to Plato. "We'll return to this question again, if you have no objection."

Plato shook my hand, and I went out with my customer, who was going to the Boulevard Barbès. It turned out that he was a journalist. He had a mocking expression on his face, with tiny, rapid eyes. After he had got in beside me and told me the address, he asked me, once the car had moved off, "Would you mind telling me, if you'll excuse me being so direct, what exactly you were planning to talk about with your friend?"

"About Nietzsche," I said bluntly.

"Have you fallen out with your family?"

"Me? No, I've never had an argument with them."

"Then why are you driving a taxi?"

"I'd prefer to be driving a Rolls-Royce, but, unfortunately, I'm not lucky enough to have that possibility."

"All right, all right, forget it."

And when we were driving up to the place where he had to get out, he suddenly asked, "Are you a foreigner, perhaps?"

"No," I said, "I was born on the Rue de Belleville; my father has a butcher's shop there at number 42; perhaps you know it?"

"No," he replied.

And he walked away, shaking his head. I set off back down the Boulevard Barbès, then drove on farther to the Place de la République. One after another, round streetlamps appeared and then disappeared in the dark air, stars showed in the distant sky, and on the glass in front of me, as in a child's optical instrument, the lights of cars flickered and gleamed, now drawing closer, now heading away, and the dancing lines of light they made were reflected against the transparent, blue-black background. The more time passed, the more effort I had to make to master myself so as to notice, if only for a moment, the beauty of this nocturnal conjunction of luminous lines, or the straight vista of a boulevard, or, finally, sharply lit up by car headlights and then vanishing into the darkness, the dark green branches and leaves of the Bois de Boulogne at the turning of a black avenue. Paris was slowly fading before my eyes; it was similar to how things would be if I had started gradually to go blind, and the quantity of things I could see began to reduce little by little, right up to the moment when complete darkness overcame me. This blindness, however, would suddenly disappear on my free days when I was not working and would walk around Paris on foot; then the city seemed different to me, and those same street corners and slanted ends of buildings I knew by heart appeared before me in a different guise, in which there was an unfamiliar stone attractiveness. Even when I took a taxi myself and sat inside the car and not at the wheel, everything seemed different to me, and it took me a long time to get used to the thought that one aspect of Paris or another ultimately depended on these kinds of insignificant shifts, and that this whole urban world could be transformed simply because of some insignificant changes of position, no greater than a yard and a half in length or an inch in height.

This thought brought after it its logical and irrefutable continuation: the existence of a gigantic quantity of people and the improbable fact that this entire artificial and unjust system of persecution, slavery, and poverty, the rickshaws, the laborers on rice plantations, the miners in mercury and sulfur pits, the millions of slaves, and the tens of millions of workers could yet continue in relative calm for many years, and the immense factories and luxurious city quarters had not been blown up into the air; this entire fragile and accidental, and yet, in its accidental equilibrium, this unchanging order was, in the final analysis, also founded on the subconscious utilization of that same law of infinite spatial shifts of an inch at a time, which determined the entire lives of immense masses of people. But I tried not to dwell on this; it seemed to me beyond comprehension to the same extent as the concept of infinity did, long ago, in my secondary school years. And not infrequently I would, quite suddenly, in the space of a single day, feel the need to forget everything I had had occasion to see, experience, and know so that this painful vision of the world would disappear and be replaced by some radiant and harmonious idea, something like a complex and elegant symphony of happy humanity, or, as a last resort, that naive plan that so many people believed in—among them many intelligent people in their own right—that idyllic and pathetic construct: hopeless socialism.

Meeting as I did the most widely different people, I would frequently envy them their naive convictions; the majority of them
had fixed views on everything: politics, the role of culture, art. I
was astounded by the speeches of professional political orators, who
were more often than not simple and ignorant people who believed
just as firmly in their programs as my elderly professor did in the
nonexistent laws of the pseudoscience that he taught for his whole
life. They all reminded me of a Frenchman of a certain age, a driver
I used to see almost every night at the taxi stand. He had begun his
career a very long time ago, when there were extremely few cars—
at that time he had driven a horse. He had never learned to drive
a car properly as a result, and he never would exceed his constant
speed of twenty miles per hour. In spite of the difficult life he had
led, he had never lost his love of reading and philosophizing, and
in his reckoning all questions could be resolved extraordinarily
simply. He was troubled by the way that people were so wicked and
lived in constant conflict with one another; all of this happened,
in his opinion, because the earth's surface was not exploited in a
rational way. "If it were up to me," he used to say, "I would say to
people: do you want to work? Then go to Siberia, go to Argentina,
there's virgin land waiting for you there, enough for everyone."
What could be simpler? Any other notions—nationality, language,
heredity, the correlation between industry and agriculture—he
considered to be things of secondary importance. "That's all been
thought up by capitalists to oppress us," he would say to me. "You
don't understand it because you're young; but when you've been
driving for thirty-eight years like me, then it'll all be clear to you."
In his words, it turned out that all this uncomplicated political wis-
dom he had attained could be explained by that very same lengthy
horse and car driving experience of his, and if one were to suppose
that every statesman be made to undergo the same experience,
then one had to presume that everything would be a lot better than

it was now. Overall, in his conception what emerged was a hazy and beautiful agricultural republic governed primarily by elderly people, and preferably drivers. Then changes would also be made to both laws on and the correlation between corporations, so that professional rag pickers would not hate him with such vehement hatred because he, who was not a member of their syndicate, could never deny himself the pleasure—on his way home in the early morning, after his night's work—of carefully going through those rubbish bins, which, for some reason or other, caught his attention. "You see how unfairly the state is organized," he would say, "how unequally privileges are distributed. He is entitled to dig around in rubbish bins because he is a professional rag picker, but I cannot because I am a driver. That's not good, is it? If I were in the government, I would allow all professions to do this without any exception."

And in the same way, or almost the same way, that in his conception all the most complex human problems were essentially reduced to the satisfaction of his own private desires—he was an amateur vegetable gardener, an amateur rag picker, even an amateur architect because he had built his own house himself out of old boxes, half bricks, bits of wood, and pieces of iron and tin—and he would say, "You see, you shouldn't look down your nose on garbage; I built my house out of it." And his dwelling really was slowly being built and taking shape, growing out of rubbish bins, and if they had not existed, then there would have been no house, either; in this same way, without doubt, the majority of theoreticians of these problems also constructed their imaginary future world, just like him, out of the same haphazard and incomplete material.

Of all the days of the week, the most unpleasant and the most lucrative day was Saturday. In the winter I would spend whole nights in taxi queues beside brightly lit entrances, where balls were taking place. Along with the drivers other people congregated who also sought to make a living there but in a somewhat different way: malodorous, unshaven beggars who opened the car doors for people, a flower seller with three or four bunches of violets that she attempted to sell to men as they came out with their ladies, a man in worker's clothes who would purposefully offer to help start up a cold engine. At Russian balls, besides these, several Russian scroungers, whom we all knew, would invariably show up; a red-bearded man stood out from the others and was always surly when he started work. But once he had received a few francs and drunk a few glasses of wine in the nearest café, his mood would improve; he would waggle his head about, dance around in the frost, and say in a loud voice, "Hey, Moscow's come to Paris!" and would charge up to people coming out of the ball almost shouting, "Spare a franc, your honor, for a former Petersburg university student, I swear!"

And when I had occasion several times to emerge myself from these same brightly lit entrances late at night and looked at the cars parked there and recognized drivers whom I had worked with yesterday and would work with again tomorrow, I felt uneasy, as if I had committed a breach of professional etiquette and taken up a place that I should not have taken.

More and more often, the longer I carried on working as a driver, I came to notice how much each category of people constituted a closed, permanently fixed world. The most telling examples of this were the Parisian destitute and the pimps. I was never fully able to get used to the mixed feelings of curiosity, revulsion, and sympathy which these people aroused in me. There was of course something common to them both, in spite of the fact that the destitute retained

the appearance of medieval vagrants while the pimps dressed most
fastidiously. The clothes the destitute wore were distinguished first
and foremost by their astonishing shapelessness—it was hard to
discern where an overcoat ended and a jacket began and what color
the material which had now turned into shiny rags had once been.
They, however, had their own ideas about how to dress; I am not
even sure that they did not—in certain cases—follow their own
peculiar fashions, which was such an obvious trait in the pimps.
I saw an old beggar who was reduced to tears in his distress at
having lost his hat and who complained to me: "It was a perfectly
black hat, a beautiful hat! What am I to do now?" And it seemed
that he was suffering precisely because some kind of etiquette was
no longer being observed, that he was not correctly dressed and
that he felt more or less like a man wearing a jacket when he should
be in evening wear.

There were various kinds of people among them; in most cases
they were gloomy, and I rarely saw tramps laughing or smiling. But
their gloominess certainly did not result from them understanding just how terrible their situation was. They did not suffer in
the least from this; they had no capacity for making comparative
judgments; the word *world*, if it occurred at all in their thoughts,
would have contained nothing which lay outside the limits of their
own existence. Their gloominess was characteristic of them in the
same way that viciousness is characteristic of certain animals, or
rapidity of movement characteristic of certain rodents. But in just
the same way that albinos occur in zoology, there were some cheerful individuals among them.

One night in winter I was parked on the Place du Trocadéro;
it was very quiet, and suddenly, from the direction of the Avenue
Kléber, I heard a loud, hoarse voice singing the famous aria from
Faust. It turned out to be an old tramp; he came over to my car and
asked me for a cigarette. I asked him how he came to know opera

tunes and why he sang them. He explained that he had selected that particular aria because, in his opinion, it impressed the police. "When they hear you singing it, they think straight away—that's no ordinary person if he knows opera." He even gave me a brief account of his philosophy: "You shouldn't hold anything close to your heart; don't give a damn about anything, then everything else will take care of itself." When I asked him how long he had been a tramp for, he told me thirty years. "And you're not dead yet?" No, he had never been ill, had never even had a cold, even though he usually spent the nights on building sites or on the steps of the Metro; he slept on boards or on the stone floor summer and winter and had long since forgotten what a bed was like. He had worked at one time in a plush Parisian hotel bottling wine in the cellar, but then had taken to drink and become a tramp, and now, in his declining years, he found this to be much better.

I met carefree tramps, but I also knew others who saved up their money. I saw one stinking old man muttering gloomily at the counter of a café that he had no money to pay and that the waiter was cheating him—because he was unwilling to change a thousand-franc note; he carried his capital, fourteen thousand francs, around with him. I do not know which was the greater accident in his life—that he was a tramp or that he was not a banker. He was dressed in the same way as all other tramps, like them fed on rubbish he collected at Les Halles, and like them he slept on the steps of the Metro. But I think that in him the corporation of money lenders or shareholders lost a valuable member of their society.

Many of them did not even ask for charity; others held out their hands, complaining that they had nothing to feed their sick wife or numerous children with. One such—for some reason his nickname was Turbigo—would show everyone a photograph of an infant that he had cut out of a newspaper and shout, "Look, messieurs, that's my latest newborn; his mother can't buy milk for him. Look, messieurs, what a lovely little thing he is! Milk for the child, messieurs!" He took this photograph from the evening paper, from the section titled BEAUTIFUL BABY COMPETITION.

Turbigo was more than sixty years old and, of course, had never been married. Generally speaking, the most ordinary concepts were inapplicable to tramps: marriage, flats, work, political views. It was always difficult to find out where exactly they had come from, from what background, from which town, and what predetermined their infinitely sad fate. It was as if they had never existed any differently, and they had simply appeared on the Earth in order to drag themselves slowly along the nocturnal streets of Paris on trembling feet on that long journey that led them inevitably to a prison hospital or an anatomy theater. Why and for whom were these thousands of cloacal existences necessary? Plato once told me that tramps were useful as "dialectical material," like biblical quotations, and were a lesson for human vanity: they could be the same as we are, we could be the same as they are, and for this, one insignificant, accidental detail, or "shade of social pigmentation," was all that was needed. But clearly on this subject he was not capable of being impartial.

And nevertheless, in spite of the tragic, animal nonexistence the tramps followed, they seemed to me worthy citizens of the universe in comparison with the pimps. Tramps, at any rate, merited at least theoretical sympathy, and they did not have in themselves the sort of moral syphilis that characterized the pimps. I was never able to get used to what I saw every night, to those poor women, so peculiarly dressed, and to their companions, who waited for them in cafés and discussed among themselves the following day's racing program and the relative merits of one horse or another. They were all fashionably dressed, with a particular chic, both pathetic and loutish at the same time. I listened to their conversations, both with one another and with those women. They all shared bourgeois ambitions—to have their own setup, to go away for the summer—and they inhabited their own special, leprous world, which no one could penetrate except them. A few of them, those more successful than the others, who did not disappear forever either in prison or in some dark settling of scores, grew rich and became respectable people. Then they would open, though not in their own name, a brothel or cabaret. But this happened extraordinarily rarely. What actually brought about their ruin was the desire to get rich; not satisfied with the earnings the women provided for them, they were susceptible to another type of activity, to thefts and burglaries, and it was precisely on this route that danger lay in wait for them. So long as they restricted themselves to "working" as pimps, they remained untouched. But when they encroached in such an illicit manner upon the sacred right of property, they came up against police inspectors, the state magistrature, and that whole gigantic, defensive apparatus that protected the material well-being, or the illusion of material well-being, of its citizens.

"Let's not delve too deeply into this question," Plato said to me, still in that same conversation. "They strive to grow rich; that is their right—that is even their civic duty. But the choice of means they have for the realization of this is very limited. When all is said and done, you can hardly ask them to write symphonies or take up sculpture. And they are not ministers, as you know."

He drank down a mouthful of wine and added, "That is, for the moment they are not ministers, though we may yet reach that stage, since the world has gone completely mad, having rejected the sole possibility of salvation."

"What exactly, dear friend?"

"King, family, and country," said Plato.

"Ah, yes, of course," said I. "I almost forgot about that."

With almost the same degree of regularity with which I went to the café opposite the station, every night I would stop at one of the taxi stands in Passy. I went there for the first time when I was attracted by a ferocious argument between two drivers; they were waving their arms around, shouting and generally in such a state of agitation that a fistfight seemed inevitable. I stopped my car and, when I approached them, could already hear from some distance away, "If you would permit me . . ."

"I cannot permit you; Russian legal reform is . . ."

I went closer and found myself presiding over a lengthy discussion; fortunately there were no customers, and I learned much that was interesting. The argument was not notable for its coherence: after legal reform came the Decembrists, after the Decembrists came opinions about the Teutonic order, after the Teutonic order came the Slavophiles and Russian historiosophy, and then Attila—his role, his cultural level—and then, finally, contemporary English literature, at which point the dialogue was cut short since some customers had arrived, and the driver who had spoken in defense of legal reform drove them off, for sixteen francs, from Passy to the Porte d'Orléans. Subsequently I got to know him better, as I did the people he usually conversed with at that taxi stand. I was genuinely sorry for this man. In Russia he had been preparing to take up a professorial position; during the war he had worked in the foreign ministry, since he knew several foreign languages; and he had spent his whole life, before he had left to go abroad, studying. He had a splendid memory and exceptional, almost encyclopedic, knowledge. But he had grown so used to operating with concepts of a different order than those which he now had to deal with that he was never able to engage in a meaningful way in the life he now led and was unable to master many simple peculiarities of the taxi-driving profession. He was so accustomed to these concepts—categorical imperatives, ethics and culture, the order of diplomatic relations, the hierarchy of values, social structure, genesis, synthesis, the evolution of legal norms— that everything which lay outside these questions barely existed for him, and, at any rate, had no significance at all. He drove his car, like his other comrades in misfortune, Russian intellectuals, and this work remained completely alien to him, work which he essentially failed to understand and in which he participated purely mechanically. After long conversations with him I noticed that he possessed a failing that is characteristic of the majority of people on whom has been bestowed an excessively good memory: the volume of his knowledge outweighed him; he found it difficult to make logical or historical constructions since he was dealing with an enormous quantity of factual information, often equally valid and at the same time contradictory. Even so he tried to tackle this, and every opinion he put forward represented a kind of intellectual tour de force since it had had to overcome the initial opposition of a great number of contradictions and mutually exclusive positions.

If this had happened during the early years of my time in France, it would probably have seemed astonishing to me that people like him could find nothing better than the taxi driver's profession. But my acquaintance with this man was preceded by several years of my living in Paris—doing factory work, office work, years spent studying in college—and at this stage I was not astonished by this and considered it completely natural. First of all, he was a foreigner; second, it was impossible to extract any commercial gain from his wealth of culture; third, I had known very well for a long time that cultural values specifically, so long as it was not possible to exploit them immediately, had no significance whatsoever. This was what led to the involuntary and unjust attitude toward France that I observed in the majority of such people; at best, it amounted to scorn and mockery. It seemed to me completely understandable; to a significant degree it could be explained by the fact that these people did not make a distinction between the country as a whole, which they did not know, and the repulsive surface of nocturnal Paris, which they knew only too well. In addition to that, their impartiality of judgment was also impaired by the fact that they were taxi drivers—no doubt, after a year or two of this work they had seen as much human vileness as would have been sufficient for ten lifetimes. This was, perhaps, the most wretched and hopeless aspect of their profession. Some of them, however, found sufficient strength in themselves to be able to resist the influence of their surroundings and of the present conditions of their existence; they devoted themselves to all manner of abstract subjects or historical researches and gradually grew accustomed to this abnormal life in which there was a significant element of selfless and, quite possibly, futile heroism. But these were a tiny minority, one in every hundred; the remainder took to drink or became professional taxi drivers. The taxi stand in Passy that I had happened upon, my interest having been aroused by the threatening gestures of the men involved in an argument, consisted almost exclusively of drivers of this unusual kind; and, listening to their conversations, I learned a great deal of things which I had not so far managed to read or hear about.

"We know," said one of them to me, the very one who had been arguing about judicial reform, "that the world in which we live continues to exist only in our imagination. Our individual lives are over; and so, as we drag out our final years, we do not want to fall into that condition in which contemporary Europe finds itself. This Europe, in its intellectual manifestations, do you know what it reminds me of? The death agony of Maupassant, when he ate his own feces. That is where the meaning of contemporary Europe is to be found. It is not us who are responsible for this. But let us not be reproached for our lack of contemporary interests; we prefer to preserve our archaic stance and turn ourselves into living hieroglyphs."

He went on to talk about the succession of cultures. I listened to him and looked at his very typical face, a broad Russian face covered with two days' growth of stubble, and at his neck, already covered with wrinkles. Hardly listening to what he was saying, I imagined him at a large writing desk in an office of half-official, half-academic appearance in which he might be conducting negotiations over some details of an agreement or the latest reform. I could imagine this so clearly that when I brought myself back under control and saw how everything was in reality, it suddenly seemed outrageous to me that he was dressed in a shabby jacket with shiny patches, that he was sitting at the wheel of a car that had long ago reached the kind of ramshackle state of a lousily built house; the night, the quiet, the tall buildings of a rich district, and behind the closed shutters—the peaceful sleep of the people who inhabited them and who belonged to that same "ignorant bourgeoisie," for whom this penniless man felt such heartfelt contempt.

Meanwhile, he continued to give me a lecture on contemporary Europe, on the reasons for Russia's military defeats in the nineteenth century, and on totalitarian systems, about which, among other things, he said, "We have inherited a particular succession of cultures; you know yourself what I mean. And now it is proposed to us, after the sixth century B.C., after Christianity, the Renaissance, German philosophy, and the nineteenth century, it is proposed to us that we should let go of all of this, that we should become radically stupid, forget everything we know, and descend to the level of semiliterate apprentices. On the other hand, of course, postwar Europe amounts to such a loathsome spectacle . . ."

At this point a drunken, unemployed man approached us and started trying to persuade my colleague to drive him for five francs somewhere in the remote suburbs. He moaned on for a long time, complaining of his difficult life, said that he had been penniless for over four years since he was ill and unfit for work; he said that his wife was also ill and that they had six young children. The commentator on judicial reform began explaining to him in polite French that, first of all, he could not take him for five francs, and second, that if he really was ill, he should not be having children. As evidence in support of his words he cited completely irrefutable arguments and was on the point of launching into a general discussion of Malthusianism, but I interrupted him and said in Russian that he was wasting his time. The unemployed man looked at me in drunken curiosity.

"Listen," I said, "first of all, there's a ninety percent chance that he is lying. Then, even if everything he says is true, you're not going to prove anything to him here; it's just as senseless as advising him to go and read Aristotle." After that I advised the unemployed man to "get the hell out of there."

My colleague shook his head and said, "How can you, an educated man, speak like that?"

I shrugged my shoulders and replied to him, in justification, that it was best, in my view, to speak to everyone in their own language, otherwise they would not understand you. "Remember the story about Hamlet," I said to him. He did not know it; then I told him how the commander of some regiment or other, having decided to further the development of his charges, booked a visit from a decent troupe of actors, who then performed Shakespeare's famous play before the regiment. The soldiers liked the play enormously: there was laughter in the hall from start to finish.

"What vicious nonsense!" he said. "What unfair slander!"

That same night, an hour after this conversation, I saw Plato, who seemed to me to be particularly morose. In response to my question about this he said that, for a very long time, even in his youth, he had been struck by *Dr. Jekyll and Mr. Hyde,* and that as time had gone by he had started to forget about the doctor, and soon, one must suppose, the time would come when Mr. Hyde alone would remain in him. It was these reflections which had upset him. To try to console him I remarked that he was not, so far as I could tell, aggressively negative and that, from a social perspective, he was entirely harmless.

"I cannot entirely share your conviction," replied Plato. "You know that in all probability I will eventually go mad, and who can be sure that my madness will take a benign form? I could set fire to a house or murder someone, although at the present moment, for instance, I would suggest that this type of urge is devoid of both interest and allure in equal measure."

After returning home and getting several hours of the deepest sleep, I woke up the next day, smoked a cigarette in bed, got up as soon as I finished, and began to do my gymnastic exercises, overcoming the most powerful urge to remain in bed for a few more minutes. I knew that after these demanding exercises, which wrenched my joints, after half an hour's worth of tensing my muscles, and a cold shower to wash the sweat from my body, I knew that after all of this I would be in the type of state where there would no longer be space for my painful and fruitless introspection, and I would go either to the swimming pool or to a cinema matinee, or I would take down a book from my shelf and settle down to read it and become, for a few hours, the obedient companion of long-familiar heroes. But the days when I nevertheless remained in bed and did not get up straight away were the most depressing days of my life because I could not stop sensing the presence of that nocturnal world in which my work took place, and I could not stop thinking about it; as the years passed I found it harder and harder to separate myself from it and to effect the transition back to that other life which, in spite of everything, I daily attempted to create for myself. Over the many years of my nomadic existence before Paris I had grown used to everything often changing: living conditions, cities, and countries. By the end I had begun to think that in this essentially mechanical but constant displacement there was some kind of private meaning and that I would stop this journey myself when I began to feel fatigue or suddenly saw that, at that period of time, there was nothing more beautiful than where I was living now. And then it all stopped in Paris in spite of and against my will. I could do nothing about it; it was a time of constant failure in everything I undertook, as it was in my inner life. What improbable concatenation of circumstances—winter, Russia, the immense red sun over the snow, the Caucasus, the Bosporus, Dickens, Hauptmann, Edgar Allen Poe, Ophelia, the Bronze Horseman, Lady Hamilton, the three-inch cannon through whose panoramic sight there had passed so many city walls and groves of trees where enemy batteries stood, and, finally, the horrible mishmash of people's faces, that regiment that bore down on our armored train in an insane cavalry attack, the mishmash of these faces I can still see in front of me all these years later, Shakespeare, the Grand Inquisitor, the death of Prince Andrei, Budapest and the bridges over the Danube, Vienna, Sebastopol, Nice, fires in Galata, gunshots, seas, cities and time rushing soundlessly on, all that irretrievable and silent movement I sensed for the last time on that occasion in a boulevard café, to the music of a chance ensemble, gazing at the uniquely beautiful and at that moment clouded face of Alice—through what improbable concatenation of circumstances had all this multitude of alien and magnificent existences, all of this infinite world in which I had lived so many distant and miraculous lives, led to me ending up here, in Paris, at the wheel of a car, in this infinite network of streets, on the roadways of a hostile city, among prostitutes and drunkards, dimly appearing before me through the vague smell of decay that pursued me everywhere? But the question of my own personal fate was neither the only nor the most important one. More and more often it began to seem to me that this soundless symphony of the world that had accompanied my life—something hard to define but always present and always changing, an immense and complex system of concepts, ideas, images, moving through imagined spaces—that its sound was growing weaker and weaker and any moment must fall silent. I felt, thinking about this, an almost physical anticipation of the tragic and unknown silence that must take the place of this enormous and slowly dying movement. Perhaps, I thought, this idea pursued me because I had so often seen the death agony of people close to me and that they had all died before my very eyes, and, thanks to a cruel anomaly of my memory, their final moments nearly always came to me when I was on my own and had the misfortune not to be occupied with anything. Particularly painful, unbearably painful for me was the memory of the death of a woman who was especially close to me. She was twenty-five years old. After several months of excruciating illness she choked to death after drinking a little water, and her weak lungs were unable to expel this last mouthful from her windpipe. Stripped to the waist, kneeling over her dying body, I gave her the kiss of life, but nothing could help her, and I went away when the doctor, touching me on the shoulder, told me to leave her. I stood by her bed, breathing heavily after my prolonged labors and looking in despair at her monstrous, wide-open eyes, with their pitiless, leaden glaze whose meaning I knew so well. I thought then that I would give everything for the possibility of a miracle, for the possibility of giving to this body a little of my blood, my useless muscles, my breath. Tears flowed down my face and into my mouth; I stood immobile until she had died, then I went into the next room, lay face down on the bed, and instantly fell asleep because over the previous months I had not once slept more than an hour and a half at a stretch. I awoke with the awareness that this had been a betrayal on my part; I kept feeling that I had abandoned her at the most terrible, final moment, while she had always thought that she could rely on me to the end.

And I had never managed to save anyone and keep them on this side of that deathly space, the cold proximity of which I had sensed so many times. And that is why, when I woke up every day, I was eager to leap out of bed at once and begin my gymnastic exercises. But even now, every time I am completely alone and I have no book that can protect me, no woman to whom I can turn, nor, finally, these smooth pieces of paper on which I write, without turning around or moving I can feel the presence beside me—perhaps near the door, perhaps farther away—of the specter of someone else's inescapable death.

I remembered that I had not seen Raldy for a long time, since that same day when she told me that Alice had left her. Looking for her, I drove several times along that part of the Avenue de Wagram, where she used always to be, but for five or six evenings in a row she was not there. I came across her where I really did not expect to, on the Place de Clichy, past four o'clock in the morning. She was standing—in her now completely worn-out man's coat and soft bedroom slippers—by the entrance to a large café, with her heavy head lowered and looking at the pavement. When I stopped the car opposite her, she looked up at me with her tired but, as ever, tender eyes.

"Hello, my dear, you have been sent by Providence," she said. She was, it turned out, waiting for the first Metro in order to return home and could not go into the café, as she had no money.

"Come on, come on," I said. "We'll talk in the café."

She nodded her head. While we were sitting at our table, she almost fainted several times; she put her hand on her heart and stopped eating. Then, after taking some deep breaths, she came round again.

"What's the matter with you?" I asked.

She replied that her heart was tired out, that she had spent forty-eight hours at home since it was hard for her to stand up; only yesterday evening had she been able to go out to work, and, of course, it was in vain. She did not want to return home on foot, although it was really not far, but she was afraid that she might not make it. She had stood there for half the night; she had been very unwell: she had felt as if in a delirium, lights shone hazily before her, and people moved around with uncertain and wavering outlines. When she told me that she had eaten enough, I drove her home and helped her to climb up to the third floor; she went into her room and, without undressing, still in her overcoat, lay down on the bed.

"Go to bed properly: get undressed," I said.

"No, no, it's all right. I'll rest a little. I'll undress later."

Her head lay on a high pillow; in the morning light, against the white linen, her face, both yellow and pale at the same time, stood out sharply.

"You ought to go to the hospital," I said. "Do you want me to arrange it? I'll telephone . . ."

"No, no. I don't want to go to the hospital."

"But it will be better for you there."

She continued to refuse.

"Understand me," she said. "There I'll just be patient number such-and-such, just like everyone else. I'm not the same as everyone else." She lifted her head up from the pillow. "I am Raldy, after all. Yes, the same Raldy, with her diamonds and her admirers and her large fortune. I know that none of that is left now and that I'm just an old woman who is dying because her heart couldn't stand the large amount of drugs I gave it. Do you understand? I'm still Raldy. I'll die alone."

I stayed silent, clenching my fingers together, sitting on the solitary chair in her room, which squeaked and wobbled.

"Don't imagine that I'm quite ready to die yet," she said. "Maybe I'll stay alive this time, too. I've had turns like this before, though I've never felt as bad as this."

I went away, left her some money, and promised to come back in a few days. For the next twenty-four hours I could not stop remembering about her and thought that I would perhaps be too late. But I was wrong. When I came to see her a day later, I found her in bed as before, but her eyes were brighter than the last time, and she complained only of feeling weak. This time I had a proper look at her room, which I had seen for the first time the day that Alice, who had been getting changed in my presence, had stood before me naked, in all the cruel magnificence of her splendid body. Now I could see distinctly the faded photographs of Raldy that had been taken during her heyday: a picture with the arms of the city of Nice overlaid with pearls, another one with a sketch in oil paints depicting the pier casino, with the caption "Carnival of Nice, first prize" and the date—one of the first years of our century. And in a satin frame, unfaded in spite of its long life, was a large photograph: a carriage decorated with white flowers, ornamental white horses, and in the carriage, standing upright, a beautiful, smiling woman with a garland of flowers on her head. It was Raldy as she was then, at the beginning of the twentieth century.

"I keep that," she said. "It must seem amusing to you because that was the best year in my whole existence."

Then she looked me in the face so closely and intensely that I began to feel uncomfortable, and I averted my gaze so that she would not understand what probably showed in my eyes and would be better for her not to understand.

"Are you married?"

"No."

"Do you have a lover?"

"Yes."

"Do you love her very much?"

"Yes."

"And does she love you?"

"No."

I controlled myself, smiled, and said, "Why are you asking me about that? This dialogue is like an exercise from a French language textbook."

"No, I'm asking because there's one thing I want to understand; maybe if I get to know more about you than I do now, it will help me. I even think I'm beginning to understand."

"But what exactly?"

"I had a lot of lovers," she said, without replying, and her eyes filled with tears. "They all owe me so much because, were it not for me, they would never have known what happiness is, or what pleasure is. And now, in what may be the final days of my life, none of them remembers about me; I'm alone, and only you, who came a quarter of a century too late and don't owe me anything, here you are sitting on my bed beside me. If only you had known how beautiful I was and how I could love! But that's something you'll never know."

I listened to her and thought that, in spite of her undoubted intelligence and her vast experience, she could imagine for herself only one possibility of happiness, the very thing that she had sold and dispensed all her long life and to which everything else had been a fortuitous extra. And even now, at the very end of her existence, when the muscles of her body had long since turned slack and lost their suppleness and a fatal chill had begun to slowly rise up toward her heart along a vertical line from the earth— she complained that her legs were frozen, that she could not get warm—even now this youthful burst of her long-ago extinguished, powerfully sensual outlook was reaching her with its final, dying crash. This may or may not have been the right way to understand it, but because Raldy was speaking of it now in particular, it was clear that the possibility of this way of understanding things was beyond dispute; this had been her great and long-lasting power, which had been so vainly, so carelessly squandered by her. And once again I saw that clear spring night when Plato and I had walked back to Montparnasse, and I recalled what he had said then about Raldy.

"Now I know," she said. "I think I know why you are here, and why it's you in particular. It's because you are unhappy in love, my dear. You have more to give than is demanded of you. And what's left over, you bring to me."

She reached out her hand toward her bedside table and took a glass of water. But her fingers were trembling so much that she was unable to raise it up to her mouth. I began to give her water from a spoon and leaned over her. In the damp darkness of her room I could hear only her hoarse breathing and the faint gurgling of the liquid in her throat. It was precisely at that moment that I sensed with unusual clarity that her imminent death was now inevitable. This was obvious before now, of course; but in order for this to cease to be an idea and to become a feeling, for some reason it required these seconds of cruel silence, the wheezing of these lungs, the gurgling of this water.

When I was leaving, telling her that I would come back tomorrow, she asked me to turn on the switch of the small radio set that stood on the chest of drawers. She said that this was her only form of entertainment and explained that the radio had been given to her by a young electrical engineer who had lived for a while in her building. I switched on the radio, and when I was saying good-bye, a high male voice, sounding very quiet and pure, sang an aria from "La forza del destino" in Italian in Raldy's room. It was already getting dark; the outlines of objects were losing their sharp definition; the tiny wavelets of satin from Nice were no longer visible; on the photograph of Raldy in the flower-strewn carriage, the endless combinations of white grew dim and dark, and it was hard to distinguish the curved line of the gigantic garland from the bend of the horse's picturesque neck. Through the high and narrow window, which in its form recalled one of the component parts of a stained-glass church window, I could still see the solid wall, different-colored patches of brickwork, and a piece of sky, bounded by the irregular lines of buildings of different height, and where the immobile blueness grew ever darker and darker.

"Until tomorrow, dearest," said Raldy. "I feel much better now."

One of my friends was a young and very gifted doctor, to whom I made a request to examine Raldy. I told him her story in brief and described her illness as best I could. The next morning, in his car, we set off to visit her. When we had climbed up the stairs and had paused for a second at her door, the sound of music from her radio set reached us. I knocked, and no answer came. Then I opened the door, and we went in.

Raldy lay on the bed in all her horrible, final immobility. Beside her, on the bedside table, lay a glass that had been knocked over and broken and from which the water had spilled out. Her dead, wide-open eyes had rolled backward and gazed up at the ceiling; her lower jaw hung open, after she had breathed her final breath. Melody continued to flow from the radio, and its pointless charm failed to disturb the irreparable silence of the room; the sun shone weakly through the high and narrow churchlike window. I looked for a long time at Raldy, and through the heavy grief I felt, I noticed nevertheless that her white, broad face had hardly changed, and what gave her this extraordinarily terrible and dead appearance was the disappearance of her tender eyes, in place of which, with a stony and dull immobility, the blind whites of her eyes could be seen in their full extent. I covered her face with the sheet, and we went out, trying not to make a noise, as people always walk in the room of a person who has died. Once we were downstairs, the doctor went in to the concierge and told her that Raldy had died.

"That's impossible!" the concierge replied and, throwing on a coat, ran off somewhere; the water in a pan that stood on the stove in the kitchen next to her room boiled and spilled over and finally extinguished the flame with a hiss.

The doctor drove me home; we stayed silent the whole way. Then I went up to my room. The wooden shutter was partly lowered; it was only half light in the room. I sat down in an armchair, lit a cigarette, and suddenly the melody that had sounded in the dead Raldy's room and flowed through the damp air beside her corpse came to me again. In it I could hear the sounds of water and the cries of birds; I saw a retreating shadow moving after the sun, the glittering dew on the green grass, and a light mist above the trees—that whole morning world she had lacked the final reserves of air in her lungs to live to see. It was Grieg's "Morning."

A few days later, in the evening paper I bought, a headline leaped out at me: JEANNE RALDY, WHO WAS IN HER TIME ONE OF THE QUEENS OF PARIS, WAS FOUND DEAD YESTERDAY IN A CHEAP HOTEL ROOM.

This was inaccurate: the building she was living in was not a hotel. But this was of no significance. The article told the story of her life; in it I read about everything she had spoken of to me, even Dédé the roofer featured in it. It described the beginning of her career, her parties in Ville d'Avray, and then once again all those princes, senators, bankers, then the *maison de passe* she had owned, then her arrest on suspicion of dealing in narcotics—she had never told me about that, not, I do not think, because she considered it necessary to conceal this but because she did not grant it any significance—then her gradual and slow fading away, the sidewalks of the Avenue de Wagram, that same Avenue de Wagram along which she had once driven in her own carriage, and, finally, the no-less classical, traditionally effective death in poverty: in short, a ready and grateful subject for a cheap novel. And, reading the article, I thought that Raldy deserved better. Her misfortune consisted in her having fallen in with a set of exhausted and ignorant debauchees, among whom every one strove to live like the hero of a fashionable book, and in the mediocrity of this cheap aesthetic and this set she had no other choice to make. And besides, of course, as Plato said, there had always existed within her that destructive inclination toward unhappiness, that constant awareness of being doomed that made up her incomparable, tragic allure. And

I remembered her words: "But I'm not the same as everyone else. I'm still Raldy. And I will die alone."

She did die alone early one summer morning or, perhaps, during a light and limpid night in the hours before dawn. And along with her a whole world disappeared which she had created: suicide attempts, duels without a deadly outcome, a few bad poems, the see-through blue nightshirt in which she lay as Prince Nerbatov wept kneeling before her bed, the unfaded satin from the carnival of Nice, like the *peau de chagrin,* as yet untouched by any wish, and then perhaps the only thing she had managed to achieve in her life—that distant sense of pity, slowly growing weaker like fading music and familiar to everyone who had felt the sad and unforgettable quality of intimacy with her.

One of the reasons for my constant and pointless irritation was the fact that, being compelled to live in the way that I did, I could not allow myself the luxury of giving myself up to a particular set of feelings, I could not read as much as I wanted to, and I could not devote the necessary amount of time to whatever subject interested me at any given moment. With the aim of managing to accomplish what seemed to me most essential, I gained time by sleeping less, and over the course of many years I slept for five hours a night and sometimes less. It is possible to get used to this, but once every two or three weeks I would wake up at the normal time then decide not to get up and rise only the next day and in this way would sleep heavily, without waking, for sixteen to twenty hours in a row. It was always like this when I had to work, and there was an irritating stupidity about it to which I could never reconcile myself. The majority of my fellow drivers experienced no need for free time; on the contrary, for them leisure time was a burden. I had seen people like this in factories and in the other circles with which I had happened to come into contact; some of them could not settle to anything on their days off. I knew Pierre, an old worker at one of the first factories I went to work in; he lived very far away, four or five miles from Paris, and every day he got up at four o'clock in the morning to get to the factory on time at seven. He had worked at this factory for thirty years. On Monday mornings he was the first to show up, his face aglow, and he would invariably complain that he had been bored to death the whole of the previous day. The most astonishing thing, however, was that, like the majority of old French workmen, he did almost nothing: he would walk from one workshop to another, chat, and spend ages rolling cigarettes with his fingers from which nothing could wash off the many years of metallic dirt; when he had rolled one cigarette, he would put it behind his ear; when he had rolled a second, behind his other ear; and he would only light up the third, evidently, because he had no ears left. In general, people who had been settled in a job for a long time were usually paid their wages for doing nothing, and this was what amounted to the goal of each of them. It was understandable: before they could reach a more-or-less decent position, they had to work for many years, and when they finally did reach it, then neither their age nor their physical strength permitted them to undertake any wearisome exertions. But the less they labored, the more they talked about it. When I came to France, I was struck by the two words I heard most often and more or less everywhere: *work* and *tiredness*—in different variations. But it was those who really did work and really did get tired who uttered them least often.

When I was working in different factories, my whole life consisted in waiting for the howl of the siren that heralded the end of the working day, and I took little interest in what was going on around me. And even so I could not help noticing how badly and irrationally the work was organized in any factory, how much time was wasted, and what enormous sums of money were paid out daily to hundreds of people who did nothing or next to nothing. But even so this had to be considered ideal organization in comparison with the huge semi-state establishment that dealt with the dispatching of books, newspapers, and magazines to all towns in France and to all the countries of the world, and where I went to work some time later. I worked there in the office for three months, and this was the most useless waste of time of my entire life.

When I arrived there a small lacquered table was brought over for me at which I was made to sit, and after an hour of tediously waiting I was summoned by my immediate superior, a little elderly man with a black beard whose face was waxen and the whites of his eyes yellow.

"I am entrusting you with a fairly important job right away," he said. "Here, please draw up a list of our representatives in

Constantinople and its environs from the information in these copy books."

I copied out these names: there were exactly forty of them. But when I brought this list to him two hours later, he looked at me as if he had seen a lunatic standing before him.

"Do you mean that you have completed that list? That is to say, in other words, the task which I gave you has been completed?"

"Yes."

"But you must understand that this cannot be!" he cried. "Do you understand, it cannot be! There is a week's work here, young man. Go away, go away."

I shrugged my shoulders and returned to my desk. The other workers looked at me with sympathy. Once again I became absorbed in my list: Arabagi, Avrikides . . . I sat over it until evening, reading over and over again these Turkish and Greek names, from the repetition of which my ears were beginning to ring. When I was leaving, my superior clapped me on the shoulder and asked, "Well, how is the work going?"

"It's going fine," I replied. And the next morning I once more sat over this list. I learned the order of commas and periods by heart. I underlined the surnames and first names, and when, at around eleven o'clock in the morning, I took this list once more to my boss, he looked at me again with his eyes full of reproach.

"You probably mean to tell me that your list is ready?"

"Yes, completely ready."

"Splendid," he said with a smile, at which his face took on an expression uncharacteristic of him, at once concerned and sly.

"Splendid. So, this will be your next task: look through it carefully and check to see, please, whether any mistakes have found their way into this list. Look through it properly; don't rush. I've noticed that you're rather nervous when you're working. Ah, you young people!"

And I went away in a state of complete despair. Arabagi, Avrikides . . . I sat over this interminable list, read for the hundredth time the addresses of these firms, closed my eyes, and saw Constantinople before me: Pera, Galata, Stamboul, Besiktas, Nisantas, the Bosporus, the clanging trams, the evening lights of the ships over the bay, Bayazet Square, Taksim, the mosques, the graveyards, houses with wooden gates, the wind coming off the sea, night, and immense stars in the sky. I worked for five weeks over that list. Every morning I would get up with a feeling of mortal dread which I now knew by heart, like an oriental melody from some absurd *Sheherazade:* Arabagi, Avrikides, Baranopoulo, Bakribei . . . Finally, at the beginning of the sixth week of the Constantinople list, my boss called me again and told me that, although this work was nearly finished, it needed to be put to one side so that it could be checked definitively some time later, and meanwhile he would give me another task.

"Here is the file on our Amsterdam representative," he said. "He is unhappy with something and has been writing letters of complaint for more than six months now. Try to find out what the problem is, please."

The problem was an extraordinarily simple one. Eight months ago the Amsterdam representative had sent to Paris, addressed to our establishment, five hundred francs, asking to have sent back the equivalent quantity of a particular type of postcard which I knew about; he had indicated the series and number: the postcards were photographs of completely naked women in various poses but with just one obvious blemish, which was explained, however, not by some physical abnormality, but by the demands of censorship—on all of these bodies there was not a single hair to be seen because the existence of hair was considered acceptable only on the heads of the women who had been photographed. The dispatch office had sent only three hundred francs' worth of these postcards to him. And so over the course of many months this man had been demanding that either two hundred francs should be returned to him or he be sent goods worth this amount. The first few letters were written with the formal politeness of commerce and in none-too-elegant French, and to each of them was attached a reply with always the same unchanging content: "Dear Sir, we write to inform you of the receipt of your correspondence of such-and-such date. In reply to the request which you set out therein, the management is glad to inform you that it has been noted and that those measures which fulfillment of your request will entail, will afford you, as we very much hope, complete satisfaction."

As time went by, however, the Amsterdam representative wrote more and more energetic letters in which there remained nothing commercial or bureaucratic. "The breach of elementary principles of decency," he wrote with exclamation points, "which your world-renowned firm has permitted itself is completely disgraceful! I would like to think that it is some irresponsible rogues who, with the purpose of provocation, are dragging out this conflict which is gradually turning into swinishness!" But in reply to all of his exclamation points the management calmly retyped the text of its first letter: "Dear Sir, we write to inform you of the receipt of your correspondence of such-and-such date. In reply to the request which you set out therein, the management is glad to inform you that it has been noted and that those measures which fulfillment of your request will entail, will afford you, as we very much hope, complete satisfaction."

The Amsterdam representative replied: "Messieurs, I cannot rid myself of the impression that your world-renowned firm has hired some shameless parrot who has learned to write and who is now replying to my letters. Please understand, sirs, that what is happening is a disgrace to French prestige abroad, and in particular in the Netherlands, where I am no longer able to conceal from my numerous friends that I have been the victim of this inexplicable, this shameless thievery."

"Dear Sir," replied the firm, "we write to inform you of the receipt of your correspondence of such-and-such date. In reply to the request which you set out therein . . ."

In the file there was one letter missing, the very first one, which I wanted to read in order to have a clear conscience. I was told that it was to be found in the archives, from where I would have to fetch it. The archives were kept in a three-story glass building situated opposite my window, several dozen yards away. I made my way there; inside there was complete silence; and after I had shouted out several times—"Is there anybody here?"—the shuffling sound of slow footsteps reached me from out of that dusty silence, and a little old man, like someone from a German fairy tale, came down from the iron staircase that wound between the tall bookshelves.

"There was no need to shout like that," he said to me in a quiet but stern voice. "I am not deaf, thank God. But you, evidently, fail to take into account that a person may be busy with his work."

"Please forgive me," I replied. "But the fact is that I need a document, and I have come to get it, with your permission."

The old man pushed his spectacles up onto his forehead, came up closer to me, and looked me over very carefully.

"That is to say you think, perhaps, that I will fetch this document right now and hand it over to you!"

"That is exactly what I imagined."

"Well now!" he said with astonishment and indignation. "Would you take a look at this, if you please! Do you think that I give them out just like that, left, right, and center?"

"Excuse me," I said, "there must be some misunderstanding here."

"That is my feeling, too, young man."

"And are you in charge of the archives?"

"For thirty-two years, monsieur. When I started in this job, you were not even born."

"Very good. I need a document; I will tell you exactly what it is. Can you get it for me?"

"No."

"What do you mean, no? What are the archives here for, then?"

He looked at me once again and asked if I had been working there for long. I told him. Then he shook his head and explained that I must write a letter to him, send it to him in the internal mail, and only then would I receive a reply and the document—should the archives consider it possible to do this.

"I'm sorry," I said. "How much time will this take?"

"From two to four days."

"Listen, I work just over there," I showed him my window. "Why should I have to do this by correspondence?"

But he shook his head once again and replied that I would do better not to try to break the firm's rules, which had come into being, as he put it, before I was born and would continue to exist after my death. Then he added that he would not keep me any longer, climbed back up his iron stairs, and disappeared like a little old wizard.

When I got back to my office, I told my boss that the old archivist had lost his marbles, and I related the results of my visit.

"He is right; he is entirely right," said my boss. "Write him a letter, and then after that you can tell me whether you have managed to resolve this matter with our Amsterdam representative."

"It's a very simple matter," I began, but he cut me off and observed, not without a certain moralistic tone in his voice, that one should avoid premature judgments: "There might be information in the first letter which . . ."

The first letter, which I received three days later—in the internal mail—differed from all the others only in its politeness. I told the boss what had happened and expressed my astonishment that such an obviously ridiculous thing could drag on for such a long time.

"He needs to be given either two hundred francs or goods to the value of that sum."

"That is just what I thought." He uttered this without a hint of irony in his intonation. "Yes, that was very much the impression that I had."

"So why did you do nothing about it?"

"You know, so long as he does not go to court . . . And that sum of money has been received by us, so this increases the firm's revenue."

"But the firm's turnover is in the millions; what does two hundred francs matter to it?"

"Those millions are made up of francs, young man. In any case, you have handled this business very well; I am grateful to you."

I felt like rubbing my eyes.

"Now, please, if you could make a final check of the Constantinople list."

I did nothing more in this establishment. There was, it is true, a plan to entrust me with the classifying of some documents or other, and my boss even gave me an entire lecture on the principles of classifying documents, but it went no further than that.

I noticed that I was not an exception among the employees. In the office I was working in, there were fourteen of them, but a single person would have been able to manage all of the work— and he would still have had time to spare. How this joke of an establishment could exist and earn huge profits I could not understand, so wrong and ridiculous was everything about it. I remember how a young man came into the office one day and said that he had brought samples of goods.

"Take them upstairs."

"I've got them in a lorry."

"In a lorry? Why?" I asked. There was only one thing these goods could be, postcards, and in order to obtain samples of them, a whole lorry was certainly not needed. I went downstairs with him; down below, by the gates, there really was a vehicle, on which a whole mountain of metal furniture had been carefully stacked.

"What's all that?" I asked in astonishment.

"Samples of goods."

"What goods?"

"Metal furniture."

"Who ordered you to bring it?"

"I don't know. The order was made over the telephone."

Then I went into the downstairs office and established that the phone call had come from a most respected employee, a distinguished and elderly man who had been awarded the Legion of Honor and who was very hard of hearing but did not want to admit this at all, even to himself, and who, in order, as it were, to confirm the groundless nature of such a suggestion, often went to answer the telephone. This is what had happened on this occasion. His colleagues informed me that this was not the first time and that on one occasion they had had a delivery of sausage from a grocer's shop, on another of electric lamps, and now, this time, of metal furniture.

"But how can this be possible? Surely this man is nothing but a complete disaster."

"He is a most respected person; he served with great distinction in the war."

And so, for year after year, these phenomenally ignorant and phenomenally blasé people had managed this business, had grown old, earned their pensions, and died. In my department there was a particular muddle as well because the employees had to deal with foreign names; they did not know a single language other than their own, and every non-French word was for them difficult to read and almost unpronounceable. When, in order to escape from my deadly Constantinople boredom, I helped them a few times, they were astonished that I could read German or English or Bulgarian names without any great trauma; all of this seemed to them incomprehensible. I explained to them that I was a foreigner and had lived abroad for a long time, and then they ceased to be astonished and began to find it completely natural.

One fine day I received my monthly salary, left, and never went back again to that establishment. They brought an action against me, went to court, and sent their own solicitor there, a typically litigious character in a black suit, who shouted right in the face of the judge, a quiet, little old man, that the company would not just leave things as they were, that I had left without notice, that they demanded that I make a payment of one thousand francs, as well as legal costs, that my conduct was disgraceful, and that he could find no words to describe it. I shrugged my shoulders and replied that, whatever else, there was no need to shout and that if he thought that this shouting would have some effect on me, then he was mistaken, and that if the firm set great hope on getting my thousand francs, then they were quite obviously deluding themselves. Since I put my departure down to illness—nervous exhaustion—the little old judge suggested that I go and see the court doctor and be examined by him. I agreed to this, and another month and a half later I received a summons to the doctor's, where I appeared and then waited for a long time in a deserted waiting room; on the table lay last year's issues of *Illustrations* and Hugo's *Les Orientales*, which, out of boredom, I began to read. Finally the doctor came; he looked at me in astonishment and asked what I was doing there. I explained. The doctor was an old man, too—like my boss, like the archivist, like the judge—and once again I thought to myself that in France any secure and undemanding positions were occupied by very elderly men.

"What is your surname?"

I told him.

"Wait here."

And he went away. I opened *Les Orientales* once again and carried on reading. About forty minutes went by. Then he quietly came in again and said, "Excuse me, please, but what was your surname again? It was something foreign, wasn't it?"

I told him again.

"Good, wait here, please."

Another hour went by; I smoked three cigarettes, read several articles in *Illustrations,* and was about to take up *Les Orientales* once again, when he finally came in, for a third time, and explained that he was going to examine me. But then he remembered that he had not brought a towel with him, so he went out to get a towel and vanished for another ten minutes. After returning to the waiting room, he instructed me to follow him, and we went over to his office, on the desk of which a book lay open; I glanced over at it and read one sentence: "The Count, as we will recall, ate very little at mealtimes."

It was *The Count of Monte Cristo,* and it was then that I understood why the doctor had been absent for so long: he had been reading this book, from which, evidently, he was unable to tear himself away.

He listened to my breathing, sighed, and then asked, "What is the matter with you?"

"Nothing at all," I replied. "I came here because you summoned me. I have been sent to you by the judge for an examination, since this visit is not of a private, but rather a judicial nature, do you understand, doctor?"

"Ah," he said. "That is a different matter. Excuse me, please, but I have forgotten again, what is your surname?"

I had a sudden desire to go right up to him and, after a tragic pause, to whisper meaningfully: "Edmond Dantès." But I restrained myself.

"The examination is over; you may go."

"Thank you, doctor. May I know the result of the examination?"

"No, m'sieur, but it will be sent on to the judge."

It was indeed sent on to him, and when later on I went to see the judge again, I saw in his hand a sheet of paper with illegible words opposite each section, and the only thing I could decipher was "general state of health—excellent."

The company solicitor was triumphant, and it proved impossible to trouble his unwarranted delight, even though I told him that the result of the medical examination was merely a detail of no great significance that would alter nothing. Time passed by, and the judicial process took its course; I received a summons to the court, but that day I slept in and did not go. Then I began to receive letters from the bailiff, in which it was explained to me in clumsy legal language that he was empowered to demand of me such-and-such a sum, I think around fifteen hundred francs, and I was required to pay it—first of all within a week, then within three days, and then two; the last of these letters warned me that the following morning my property would be impounded. But I had no property: I was living in a hotel. I was not home for days at a time, and so I never found out whether this property of mine, which existed only in the suppositions of the French judicial system, was ever even symbolically impounded.

Of this time, this office work with the list of Constantinople representatives and the Amsterdam correspondent, another memory
has stayed with me: every day for the whole of those three months
I desperately needed to sleep. At that time I was renting a room, by
some absurd chance, in a Jewish quarter in the north of Paris, close
to the Rue Marcadet; I would eat my dinner in various restaurants,
and almost every day I visited the Latin Quarter, where the woman
who at that time was worth more than the world to me lived. I
would return home on the night bus after three o'clock in the
morning, get up at seven, and travel to work; after breakfast, when
I arrived at my office, everything would be ringing in my ears and
swaying in front of me, and I would come back to life only toward
evening. Sometimes I would find myself hearing and understanding nothing of what was going on around me; one time, on Sunday
morning after being out on Saturday night, when I was walking on
foot across Paris, I fell asleep two or three times on my feet and
woke up again only after several steps, like a soldier on a long, nighttime march. This was a time of never-ending spiritual torment for
me, probably not to be repeated in my life, and the places where I
spent time then I see clearly and precisely before me as soon as my
thoughts return to that period: the Boulevard Arago and its dense
trees which covered up the round street lamps, Fontainebleau and
Marly-le-Roi, where I would go on Sundays, nighttime cabarets
and the musical waves of those trashy songs and melodies in which
I found a hopeless and mournful charm which existed, I think, not
by itself, but which arose because it was past two or three o'clock in
the morning and next to me were those unforgettable, distant eyes
and that face exhausted by the night and the music.

And nevertheless that time, in spite of my chronic lack of sleep
and work in the office, was on the whole remarkably beneficial for
me in the sense that everything then was concentrated on a single

idea, the idea of personal and illusory happiness, and the rest of the world ceased to exist. At that time this was fuller and stronger than anything; it did continue afterward for many more years, but later on my work got in the way, work to which I had to give up too much time, as well as a whole series of minor failures; but even then for a long time still what I saw, learned, and observed seemed to me imprecise and confused since it was masked by my stormy private life, which was so egoistic and intense that I was incapable of seeing and understanding even a tenth of what I would have understood and learned had I not been so spiritually encumbered and absorbed. It was beneficial for me because later, when, for countless and complex reasons, I realized the undeniably chimerical nature of my lengthy and futile expectations and the almost glasslike fragility of everything I had thought I could rely on, when I began to come to my senses and saw the world differently from how it had appeared to me earlier; it was as if it was slowly emerging from darkness. It was similar to what it would be like if, after a long absence, I returned to a country that had changed beyond recognition over this time.

Until then I had had to begin my life all over again many times because of the unusual circumstances in which I had found myself, like all of my generation—the Civil War and defeat, revolutions, departures, journeys in the holds of steamships or on deck, foreign countries, conditions that changed far too often, in short, something sharply opposed to what I had grown used, long, long ago, as if in some book I had read, to imagining to myself: an old house with one and the same porch, the same front door, the same rooms, the same furniture, the same shelves in the library, and trees which, like the archive in my bureau, had existed before my birth and would carry on growing after my death, an oak tree as in Lermontov's poem above my quiet grave, snow in winter, greenery in summer, rain in autumn, and the gentle wind of an unforgettable

Russian month of April, many books read many times, travelers'
returns, the slowly unfolding charm of a family chronicle, a single
powerful and sustained breath, growing weaker as the rhythm
of my own life grew slower, my voice lost its resonance, my tired
limbs stiffened, my hair turned gray, my eyesight worsened. Then
one fine day, glancing behind me for a second, I would see myself
looking exactly like my grandfather, sitting on a bench on a warm
spring day beneath a tree in a fur coat and glasses, and I would
know that my remaining years were numbered and would listen
intently to the sound of the leaves so as to remember it once again
forever and not to forget it when I died. Then, if it really had been
so, I would probably know and understand a great deal more than
I knew and understood now, and I would look on the world with
calm and attentive eyes. But now, far away from my own country,
from the possibility of any kind of calm understanding, I would be
doomed to the slow and gradual onset of blindness, to a gradual
loss of interest in anything that did not concern me directly, and
the changes that occurred would probably be insignificant—a
series of trivial deteriorations and nothing more. Yet after this
inner anguish, after I had spent a long period of time without any
considerations that were not individual ones, and all the more powerful and all-consuming for being narrow and selfish, after this I
once again began to see and hear what was happening around me,
and it appeared to me different from before.

I thought then that all my reflections on the life I had observed,
and all my judgments on it were a result specifically, to a significant
degree, of my work as a taxi driver, of my finding myself on the
other side of things, always the least attractive. But it was impossible to assume that all of these things were merely accidental,
merely deviations from some kind of rules. And it seemed to me
that the life which my nocturnal clientele led had no justification in
anything. In the language of the people who lived in this way, it was

all what they called work. But in France they call everything work: pederasty, pimping, fortune telling, funerals, collecting cigarette butts, transactions of the Institut Pasteur, lectures at the Sorbonne, concerts and literature, music, and the sale of dairy products. When one day I took some passengers to the famous brothel on the Rue Blondel—its address was known to thousands of people at all ends of the earth, in Melbourne and in San Francisco, in Moscow and in Rio de Janeiro, in Tokyo and in Washington—I saw a man who was selling pornographic postcards and whom I, of course, knew, just as I knew most nocturnal professionals in Paris.

"Is business going well?" I asked. He replied indignantly, "No, old fellow, no, it's not going well at all. Yesterday they arrested me; the day before they arrested me; three days ago they arrested me. What kind of work is that?"

I never used to stop in Montmartre; there every establishment had its own taxi drivers, something like a small clan; they did not permit any competition. Besides, this type of work was boring and repellent. I generally preferred remote districts of the city, where there were no long lines of taxis. The easiest places to work were the rich, quiet districts of Paris, where there were fewer cars than in the center of the city. On Saturdays a special category of client would appear there; these were respectable, elderly men who would see young and beautiful women out to their taxis; this would usually take place late, after two or three o'clock in the morning. "Driver, will you take mademoiselle to the Boulevard Arago, number 34? Good-bye, my dear. So, till Wednesday, then?" "Yes, I'll phone you at your office." "Splendid. Be a good girl, sleep well." "Good night." And as soon as the car set off, an altered female voice would say abruptly, "Pigalle."

Sometimes it would be Blanche or Montparnasse. And it was in Montparnasse, after one of these journeys, that one time a couple stopped me, a man and a woman, coming out of a private house on the Rue Saint-Beuve; this was a house I knew very well. The woman, who was well-dressed and very young, looked awful; one look was enough to understand that this was the first time she had been in a *maison de passe,* probably with her first lover. Her hands were shaking, her eyes were blinking, she was breathing fast. After saying good-bye to her companion, she gave me her address; her flat was right on the banks of the Seine. Once we had arrived there, in her agitation she was completely unable to take any money out of her bag with her trembling fingers; finally, she pulled out ten francs, but I in turn could not find any change. "Hurry up, hurry up!" she said hysterically. "Hurry up. My God, what's going on? Be quick!" I looked at her and replied, "Don't get so worked up, madame; it's too late now. What's done is done; there's nothing you can do to change it."

"Bastard!" she shouted, sobbing, and ran off without waiting for her change.

At night Paris was inundated by people like this who were in a state of sexual frenzy. Quite often in the car, as we were driving along, they would behave as if they were in a hotel bedroom. One day I was driving a tall young woman in a fine fur coat after some ball; she was accompanied by a man who looked to be about seventy years old. He stopped me in front of a building on the Boulevard Haussmann, and since they were not getting out and were not talking and since, on the other hand, I did not suppose that this candidate for the Père Lachaise cemetery was capable of any kind of indecent behavior, I turned around to see what was going on. She was lying on the seat, her dress was up around her waist, and moving slowly upward across the dazzling white skin of her thigh was his dull red old man's hand with its prominent veins and its fingers gnarled with rheumatism.

I was frequently shocked by the attitude of the taxi drivers to people from Auteuil and Passy; while cultivating something like class hatred toward them, the drivers silently and subconsciously acknowledged their imaginary superiority. I had a number of conversations with drivers on this theme. One time I was standing, waiting for a theater to empty, with some fellow drivers. We knew that there would be plenty of clients; this is always easy to tell from the number of private cars waiting for their owners. *L'Arlésienne* was on, and I said that it was remarkable that a play like that could attract so many people. The old driver to whom I had said this replied to me, "Listen, old man. They're not like us, these people. You can't understand this play, and nor can I. For that, old man, you need to be educated. There's probably the kind of words in it you've never heard of. All that's just rubbish to you. For them it's another matter, and we'll never be the way they are. There's no point getting worked up about it." Another, a heavily built man around fifty years old, whom I had met a number of times at the taxi stands, said to me, "Look at those Russians, they'll say. But I feel sorry for them, do you know that? I'll tell you why. People like us have been working since we were children. I, for instance, started when I was fourteen, and you were probably the same. But I know what those Russians are like. You see them and look at them like you would everybody else, and you don't understand how unhappy they are. Man, they used to be lawyers, doctors, officers; they had servants and everything you'd expect rich people to have, and now here they are driving taxis like you and me. That's hard, man. I think it takes courage to do that. I know what I'm talking about, man."

And he told me how before the war his wife had been a maid for some Russian in Paris and that now he had met this same Russian, who was working as a taxi driver. "That, my friend, is the end of the world!"

And it never entered the head of this simple and good-hearted man that he might be entitled to live no less well than them, or at least to aspire to doing so. But neither he nor his fellows ever reflected on questions like this. Nowhere else was I able to see so closely the sharp social differences between people and, most importantly, such complete resignation to one's lot in life, and I could never get used to this. I felt that even if I were to live here another fifty years, it would alter nothing. I remember with what wild eyes my clients would look at me when I replied to them in what in my understanding was the most normal manner; because of my way of speaking to them I ended up in the police station several times, though fortunately it always ended happily.

These misunderstandings, of which there were a large number, began when one passenger of mine, who was going to the station with two large suitcases—he was a doctor by profession, as it later transpired—announced that the meter was showing too much for the fare. I replied to him that he was mistaken and that, in addition to the sum indicated on the meter, he would need to add two francs, one for each suitcase. He then made a scene and began shouting that this was daylight robbery and that in any case, under no circumstances would he pay the two francs.

"This is daylight robbery!" shouted the doctor. "You will not get a single centime of those two francs."

"Fine," I said. "Do you want me to give them to you? I'll give two francs to the first beggar I see when he asks for money from me. So I don't see why I should refuse to give you the same sum. But you'll have to ask for it from me, like beggars do."

He looked at me in astonishment and eventually said that there must be a misunderstanding, that he was a doctor—this is how I found out—and that I understood nothing.

"You're a doctor," I replied, "but you have the psychology of a beggar; that's paradoxical, but normal enough, I suppose."

"No, no," he said in confusion, paid the money, and left, looking round as he did. One of the policemen who had been close by during this conversation, just in case things got out of hand, looked at me and asked, "Tell me, please, you wouldn't happen to be mad, would you?"

"I don't think so," I said. "At any rate, not as mad as my clients."

Then there was an incident with another man, who had five suitcases and whom I drove to the Avenue Victor-Hugo early one morning. He got out of the car and said to me, as if it were the most natural thing in the world, "Now take these suitcases up to the fifth floor."

He did not even take the trouble to add "please" or "if you would be so kind," and in his voice there was not a hint of either doubt or pleading.

"Listen, old boy," I said, and he turned round as if stung. "Your arms aren't paralyzed, are they?"

"No, why?"

"I just don't see why I should suddenly start carrying your suitcases up to the fifth or any other floor for that matter. If I had to change a wheel, do you really think I would turn to you and ask you to do it instead of me? I wouldn't, would I?"

He looked at me and then asked, "Are you a foreigner?"

"No," I replied.

And every time that misunderstandings like this arose, everything was resolved as soon as it became known that I was Russian, and it became clear pretty quickly that all I had to do was hand over my papers to a policeman. These misunderstandings were without consequence because, essentially, I had committed no crime, and the people who made complaints to the police against me did so not in defense of their own interests but exclusively because of my disdain for the firm views they held about what kind of relations there should be between different categories of citizen. With ordinary passengers—workers, small businessmen, women street traders—I never had any conversations of that kind; they treated me as an equal, and if they argued, then they argued with me as an equal. But clients in evening wear from those districts of Paris with expensive apartments could at times provoke a fit of rage in the most peaceful of men, like one lady whom I was driving one day to the Avenue Foch and who, after traveling a few hundred yards, knocked on the glass separating her seat from mine with her umbrella, and yelled, "We're not driving to a funeral, are we? Faster, please."

Usually in situations like these I braked as hard as I could and said, "If you're not happy, get out and take another cab."

But on that day I was in a particularly bad mood. I put my foot down on the accelerator and drove the car as fast as I possibly could. We overtook other cars, shot across junctions, almost crashed into a bus; she cried out that this was suicide, that I had lost my mind, but I paid no attention to her cries. Finally, having reached Avenue Foch, I slowed down.

"You are insane!" she cried. "You wanted to kill me! I'll complain about you!"

"You need to see a doctor, madame," I said. "It seems to me that the state of your nervous system cannot but inspire a certain concern. Would you like me to give you the address of a clinic?"

"What kind of nonsense is this?" she was beside herself with indignation. "Perhaps you don't know who I am?"

"I really don't know who you are."

"I am the wife of ———." She said the name of a well-known lawyer.

"Very good. But why do you reckon that should make some kind of impression on me?"

"What, don't you recognize my husband's name?"

"I might have heard it, is he a lawyer or something?"

"Yes, and at any rate, he's not a taxi driver."

"I would suggest, madame, that of these two different professions, that of taxi driver is possibly the more honest one."

"Ah, you are a revolutionary!" she said. In spite of the unpleasant turn the conversation had immediately taken, she did not leave and did not pay me; the meter continued to tick away. "I hate that breed of people."

"Because, most likely, you know nothing either about revolutionaries or about social and economic questions," I said. "Please note that I have very little intention of reproaching you for that. But at least have the decency not to speak of things about which you are ignorant."

"Never in my life has anyone spoken to me like this," she said. "What astonishing insolence!"

"It's very simple, madame," I replied. "Everyone you know is trying to preserve your acquaintance, or your friendship, or else your good will. All of that is a matter of total indifference to me; in a few minutes I'll drive away, and I hope I'll never see you again. Why, taking account of these conditions, shouldn't I say exactly what I think to you?"

"And you think that I'm nothing but a fool and ignoramus?"

"I wouldn't insist on the first description, but I would find it hard not to admit that the latter does, to my mind, correspond to reality."

"Fine," she said. "I'll just pay you then, and I'll even give you a tip."

"You can keep the tip, madame. I'd like to give it back to you."

"No, no, you've earned it, if only for your charming conversation."

"I am delighted, madame, that you enjoyed it."

And then she asked me one final question, "Tell me, please, you're not a foreigner, are you?"

"No, madame," I replied. "I was born in 42, Rue de Belleville; my father has a butcher's shop there, you might happen to know it?"

When thinking back to this time, I would often recall those drawings that show a vertical section of an engine or a car. Thanks to innumerable chance occurrences—which included, to an equal extent, both historical events and geographical factors, as well as all manner of trivia, and which can neither be reckoned up, nor foreseen, nor can one even imagine the likelihood of them arising—I ended up living in several different social spheres, none of which came into contact with any other. Frequently, during the course of a single week, I would find myself at a literary and philosophical debate, spend an evening talking to the former foreign minister of one of the Balkan states and listening to his diplomatic anecdotes, dine in a Russian restaurant with once-influential people who were now laborers or drivers, and, on the other hand, I would end up in districts populated by the miserable Parisian poor, chat with Russian "scroungers" or French vagrants—from whom one had to keep a certain distance since they all gave off a sharp, acrid smell, and it was just as constant and inevitable as the musk of certain species of animal—or I would transport prostitutes who complained about their poor earnings, stand at a zinc counter alongside the pimps continually coming and going, who were my Montparnasse acquaintances, and, finally, sit for hours in a comfortable armchair in that flat in Passy and hear a female voice—I had known it for many years and never forgot a single one of its intonations—saying, "Remind me of that sentence you quoted to me recently, from Rilke, I think, about feeling. Feelings are the only subject you know something about; you are deaf and blind to everything else."

And the next night, when I stopped my car on the Rue de Rivoli and closed my eyes, remembering this conversation and resurrecting in my memory every sound of that voice, I was approached by a shabbily dressed black man, who asked me for a cigarette, lit it, and said, "Just think, I used to give out cigarettes by the pack, and now

I have to ask you just for one cigarette." And all at once, turning his head to the right, he added, "Here she is again, the bitch!"

A woman, limping very heavily, was walking past us along the sidewalk.

"Just look," said the black man scornfully. "Call that a woman!"

"What's your problem with her?"

"She's an alcoholic, m'sieur, is the problem; drunkenness, that's what the problem is with her." And he shouted after her, "Are you drunk again?"

"Black piece of filth," she replied.

"What? D'you want your face slapped?"

He shouted this with real ferocity but did not move from where he was, and when he turned back toward me, he looked at me with his lazy black eyes with their yellowish whites.

"Do you know how they go about their work here?"

"No, old fellow, I don't know."

"Well you see, m'sieur, there's no hotels here. It's that kind of district. There's the Ritz and Le Meurice, but they're for kings and dukes; you can't rent a room there."

"So?"

"So they have to go on the benches in the Tuileries. The client sits on a bench, and the woman sits on top of him."

"And?"

"Yes, that's how they work here. And that bitch was so drunk last night . . . Her client was sitting waiting for her, and she couldn't sit on him properly. It was shameful to watch, m'sieur, a woman in such a state that she couldn't even do her job properly."

Sometimes, once every few years, in the midst of this landscape of stone there would be evenings and nights filled with the kind of disquieting spring charm I had almost forgotten since leaving Russia, and which was matched by a special limpid sadness in my feelings, in such sharp contrast to my customary mixture of deep melancholy and disgust. At these times everything was altered, like a piano that has just been tuned, and in place of the coarse and powerful feelings which usually tormented me—unquenched and protracted desire, which caused my muscles to grow heavy and engorged; or blind passion, when I did not recognize my own face if my glance should fall at those moments on a mirror; or the insuperable, unceasing regret caused by everything being other than it should have been, and that continual sense beside one of someone else having died—and I would enter, not knowing how or why, into another world, light and glassy, where everything was resonant and remote and where I could finally breathe this astonishing spring air, without which I think I would have suffocated. And on days and evenings like these I would sense with particular force those things of which I was always dimly aware and about which I very rarely thought, in particular, that it was hard for me to breathe, as it was for all of us, in this European air, where there was neither the icy pureness of winter nor the infinite smells and sounds of the northern spring, nor the vast spaces of my homeland.

But at the same time, here in Paris there existed dozens of Russian shops and restaurants. In the shops Russian goods were on sale, and in the restaurants there were Russian dishes: *bliny, golubtsy, pel'meni,* and the inevitable *borshch.* Over the many years of my Parisian life I had visited the majority of these restaurants and knew by sight the waiters and waitresses, who moved from one district to another; sometimes they became proprietors themselves and opened their own restaurants, drank champagne on the opening day, and put out announcements in the Russian newspapers: "Petr Vasil'evich Sidorov has the honor of informing his dear friends and clientele that he has opened his own restaurant Petushok on such-and-such street. Head chef—Vasilii Ivanovich Komarov. Substantial artistic program. Daily performances by the public's darling, Sasha Semenov. Large selection of hors d'oeuvre. Plat du jour. Today: *rasstegai*. Tomorrow: suckling pig in sour cream."

I would close my eyes and imagine to myself the immobile, steel-and-glass flowers on the tables, the little lamps with shades, Petr Vasil'evich Sidorov very smartly dressed, the classically languorous eyes of his wife, the band, and the public's darling, Sasha Semenov, a heavily built, balding man with a rich, slightly hoarse baritone, and with his bald patch carefully covered by a few strands of hair; as he sang he reached out his arms with rather wooden, uncertain gestures in the most tear-jerking passages, and he told his close friends, in the early hours of the morning before the restaurant shut, that he was a devotee of the Italian school, and the friends would agree with him and also believe in this Italian school, although they knew perfectly well that Sasha Semenov had previously been a staff captain in the horse artillery and could not have had anything to do with any Italian school but had a great weakness for the female sex and had been the hero of numerous love affairs. Everything he sang had the same minor tonality, regardless of the words, and his voice quivered with powerful and, as his female admirers would say, invisible tears. As the years passed he grew fatter and balder and found it harder to get warmed up, but his voice stayed just as strong and did not change in spite of his long-standing drinking habit. Sometimes he himself would say, "Of course, it's not the same voice; my voice didn't sound like that in 1922, did it?" but this was not true; I had heard him then, and his singing was exactly the same as it was now. Everywhere he went—in any city in Europe, in the Balkan capitals, in Shanghai, or

America—he would see exactly the same things, in spite of being in different countries: the restaurant walls, the band, the stage, the same words of the same songs, the same music, the same *wiener schnitzel,* the same vodka; all that changed were the women's faces, and the expressions in their eyes, and their hair, and their bodies. He himself said more than once that when he thought about his life he had the impression that he was traveling all the time in a cabin on some ship, passing various shores and countries, but while they changed, everything in the cabin and on the ship would remain the same. And he would complain of the monotony of his existence— usually having had a good deal to drink and almost breaking into sobs as he spoke about it—and his friends would shrug their shoulders and later, when talking among themselves, they could not help but remark on what the drink had reduced this man to: he had seen so many countries, they would say, sung in so many cities, and here he was complaining of the monotony of his existence. But it was nevertheless Sasha Semenov who was right, and not they. He had an unusual memory for faces, but, like all or nearly all of his abilities, it manifested itself only after he had already drunk a significant quantity of vodka; when in a sober state he was always listless and incapable of any mental effort. I was able to judge how good his memory was because one time, past four o'clock in the morning, the two of us were the last people left in the restaurant— the woman who was with me, and me—and he sat down with us and asked me if I had not been in such-and-such a year in a particular place in Constantinople in the company of such-and-such people. He could remember exactly their physiognomies, their clothing, their appearance. This astonished me, and I gave him an answer; he immediately became loquacious, and when I asked him why he had chosen a career working in restaurants in particular, he said with sudden candor and sincerity, "Because I don't have the talents for any other career. If I did, I wouldn't be singing in a restaurant. Look, nobody could ever imagine Shalyapin in a cabaret. But you couldn't imagine old Sasha Semenov on a concert stage or in an opera, either. In music and singing, old fellow, I'll just take what comes."

Like many Russian people, though, he was highly and quite genuinely emotional, with that pure and unselfish melancholy which it would be quite proper to assume in a poet or philosopher and which seemed unexpected in a former captain who was now a cabaret singer. What was striking about this was that these feelings were undoubtedly of a higher order and should have been matched by other, equally lofty notions, which of course Sasha did not possess. In a sense it was just as astonishing as if a simple farmer or concierge turned out to be an admirer of Rembrandt, Beethoven, or Shakespeare. But this was neither accidental nor temporary, and I noticed this same lavishness of soul, a comparatively rare thing throughout Europe, in many simple Russian people. Nature had bestowed on these Russian people a certain ethical sense, an essential precursor to the emergence of artistic culture, the possibilities for which seemed almost completely stifled here in the West.

Speaking one time with my regular companion, Plato, I said that in this sense everything here seemed to me just as wrong as in music or singing, in the terminology of which I had been struck by the expression *chanteur à voix*, untranslatable into the language of Russian concepts. Plato then spoke at length of the fateful influence of Descartes, whom he sincerely despised, and about how, apart from Baudelaire, there was no such thing as French poetry. "But what about Rimbaud, or François Villon, or Ronsard?" But Rimbaud, in his opinion, was only the beginnings of an experiment, while he denied the significance of Villon and Ronsard; during the course of this conversation I was astonished to discover that Plato had a negative opinion about almost everything that was considered an expression of French genius. He spoke disparagingly of Hugo and Flaubert, of Montaigne and Lamartine, of La Rochefoucauld and Voltaire, whose intellect, however, he did not dispute. The only writers he accepted were Stendhal, Balzac, Baudelaire, and some other person who, in his words, was head and shoulders above them all; he told me his name, but I did not remember it; but what I do know for certain is that neither before nor since then did I ever hear of it. When I told him that I was astonished by his views on French culture, he shrugged his shoulders and replied that this expression was an anachronism and that there was no such thing as French culture, at least at the present time; before the war of 1914 the final remnants of it were still staggering along in some kind of pitiful existence, but now it would be absurd to look for it in that milieu which constituted the privileged class of French people and who amounted to no more than ignorant swine.

In what Plato said there was a certain element of persuasiveness, which could be explained by, firstly, his individual dialectical abilities, and secondly, one other reason: in his irreversible downfall the world really did seem to him darker than to other people who did not have such overwhelming cause to be pessimists. This colored all of Plato's judgments, irrespective of whether the conversation was about soccer—by the way, he had good knowledge of this question since, when studying in England, he had been goalkeeper for his university team for two years—about philosophy, industry, or agriculture. In general, his constant first line of defense boiled down to saying that the world he left behind did not deserve to be regretted. Such was, I think, the motivation behind his criticism, but apart from this, there was also, of course, an element of objective truth, without which all his despairing pronouncements would have seemed completely unfounded.

As for Sasha Semenov, I heard him many times later on. On Saturdays from seven to nine o'clock, he would sing in the little restaurant where I usually had dinner and where I knew all the clientele, the lady owner, the waitresses, all their biographies, and even the degree of wealth of these people in previous, distant times, in prerevolutionary Russia. Most of them had been millionaires, landowners, and carousers, and almost all had belonged to the aristocratic circles of society; this was also a defensive though merely comforting reflex, in essence quite harmless, since everything they talked about was to the highest degree implausible and would not have deceived even the most naive person. My constant table companions were two Russian taxi drivers, both no longer young and very busy people, Ivan Petrovich and Ivan Nikolaevich, and when speaking with them, I was astonished at the pointless waste of energy that was typical of both of them. Ivan Petrovich was an organizer of political parties. He had fifteen or so people close to him who made up the kernel of an organization that was constantly changing its title but was in essence one and the same. In his plans for unification Ivan Petrovich's imagination was tireless. He was successively head of the Union of Junior Officers of Lancers' Regiments, then the Committee for the Salvation of Russia—without any kind of elaboration or detail—then the Union of Former Pupils of the Northern Cadet Corps, then the Brotherhood of Engineer Units, then the Coordinated Society of Motorized Traction on the Western Front. He wrote up statutes, which were discussed in a constitutional committee, kept a tally of expenses, determined the amount for monthly contributions, and then went off to the prefecture to register the new organization. After this, presentations, discussions, and lectures were organized: "The current situation in Europe," "The current situation in Russia," "Russia and Europe," "The economic factor in contemporary politics," and so on. A little later, at dinnertime, his old friend Ivan Nikolaevich would arrive at the restaurant, his former comrade in the army and fellow pupil from the military academy, a small, rather thin man with an unremarkable face. He would sit down at our table, order himself a cup of coffee, and say, "Ivan Petrovich, I've come to clear something up. As a member of the controlling committee I have no choice but to say to you, in the name of all of my colleagues, that you have been overstepping your authority. You know that cannot be tolerated."

There would begin a lengthy argument, after which a splinter group would emerge in Ivan Petrovich's party. The splinter group would send all the members of the organization typewritten explanatory leaflets setting out in very pretentious style the reasons for the conflict, which had long since been brewing, in the words of the composers of the leaflet, but which was still in the latent stage. Then Ivan Petrovich would undertake individual discussions with each of the members separately, and after these consultations the constitutional committee would meet once again, statutes would be drafted, and everything would begin all over again. Ivan Petrovich was always badly dressed and earned very little since the greater part of his time was devoted to this idiosyncratic political *perpetuum mobile*. At the dinner table he would explain to me all the springs of the political mechanism, the principles of propaganda, and even the secret of success, but generally speaking he knew very little about it all, since apart from this he never spoke about anything else and only once did he let slip that he considered Gogol a good writer.

Ivan Nikolaevich was not involved in politics in the true sense of the word, but he was consumed by a very strange mania for administration. His whole life consisted of membership in all manner of joint-stock companies organized, of course, by Russian émigrés; he went to all the meetings, voted, abstained, gave explanations, demanded explanations, became a shareholder himself, and then, eventually, a member of the board of directors. This concluded the positive part of his program, after which, with an inevitable and inexorable logic, the second, negative part would commence. He would suddenly discover, or it would suddenly start to seem to him, that he had become the victim of some kind of swindler's scam, along with most of the other shareholders in the company. This period of suspicions would give way to a period of certainty. Ivan Nikolaevich would leave the board of directors, would make a point of not appearing at meetings, and would hire his lawyer to bring a lawsuit against the company's directors. On all of those who were numbered among those people whom he held to account, he gathered all manner of information wherever he could and compiled a dossier for each of them. Then he would sit down to work: he would make deductions, comparisons, cut articles out of newspapers, and write dozens of extremely long compositions, which he would then type up and bind together and pass on to his lawyer. The majority of those whom he pursued represented—if one were to judge by his dossiers—an extremely dangerous element both in the moral and the political sense. And when, after lengthy proceedings, the judge acquitted them, Ivan Nikolaevich would hint that a hefty bribe had been paid for this. But even during the trial he would have had time to join the board of directors of another company. His relations with people remained good until these changed to business relations, then he would begin to prepare for a lawsuit. He struggled to get by, even though he worked hard, but he was ruined by the never-ending legal expenses, the promissory notes to friends he signed, unpaid checks, and the expenses incurred through the gathering of information. Away from this he was a helpful and charming person; he had only one unfortunate fault: whenever the amplified gramophone was playing in the restaurant, he could not resist singing along; indeed he somehow managed to do this even while eating, which created a strange impression, something I could never get used to.

The lives of these people were dedicated to essentially the same goals; at all events, their efforts were completely fruitless. It struck me more than once that it was probably from just this type of people that political cadres were recruited, or statesmen and advisers; the only thing that made them different from this category of people was their ineptitude and with that, of course, their lack of self-interest. But their blind and incomprehensible love for this pointless and unnecessary activity, which no amount of failures could disturb, and which undoubtedly expressed, though in comical form, a pure and tireless yearning for useful work, was really deserving of a better lot. I was particularly struck, at the beginning of my friendship with Ivan Petrovich and Ivan Nikolaevich, by the violence and passion with which they argued in my presence over the relationship between state and private property and about the possibility of government control over capital.

"I cannot allow this illegal intervention," Ivan Petrovich would say. "Never, Ivan Nikolaevich, never. If we have to, we'll defend our rights with guns in our hands."

"As a person who believes in government," said Ivan Nikolaevich, "I consider and will continue to consider that the good of the collective is infinitely greater and more important than the rights of the individual. You have acquired through God knows what means colossal sums of money, and then what do you use them for?" Ivan Nikolaevich lowered his voice and said almost in a whisper, "In order to implement your criminal personal power and your pernicious influence, which could ruin thousands of lives."

"I am sorry, but I bring in to your government treasury enormous amounts of tax," said Ivan Petrovich. "I am sorry, but you make me pay three hundred thousand francs for a foreign car that is worth a hundred and eighty thousand, so you earn a hundred and twenty thousand from me. I'm sorry to remind you of this, but you are robbing me over everything, starting with gasoline and finishing with postage stamps. I repeat: if we have to, we'll defend our rights with a gun in our hands, and the blood from those barricades will be on your conscience."

They would sit opposite one another at a table in that little restaurant, after a dinner that had cost each of them around eight francs, both badly dressed, in shabby jackets, in shirts that were no longer new, in trousers with a tragic fringe at the bottom, and argue over a state of which they were not citizens, about money they did not have, about rights they did not possess, and about barricades that they would not be building. And, when it came down to it, nearly all the clientele of that restaurant lived exactly like Ivan Petrovich and Ivan Nikolaevich, in imaginary worlds, and whatever the conversation touched on, the past or the future, they all had ready ideas about it, dreamy and absurd and about as far as one could get from reality. It was all about vast and nonexistent landed estates, forty people around a table, the magnificence of their previous life, French cooks, governesses, trips to Paris, or, once again imaginary, their rights in an imaginary future Russia, or altogether quite formless half hopes and half feelings—"So I'll get there, and I'll say straight off: 'Chaps, that's enough now. I've nothing against you . . .'" The Europe in which they were living was of utterly no interest to them; they did not know what was going on there; the best of them turned into dreamers who avoided thinking about reality since it was a nuisance to them, while the worst of them, that is, those whose imaginations were less developed, sobbed about their lives and turned more and more to drink. And then there were, finally, a few who made a success of what they did, so-called right-thinking people in the European sense of the word, but they were the least interesting and the least Russian, and the dreamers would speak of them with contempt and envy. The difference between these Russians who had ended up here, and Europeans in general, and the French in particular, was that the Russians existed in a formless and chaotic and frequently changing world, one which they constructed and created for themselves practically every day, while the Europeans lived in a world which was real and actual, which had taken shape long ago and had now acquired a moribund and tragic immobility, the immobility of decline and death. This was not only because of the dreamers being people who were déclassé and who had willingly left behind a reality that did not satisfy them; in this there was also a purely Slavic readiness on any morning, any day, any time of one's existence to abandon everything and to begin everything anew as if nothing had gone before this, that barbarian freedom of thought which would have offended any European. Even the dreamers' love for the past, for their beautiful former life in beautiful former Russia, was also a product of this free flight of their fantasy, so that what they described with disinterested and genuine tenderness existed, more often than not, only in their minds.

And meanwhile from the radio amplifier there came a dense and constant stream of melodies in a minor key, and I noticed with astonishment that the ugly, badly rhyming, and stupid words of the songs never really irritated me—they became lost in the music like foul things in a wide river. And, on leaving the restaurant, I was always for some reason reminded of an elderly Breton woman with a ruddy-gray face who very regularly, every two or three days, would come into the courtyard of the building where I was living and sing old French songs. Some of them I knew by heart, and there were some remarkable words to be found in them:

We met, and there was a tremor in our hearts,
Fiery dreams crowded our brows
With identical smiles on our lips,
With the sweet sigh of first promises . . .
You passed by and left in my heart
A deep trace, demanding happiness.

She was always neatly dressed in clean clothes; even the patches on her dress were carefully sewn on and pressed. She had a poor sense of pitch and an impossibly croaky voice, and even so, in her uncertain singing and in the stupid selection of well-worn words telling of tragic idylls and in the unchanging effect caused by the combination of her gray hair and her ruddy-gray face, there was something which evoked both sympathy and interest. All of this aroused in me a strange and persistent feeling, hard to define and unlike those I had experienced before or about which I had ever heard or read. She was businesslike and conscientious; she would come into our courtyard, would stop and begin to sing, never smiling or making any gestures. She reminded me of a singing wooden statue; after singing three or four songs, she would collect her money, say, "Merci, messieurs-dames," and would walk away, carrying off her extraordinarily immobile, unbending figure without turning her head.

I was living at that time in a building which passersby could hardly miss, as it was built in the Moorish style, which seemed at the very least unexpected in Paris; but this had been the desire of its owner, a fat old Jewish contractor who had grown rich and who had his own strictly defined tastes in all forms of art. In architecture for some reason the Moorish style appealed to him. I was renting a room in a private apartment from a rather beautiful young woman who had an extremely chaotic lifestyle. I was struck, when I first lived there, by the way she kept dropping things over a period of several days; she broke a salad bowl, several plates, a saucer, and three glasses. Every time, after the crash of broken crockery, I heard her quietly saying the same word—*swine*! It was only later that I found out the explanation for this quantity of crockery falling from her hands; she told me about it herself. This question interested me because these misfortunes befell her three or four days each month, and the rest of the time she did not break anything. She explained to me that it coincided with her monthly indispositions; it was, in her words, just as unavoidable as headaches or fatigue. I had no particular reason to have lengthy conversations with her, but after several of Suzanne's visits to me, one day she knocked on my door and began to expound to me in detail why she did not like my conduct and the fact that I received women in my room. She found that this was bad in general terms, that moreover my choice seemed to her strange to say the least, and that this was not the way to behave. Her passion for confrontation was completely inexhaustible. She came up with her own individual and quite definite idea of a person, according to which it followed that he should live in one way and not another, that he should like one thing and not another, do one kind of work and not another, and so on to the end, right up to his way of dressing and his choice of ties. And once it became apparent that the person in question, who frequently did not even suspect that she had some kind of opinion on the subject, was not doing what she thought he should be doing or was not dressing in the right way, it aroused in her at best irritation and at worst fury. I happened to witness several of her love affairs and heard the conversations she had with her lovers, and it was always crazy and ridiculous. One of them was a doctor specializing in female complaints, and one time, after waking up at night and lighting up a cigarette, I heard their conversation through the thin wall.

"Understand me, Seriozha," her voice said. "I don't want to upset you."

"I understand," said the doctor's voice.

"You see that bronze statuette of a woman? What do you think it is?"

"A statuette of a woman?"

"Well, it's not a rhinoceros, is it, or a sphinx, or a horse?"

"It's true," said the doctor. He was on the whole a person of a rather melancholic type, very decent, quiet, and polite. He replied to her in an even tone, agreeing in advance with everything she said.

"Well, then. And you're a doctor who specializes in female complaints."

"Yes."

"And that's where you went wrong."

One of them turned over on the bed, and beneath them a spring twanged and resonated, and above the voice of my landlady I could hear for several seconds more its sound dying away.

"Why?"

"You should be a surgeon."

"Why should I be a surgeon? I've no leaning toward that at all."

"Well, how can you not see it?" she said with some irritation. "How can you not understand? You should have been a surgeon; it's completely obvious."

"Well, Lenochka, that's just your whim."

"No, my dearest. So you think it's good that women come to see you every day, sit in your disgusting chair, and show their charms to you? What's good about that, I ask you?"

"But that's my job, Lenochka."

"How can you not understand?"

"Quiet, Lenochka, you'll wake the neighbor."

"That animal?" she said. "He sleeps like a log. Do you know that he falls asleep with a lit cigarette in his mouth? He's burned two of my sheets; thank God there wasn't a fire. But let's go back to what we were talking about at the start."

"I've nothing against that," the doctor replied. There was a movement, the sound of the spring rang out again, and a few seconds later her laughing and irritated voice said, "Wait, I need to explain to you. You ought to be a surgeon. Ah, you're hurting me!"

Then I fell asleep, after finishing my cigarette, and heard nothing more.

Soon after this a very strange thing happened to her: she disappeared. Days and weeks went by, but she did not return. After a certain time various people began to appear: an agent from a sewing machine company, an insurance company agent, a representative from a furniture shop who brought two unpaid promissory notes, then the *boulangère,* then the manager of the building; all of them came mainly in the mornings, when I was sleeping. I would get up, put on my pajamas, open the door to them, and give the same explanation, that it had nothing to do with me. I spent about three months in this way, completely alone in what was effectively someone else's flat, and I finally moved out because the constant visits from all manner of agents and all the explaining became unbearable; and when I stopped opening the door to them in the mornings, they started coming in the afternoons.

I met her two years later in the south of France at the seaside. She was sitting half buried in the sand, in a swimsuit, and was staring into the distance. I had barely had time to greet her when, without replying to my greeting, she said irritably, "I told him he mustn't swim out so far; anything could happen—and then I'd really be in a stupid situation, wouldn't I?"

I looked out where she was looking: far out to sea the head of a person swimming would come into view and then disappear again. "But you don't know anything about it. And you owe me money for the room."

And she told me how she had suddenly got married and gone away to the south of France; that is, more accurately, to start with she had gone away to the south of France, and then she had got married and had abandoned the flat because there was nothing in it of any value. "After everything we lost in Russia, you understand . . . And don't look at me like that. And why are you wearing that idiotic cap on your head; do you think it looks good or something?"

"So you married a surgeon?"

"Why do you think it had to be a surgeon?"

"I don't know; for some reason I thought it would be a surgeon."

"Your head's full of rubbish, my dear. Are you still leading the same dissipated life?"

I had no time to reply; she ran into the water, dove in and swam off in the direction of the man's head, which was now nearing the shore. I lay down on the sand, closed my eyes, and lay there for about ten minutes. When I opened them again, she was no longer there.

I do not know if I will ever meet her again, and if I do, then where it will be. Sometimes in my imagination there appear the vague outlines of some building of an indeterminate style; I hear the barely audible sound of the bed spring beneath her body, and I see the sorrowful shadows of her creditors and the sad faces of her lovers. Her life intersected with mine—in headlong and absurd motion—and then she departed again into her trashy world which flew by me like an excerpt from someone's protracted and inexplicably laughable madness.

I often thought that in the life I was forced to lead the most important and constant particularity—always and everywhere—was
uncertainty about the future, its unavoidable obscurity. Just as in
other countries, where I had been at different times a drifter, a soldier, a schoolboy, an involuntary traveler, I had never known what
would happen to me and whether I would end up, as a result of all
the monstrous upheavals I witnessed and took part in, in Turkey or
in America, in France or in Persia, so it was here in Paris where,
in spite of the monotony of doing always the same job, every day I
experienced the kind of sensation one would experience following
a stream that vanished in the sands. During the course of my long,
nocturnal years there passed through my life people with whom I
traveled a certain distance, sometimes long, sometimes short, and
in the same way a chance passenger became my companion for a
short space of time, and while this journey lasted we would both to
an equal degree be either threatened or not threatened by a routine
car accident, and eventually, it could well happen that my unknown
male or female companion and I would end up lying on the pavement of the same Paris street, with broken ribs and close to our
last gasp, and for this second there would be something that united
us in our common fate that was stronger than any friendship or
family ties. But these journeys ended safely, and all of my clients
would disappear in the darkness; each of them possessed their own
private life, unknown to me, and which I traversed blindly for the
few minutes of our shared journey. So it was always, and therefore
the fate of those people whom it was given to me to know fully
attracted me so irresistibly and powerfully, even in those cases
when by itself it might have seemed unable to arouse any personal
interest in me. In that vast and silent motion, carrying me along
as in a whirl of darkness, in a world that was born and died again
each day, in which, naturally, there was no concept of beginning or
end, nor any idea of meaning or direction, and of whose powerful,

unceasing, and unpleasant rhythm I was impotently aware, any life that was fitted into some kind of normal and artificial and false schema—beginning, development, and ending—interested me acutely, and any event which had to do with these things was forever imprinted on my memory, along with the hour of the day or night when it happened, the smells in the air, the faces of the people around me, sitting in a café or passing by along the street. And over these things, in the form in which they remained within me, time had no power, and they were perhaps all I was able to hold on to out of the constantly disappearing, shifting world, which grew ever greater with the passage of time and in whose bottomless expanses had perished whole countries and cities and an almost incalculable number of people whom I would not see again.

I thought about all this when one afternoon in spring I saw, in one of the central *quartiers* of Paris, the terrible face of a person whom I knew, and I was astonished by his appearing here in particular. He was a tall, fat man who suffered from a cruel form of dropsy; his head looked like a huge ball filled with yellowish liquid, his face was so swollen that his features had more or less vanished, his eyes seemed tiny, and he seemed more like a monster from a bad dream than a living person. I had seen him for several years in a row; he was always walking along the Rue Saint-Jacques, not far from the Russian library in the Latin Quarter where I lived. And now I had met him on a quiet street parallel to the Grands Boulevards that was almost deserted in the daytime. I stopped and watched him walk away for the umpteenth time and, for no apparent reason, suffered inwardly on his behalf, because walking was hard for him and evidently caused him pain. When he finally disappeared round the corner and I walked off again, the first woman I happened to see before me was Alice.

She was walking along the boulevard straight toward me, very well dressed, heavily made up, pulling along on a taught lead an elaborately and hideously tonsured dog of medium size. From a distance Alice was just as beautiful as usual, but I thought that there was not the same magnificent litheness in her walk that I knew from before. When I came up close to her, I noticed that her eyes seemed to be duller, but none of this would have been detected by a person who had not known and remembered her from before as I had.

"Hello, Alice," I said.

"Hello, love," she replied in her measured voice, in which there was a brief note of excitement that was generally unusual for her. "I'm genuinely happy to see you. What are you up to? It's so long since I saw you."

"Everything's pretty much as before," I said. "Would you like something to drink?"

We went into a café together.

"Is your dog called Bobby?" I asked.

"Yes, that's what I called him, but now he's called Dick."

And she explained to me that she had named the dog Bobby but that the person who had given him to her insisted on the name Dick. "Well then, let him be Dick; isn't it all the same to me?"

"What are you doing?"

"I'm an artiste now."

"An artiste?" I said in astonishment. "Tell me, please, what kind of artiste?"

"I'm in a music hall." She pronounced it "musique-all."

"What do you do there?"

"I do a bit of dancing."

"Nude?"

"No, how could you think that? You wear these little things on your . . ."

"Yes, I understand. What's the money like?"

"Oh, that's not the point; artistes are not at all greedy people. I don't know why . . ."

"Yes. And your old man—what does he do?"

"I don't know, some kind of commercial enterprises."

"Tell me what's happened to you since we parted. You know I'm interested in everything about you."

She told me. To begin with she was happy with chance clients whom she chose herself, then she had gone through several regular—more or less regular—"protectors." She explained that she had not stayed with any of them because she did not like any of them, but this struck me as being untrue.

"Tell me the truth," I said. "You know you can tell me everything; it's a rare opportunity for you to be open."

"All right," she said. "Well then, I don't want to hide it from you. It makes me feel disgusted."

"What do you mean by 'it'?"

"Sleeping with a man. I'm not remotely interested in that."

"And your old man?"

"That's another matter. I'll explain it to you."

And she explained to me that her current "protector" was an elderly and sick man. "He doesn't need much, and then, he's not quite normal."

"What do you mean, 'not quite normal'? Why?"

She sat with her elbows on the table, looking straight at me with her beautiful, calm eyes, and spoke about how her "friend" would, every time he saw her, fall into an impotent and quiet frenzy.

"He always says, 'What a dream! You're the queen of dreams.' Do you understand—he pays me money for these dreams. And then he says 'languor,' and then 'intoxicated with possession,' and all kinds of other drivel. But as for results, that's another matter; he manages to do it once every four times."

"At least he's not demanding."

"That's true," said Alice enthusiastically. "That's why I like him. If he was like the others, it wouldn't last long."

She was now living in a good apartment not far from the Boulevard des Invalides, she had some money, sometimes she went out into the country with her "protector" in his car, and on the whole it seemed that she had all she needed to feel happy. But she was not happy: nothing interested her. She had tried reading, as she told me—and I remembered about Flaubert, which I had brought to Raldy for her—but books seemed boring to her. "It's so long! It's so long!" she said. "He describes to me how a man meets a woman and how they loved one another, then he sleeps with her, and it goes on for three hundred pages. And what comes after that? And he says the air was limpid, and that she had on a dress with a flower, and that she spoke to him, and they remembered a whole pile of different things. In the end, she sleeps with someone else, and he suffers; that's how it's written there, and then he goes off on his travels, meets her again three years later, and she understands that no one ever loved her, apart from him. Well, tell me, please, don't you think that's an abuse of trust?"

"Did he give you this book?"

"Yes, of course. But he's dying from pleasure when he reads this stuff."

She told me about her life, and the more she told me, the more it began to seem to me that her fate had a definite and consistent meaning. In the days when I had first seen her at Raldy's apartment, Raldy had been able to arouse in her—evidently through stories about her earlier glories—a desire for a new and luxurious life, and I would suggest that this was the strongest feeling that had ever appeared in Alice. Therefore she had abandoned Raldy, and back then she really had wanted a good apartment, a car, dresses, and furs. But this desire had been accidental and untypical of her; on the whole she had no desires of her own.

"I would like to lie quietly and for no one to bore me with their intoxication or languor or anything else."

It was as if the creative force which had called forth her existence out of nonbeing had made this perfect body and beautiful face—and had exhausted itself, and this was all that befell to Alice, and nothing more: neither desires, nor passions, nor even intentions. What would have aroused in others agitation, or impatient expectation, or burning desire, left her indifferent. Books, entertainment, the cinema—all of this merely tired her out. It was this calm disgust at everything which might have interested her that forced me to say to her: "I get the impression that you are just dead meat, Alice; forgive me if I'm perhaps exaggerating a bit. Is there anyone in your life?"

"But you already know—the old man."

"No, someone else, someone you love, whom you can't live without?"

"I don't love anybody; that's the last thing I need," she said. "I have a friend, but I don't sleep with him; that doesn't interest either me or him."

"With you that's understandable, but him? It's not normal."

"No, for him it's normal. He's a musician; he plays the piano so well. It's just he's a homosexual: that's his job. So, you understand, women for him . . . But I really like him; he's terribly nice."

"A strange friend!" I said. "Still, if he's right for you . . ."

"Oh, yes. He doesn't need anything from me; he plays all sorts of tunes; we get on so well just the two of us."

"Do you know that Raldy's dead?" I asked suddenly.

Her calm, beautiful face remained immobile.

"Yes, there was even an article in the paper. I read it."

"And it didn't have any effect on you?"

"She was old."

"So you, for example, won't live to that age."

She suddenly frowned, and for the first time the expression in her eyes altered.

"What's the matter with you?"

"I don't feel well," she said, looking away to one side. "Haven't you noticed anything?"

"Yes, I thought that . . ."

"I spent three months in a sanatorium," she said, "because of my lungs. I get tired quickly, I've no strength."

"And so?"

"Well, I don't know how it will end."

"But that's obvious."

"Oh, no, I don't want to, I don't want to, do you understand? I haven't begun to live yet."

"You want to live that much? What for? For your old man, or for your little homosexual, or perhaps for music and reading?"

She was silent.

"Do you remember," I said almost in a whisper, suddenly gripped by feelings of malice, "that evening in the café when I spoke about Raldy with you? There's a certain justice in your fate, do you not think, Alice? I saw her die; she was alone; she didn't have a single centime. You should have been there with her. But you never stopped by to see her, as far as I know."

She covered her face with her hands, and I suddenly noticed that her fingers were wet with tears.

And then I began to feel sorry for her—just as suddenly as I had felt malice a few seconds before. Later on I felt remorse: what indeed could I have demanded from Alice, from this poor pretty girl with her glazed-over, imbecilic, and yet beautiful eyes, and of her pathetic existence, caught between an old and sentimental fool, who repeated to her the same pathetic words about intoxication and languor, and her friend, the passive homosexual, the little musician? I felt ashamed at my irritation. I took hold of one of her burning hands and said, "Forgive me, love. I'm sorry I said that to you."

"You were sorry for her; you've never felt sorry for me. You've always been cruel to me. Just remember what you said to me each time."

"You didn't forget that?"

"No, because it really hurt me."

"Well, it was just words. The main thing is not to cry."

But she carried on crying quietly. Her tears, blackened by mascara, smudged her cheeks; she carefully wiped them with her handkerchief, firmly pressing the corners of her eyes.

"Don't be upset, Alice. Give up your cabaret, don't work, eat more, and you'll get over it; it's not that terrible."

"Do you think so?"

"I'm sure of it."

I went away and thought: how could Raldy have made such a mistake? Alice had nothing, apart from her astonishing physical perfection; she had no talents in order to become a lady in the *demimonde*, which is what Raldy had wanted to turn her into; she had no intelligence, no desires, no pride, not even that warm, animal charm that is characteristic of all women who are success-ful. Her unusual beauty had an impact primarily on the aesthetic faculty, and it was for precisely this reason that it took my breath away when I saw her naked. But in this body, in spite of its outward perfection, there was an inexplicable and cold weariness, the kind of weariness which Raldy had never shown even during the final days of her life. It seemed to me, after this meeting with Alice, that her future was already now predetermined and that nothing good should be expected of it. But I was mistaken about the time, as I was nearly always mistaken, maybe because my own existence unfolded in some other space whose rhythm did not correspond to external circumstances; and in this comparatively calm and infinitely protracted delirium there were extraordinarily few things which had the same meaning, the same value, the same duration in time—in short, some analogy with what took place outside of me.

And so, night once again, and the streets of Paris, Montmartre, Montparnasse, the Grands Boulevards, the Champs-Élysées, and from time to time, the gloomy and picturesque *quartiers* of the outskirts of the city or the destitute central districts. I was driving that night at around one o'clock along the Boulevard Auguste-Blanqui; on the sidewalk a small man in a cap was hitting in the face a woman whom I could not quite see. She was shouting and sobbing loudly enough for the whole street to hear. I knew that it was wrong and that I should not get involved in this and that my intervention would be inappropriate and pointless. But I could not watch it; I began to feel crushed by a dull and listless melancholy and by a desire to stop this man, to all appearances a pimp, and moreover I felt an unbearable revulsion, almost like the urge to vomit. I stopped the car, climbed out, and set off toward that place. But I was too late to do anything. From somewhere a tall, well-dressed man without a hat quickly walked up; he pushed the fellow with the cap and said in an American accent, "Aren't you ashamed of yourself, you animal? You don't hit women."

"What?" the fellow in the cap threatened him. "I don't believe it! Do you want a smack in the gob as well?"

He raised his right hand, but in that brief fraction of a second the man with the American accent hit him in the lower jaw. I saw this from close up and was able to judge the punch, which was absolutely, faultlessly true, almost of professional quality; the whole weight of his body was thrown forward in an unusually swift movement, which began in the left foot, passed along a diagonal line through his thigh and breast, and finished in a rapid and imperceptible straightening of his right arm, with his hand clenched in a fist. The fellow in the cap howled in a peculiar sort of way and fell, his head hitting hard against the sidewalk. Blood flowed from his mouth, and he lay motionless. And then the woman whom he had been beating just before this threw herself at the American and screeched at him, "You've made him bleed, my . . . Look at him, he could be dead. You bastard!"

He looked at her in astonishment, shrugged his shoulders, and walked off with his quick and lithe step. She ran after him and shouted, already choking with tears and fury, "Bastard! Bastard! Bastard! Murderer!"

I was standing close to a lamppost. She went down on her knees before the fellow in the cap, who was still lying there with deathly immobility, and said in a voice riven with sobs, in which, to my astonishment, I detected something like a burbling animal tenderness, "Weber, can you hear me? Weber, my sweetest Weber!"

And that very second there emerged out of the darkness two slow-moving policemen on bicycles.

I got back into my car and drove on, and Raldy's words came back to me: "Yes, my dear, that's love. Maybe that's something you'll never understand. But it's love."

It was a Sunday night. The taxi drivers were lined up outside the dance halls, and beside the Hotel Lutèce, I noticed one of them whose appearance had long intrigued me; he was a little old man with a huge gray mustache. He was so much like a caricature that I could not help smiling every time I saw him. And now I spoke with him for the first time. Judging by his strong accent, he was from somewhere near Grenoble. He answered in monosyllables when the discussion touched on purely professional matters, but he unexpectedly came to life at the mention of an airplane exhibition that had finished a few days beforehand.

"Yes, yes," he said casually, "they've done a few good things, but it's all rubbish really. They're forgetting about the most important thing."

"And what's that, exactly?"

He and I were standing together, apart from the other drivers who were talking to one another about their clients. It was past three o'clock in the morning, and the streetlamps lit up the deserted sidewalk; the little old man stood opposite me, small and skinny, with his huge mustache, which would have suited some grenadier from the start of the previous century, and with an extraordinarily serious and determined expression on his face which really struck me.

"The most important thing," he said, "is that every person can and must fly."

I looked at him in silence.

He repeated, "Yes, m'sieur. Can and must."

"Must, perhaps," I said, "though I'm not too sure even about that. But he can't, that's the thing."

"Yes, m'sieur, he can. I've been working on this for a long time now, and sooner or later I will fly, and you'll see it."

And he told me that he had invented a special contraption, some kind of system of wings and gears, but that his family, naturally, did not understand the significance of what he was doing, and therefore he had to work in very unfavorable conditions.

"They don't give me any space. I don't have a workshop," he said, "and I'm forced to work in the toilet; it's very inconvenient. First of all, I'm often interrupted; second, the room is too small and low; I have to stand in a particular way, and after a while my back and bum start to hurt. Flight consists of three phases. The first one is like this," and without moving from where he was, he flapped his arms several times. "That's the takeoff. The second is like this"—he made several more of the same movements, only this time smoother and slower. "And the third is what in aircraft technology is called sideslip. Like this."

And he leaned over to the left, stretching both arms out fully so that they formed a single line, and suddenly, taking little jumps, ran off along the sidewalk with rapid little steps. One of his hands almost touched the ground, and his head was pressed against his shoulder. It was so unexpected and so comical that I stood and laughed until tears came to my eyes, unable to contain myself. He came back over to me after his flight and said angrily, "You don't understand anything; you're just plain stupid."

But I could not even answer him: tears were pouring from my eyes. For a long time afterward I remembered his little old man's figure leaning over to one side with two parallel lines making a right angle with his sloping body—the lines formed by his arms and by his gray mustache. He was a quiet and harmless lunatic; his friends from the same garage told me about him. Among the taxi drivers, as there would be in any corporation of any size, you found the most varied types of people, in particular lunatics or those who were beginning to lose their minds; the peculiarities of this profession—the constant nervous tension, the way one's earnings depended on quite random circumstances on which it was impossible to rely—all of this contributed to the spiritual balance of these people being subject to trials which it frequently could not withstand. Many of the drivers were a danger to their passengers: they were either alcoholic or ill, already afflicted by the beginnings of palsy, and their system of reflexes was losing its necessary suppleness. I even knew one driver who had leprosy; God knows how he had contracted this rare disease; his whole face was covered with enormous plasters, like a fence on waste ground covered with posters; he was very poor and very badly dressed as well, so that, when I first saw him on the street—he was walking to the garage to pick up his car—I took him for a beggar. Then I got to know him; he was an embittered person and a communist by conviction, although, like most of those people, he had no understanding of systems of government or of economics.

In this nocturnal Paris I felt every day, when I was working, something like a sober person among drunks. The whole of its life was alien to me and aroused in me nothing except disgust or pity—all of those amateurs of nocturnal cabarets or dubious establishments, those special kinds of lovers, in Raldy's terminology, who in their shamelessness were like monkeys in a zoo—all of this, as one of my colleagues in the taxi-driving profession, a specialist in Greek philosophy and an indefatigable commentator on Aristotle, put it, it made you want to puke. I could not escape from it; and the impression I was left with from these years of my life was that I had spent them in an enormous and apocalyptically foul labyrinth. But strangely enough, I did not pass through all of this without my existence connecting—if haphazardly and partially—with other people's lives, as I had passed through factories, the office, and the university.

And so, in an unexpected and scarcely probable fashion, my life turned out to be bound up with three women: Raldy, Suzanne, and Alice. My friendship with Raldy was a result of her mistake, perhaps because her visual memory betrayed her, or because I really did possess the unenviable and unflattering merit of resembling some long-since departed bastard, the unfortunate Dédé. But Suzanne and Alice, both of them had some kind of incomprehensible trust in me, for which it was extraordinarily difficult to find any explanation other than an obvious aberration, not so much mental as spiritual. And although I had never said even one merely polite word to either of them—since I had no reason to pretend or to be insincere—they both told me whatever came into their heads that seemed important to them, and even though my replies to them were invariably sharp and I had no way of helping them and never tried to, they kept on turning to me with inexplicable persistence. Perhaps, however, a partial explanation for this persistence of theirs was the fact that I was clearly not interested in paying for intimacy with them and did not belong to the milieu in which they lived. Whatever about that, a couple of months after my encounter with Alice, when it was already summer, I received a letter from her that had been sent on from my garage. To begin with I was astonished since she did not even know my surname. But there was a simple explanation for it all: she had noticed the number and serial letters of my car, asked another nighttime taxi driver where the car was from, got the address of the garage, and had written: "To the driver of car number such-and-such." The letter was properly written without any spelling mistakes, and I guessed at once that it had been composed by her friend, the little homosexual, and so it turned out.

"My dear friend," Alice wrote, "I would very much like to see you. I would be grateful to you if you could stop by to see me some time"—her address followed here—"it does not matter when, day or night. I do not leave my room and feel quite unwell. I would like to talk to you. I hope that you will come and see me; it is a small debt you have after all the unpleasant things you have always said to me and for which I do not reproach you at all. So, may I expect you? With love, Your *Alice Fichet*"

Previously I would have paid no attention either to this letter or to the invitation. But with Raldy dead, the significance of this death, of her irrevocable disappearance, was so great that all other considerations paled in comparison—and after this, was it not all the same, in essence, whether Alice had conducted herself well or not in that world which was no more and which had died at the very moment when Raldy's heart had stopped? I felt sick at heart thinking about this, but there was no longer any irritation at Alice. I came to see her after nine o'clock in the evening. She had a small apartment, clean and decently furnished, without any particularly clear evidence of bad taste. There were flowers everywhere—in the hallway, in the dining room, in her bedroom. When I got there, Alice was in bed.

"Why did you write to me?" I asked.

She did not know what to reply and turned her head away into her pillow several times.

"I wanted to tell you . . . I wanted to tell you . . ."

"What?"

"Well . . . that I regret it now."

"What do you regret?"

"That I behaved like that."

"That you wrote me a letter?"

"Of course not. You know perfectly well. I'm talking about Raldy."

"It's too late now, Alice. Raldy is dead."

She burst into tears, her whole face crumpling like a child's.

"I'd like it if you would come to see me from time to time."

"Frankly, why would you?"

"I don't know. You know, I'm all on my own. I don't have anyone in the whole world, just the little musician, but then he's not a normal person; he's like me."

She explained rather confusedly why she had asked me to come. In the small and meager reservoir of feelings she possessed—and in which there was neither love, nor passion, nor hatred, nor even anger or significant pity—there nevertheless existed certain remote suggestions of interest toward what did not directly concern or affect her. She told me that every man she had met had wanted, in one form or another, only one thing, always one and the same thing. In this sense nature had not been kind to her, in depriving her of any strength of feeling.

"For me sleeping with a man, it doesn't matter whom, is torture. If only you knew how revolting it is! But that's of no interest to you; you don't want to sleep with me. And then, when you're not attacking me, you say things to me that I never hear from anyone else. Raldy always told me that you weren't like the other drivers. Is it true that you got an education?"

I felt uncomfortable, and I was sorry for her.

"I would really like it if you came to see me. I'm not asking any more of you than that. You can sit where you're sitting now, in that armchair, and you can talk to me if you want to. You can say what you're thinking. And you can tell me why I'm so stupid. Do you want to? Forgive me for the bother I'm causing you."

And so, after this conversation, roughly once a month I would come and visit Alice. Sometimes I would sit in silence, sometimes I would tell her various stories, simplifying and refashioning them as I would have for a sick girl of twelve or thirteen. And there was still a lot she did not understand.

"And to think that Raldy used to read Flaubert with you!" I would say.

"She thought it was helpful," replied Alice. "I didn't think it was, but I didn't dare tell her."

She slowly got better and after a certain time started going outside again. But she did not make a full recovery; she did not complain of anything in particular and generally felt all right, but she quickly grew tired, ate without much appetite, and slept a great deal.

"Are you thinking of going back to the music hall?" I asked her one time.

"No," she said, "I don't need that any more."

And of course the music hall had never held any interest for her; it had made it possible for her to get to know her protector, and it had no further role to play. When all was said and done, Alice was content with her life, with her apartment, and with her protector—whose words of intoxication and languor bored her, though coming from him they were completely inoffensive—with his undemanding ways, with the melodies of her little pederast, and with the fact that she could do nothing and lie about as much as she wanted. She was able to put aside a bit of money, and she spent little, though there were always large quantities of beautiful flowers; though, as it turned out, these were sent by that same "friend," always tireless in his constant concern for her and in his own way touching.

"I know he won't give me up," said Alice. "He's fifty-nine, you understand; at that age they don't go chasing girls. I'm not worried about him."

In spite of her illness, her beauty did not fade; it became some-how a little more transparent, and it was now even more evident that she was completely lacking in that warm, living charm, which is what arouses a sensual attraction toward a woman. And it was easy to see, in the end, why the person who became her closest friend was the little musician in whom the male principle was lack-ing just as the female principle was lacking in her. One time I was sitting with her one evening in early autumn, in the armchair in front of an open window; she, as ever, was lying on her couch, with her hands behind her head, while the radio set played quietly—she did not like loud music—some indeterminate melody. In all of this, from the music to the fading scent of the flowers to the very air of her apartment, there was something soporific that made one want to slumber, weakening all the muscles of the body; I sat and felt what usually troubled or strongly interested me gradually melt away and disappear, and nothing remained except this incomprehensible, almost painfully sweet slumber. And I remembered once again how in the spring two years ago, in Raldy's room with its tall and narrow window, I had seen Alice naked, her lovely body dappled with sunlight. From this beautiful girl Raldy had wanted to make a *demimondaine*. I understood now, I thought, why she had tried to prepare Alice for this peculiar career and why she had found all this necessary. It was Raldy's final illusion and also, perhaps, an unconscious thirst for immortality of which she, of course, was not aware. Her life with all its dazzling possibilities—outside of which she could not see any sense in her existence—all of this was at an end because she had grown old, and there was nothing anyone could do about it. But all her great wealth of sensual and spiritual experience—the traces of which remained only in her huge and tender eyes—had not yet become a dead weight; what had died was merely the means of putting it to use. And so this wealth, which she no longer needed, she wanted to pass on to Alice, in whom it must continue—the tears, upsets, duels, embraces, poems, and the readiness to abandon everything for some blinding happiness which, in the end, had never existed. And the fact that, in spite of all her incomparable experience, she had been so mistaken about Alice only went to prove that she was blinded by this desire of hers to such a degree that she was unable to see the most fundamental and characteristic thing about Alice, namely that strange and unex-pected absence of life in her, which was no less irremediable in her than Raldy's own age and wrinkles, and which neither knowledge of English nor reading Flaubert nor a thousand pieces of whatever kind of advice could ever replace.

I sat there in Alice's armchair almost dozing off and compar-ing through my growing somnolence the hot, sunny day of our first meeting and the quiet evening, here, now, this very minute. Between them lay the uncertain, slow space of two whole years, like sand that soundlessly falls over everything, hills and valleys, fields and seashore. From this my thoughts imperceptibly shifted to the sea, the forest, rivers, to all the innumerable scents, the sup ple swaying of branches, the slow flight of leaves falling—of what I had for so long been deprived of in Paris. These were things whose absence I could never get used to, just as I could never get used to the expression in the eyes of most of the people whom I happened to encounter. Seeing the faces of businessmen, office workers, civil servants, and even factory workers, I found in them something I had not noticed before when I was younger, some kind of perfect and natural absence of abstract thought, a sort of astonishing and reassuring dullness in their gaze. Then, after looking more closely, I started to think that this calm absence of thought could be explained, evidently, by the succession of several generations whose entire life amounted to an almost conscious striving for willful spiritual impoverishment, "common sense" and rejection of doubt, fear of new ideas—the same fear that was equally strong in the average shopkeeper and a young university professor. I could never forget the expression in the heavy and calm eyes of the owner of the hotel where I lived in the Latin Quarter. She would tell about how decent two of her long-standing residents were, an old man and woman; they had put their savings into some shares or other that had lost their value, and when they discovered this, they had both shot themselves.

"Just think, m'sieur," she said, "they were so good and kind toward me that they did it—that is, they killed themselves—not in my hotel but round the corner here, at my neighbor's. They didn't want to get blood all over the rooms. You see I'd only just put in a new carpet, m'sieur; do you know how much new carpets cost now? It was quite new—I'd had it delivered just the day before—and they didn't want to cause me any trouble with the police. And now they've died just the same way that they lived, decently, m'sieur, yes, decently." And tears poured from her eyes. And I thought about how terrible this double death was, which nevertheless proved powerless before this love of order and desire not to cause the landlady any trouble and at the same time to do her one final favor in damaging the reputation of a competitor. I still could not get used to the way that all around me people were frantically grasping after money, which they would put aside not for the fulfillment of any particular purpose but just because that was what one had to do. And this naive and beggarly mentality was equally strong in the most varied groups of people. Even the pimps and prostitutes, even professional criminals, even the communists and anarchists I came across never doubted for a moment that the right to own property was the most sacred of all rights.

"Poor Proudhon!" said Plato one day, when I shared these thoughts of mine with him. Recently he had somehow let himself go even more; he held his tired head even lower above the bar, his raincoat was even more filthy, he got drunk even more quickly, and he would fall even more often into a dead silence from which nothing could rouse him. Only rarely he would talk just with me, having difficulty recognizing me through the permanent and almost impenetrable mist that seemed to surround him. And as his condition became more acute, and as the day when his protracted tragedy would be concluded in some way grew ever closer, in his eyes the world—and most of all France—was disintegrating and dying, and the rhythm of this collapse corresponded exactly, I would suggest, to the speed of Plato's own downfall, the steep curve of his descent. Each time, over the periods when I did not speak with him, interludes of many days or many weeks, another catastrophe would occur in his consideration: first it would be the disappearance of philosophy, then art, then poetry, then sculpture. "Carpeaux was essentially a rather pathetic person. Pascal was just sick, you know that as well as I do; and tell me, please, what's the meaning of all those ravings about Jesus Christ? And what's the meaning of that almost frighteningly banal phrase—you know, the famous phrase—that we die in solitude? And the chair he saw on the edge of the abyss? And that completely stupid 'eternal silence of infinite spaces'? Of what use to us is that silence, tell me, pray? A hospital case? Yes. Material for analysis in the field of dangerous lunacy? Yes. Only not philosophy and not science: let's be serious about it for once." And the last thing to go, coinciding with those days, days spent with Alice, which were a precursor to another disaster I was to be witness to once again, the last thing to go was music. "But, my poor friend, we never had any music. And what would we do with it if we did? We can't hear music; it's about as good to us as Renaissance paintings are to a caveman. We have Tino Rossi; that's our music!"

It was hard for me to listen to what Plato said; he was one of the few people whose fate I was not indifferent to. Therefore I sometimes selfishly avoided talking to him and limited myself to a bow. Each time I followed his every movement with pained attention. He would reply to me with his unfailing politeness and utter a few words; in the whole of my nighttime Paris he was the only person who spoke decent French—he and Raldy. But Raldy was dead by now, while he was still alive.

And apart from everything else, there was something instructive for me personally in his fate—to the extent that the fate of any one person can contain within it something of use to another, a few details in an at-first-glance absurd and perhaps, in truth, illusory comparison. Since the time of my first conversations with him— how many things had changed or disappeared in the narrow world in which my life unfolded? And at that point I remembered my old fear, based on lengthy and sad experience, which in essence boiled down to the thought that perhaps this malevolent and wretched Paris, traversed by infinite night roads, was merely a continuation of my state of almost permanent semidelirium, into which in some strange and incomprehensible way were strewn fragments of something truly alive and real, surrounded, though, by a dead architecture buried in darkness, by music that was swallowed up in some mad and opaque space, and by those human masks whose deceptive and spectral quality was probably obvious to everybody except me. Accordingly, I had no choice but to lead a double life; driving along familiar streets, it was enough for me to relax my attention for a second for strange buildings to begin to rise up before me, unknown corners and sharp stone turnings, and it would suddenly become clear that I was crossing some dead nocturnal city I had never seen before. And only a second later, when my attention once again took hold of this elusive zone of consciousness which fluttered like a rag in the wind, would I notice that I was on the Boulevard Raspail and turning into the Rue de Rennes, where I knew all the shops, all the buildings, and, it seemed, all the people who lived there. And it felt just as absurd and just as much of a double life for me to be sitting at the wheel of a car in my gray cap with a cigarette in the corner of my mouth and to be speaking in *argot* with all sorts of nighttime lowlife, among whom were friends and people I would chat to about their clients, their difficulties, their bosses, their professional interests, or else with drunken passengers or dubious characters who were transporting in my car things which were clearly stolen, and then after returning home, I would automatically and instantly begin to live in another world, where there existed none of those ideas which constituted my unreal, nocturnal, and alien life.

Each time I managed to focus my attention on some question that interested me at any given time, I noticed a strange thing: the further this went on, the more I sank into something that was like a deadly calm or a slow, imaginary death agony. I think that is how people dying must feel in their penultimate minutes, when their physical sufferings have for some reason come to an end but the external world with all its interests, questions, and sensations has already ceased to exist for them. It seems to me that it is precisely at that moment that their eyes acquire the particular leaden opacity, the meaning of which it is impossible to mistake and which I had seen many times; perhaps this happens because their pupils, as they grow dim, no longer reflect anything living, like a mirror that has suddenly grown dark, become blind. When in this state, I would usually lie in my room on the bed, and I had the feeling that if there had been a fire, I would not have moved from where I was. It was all the more surprising as it was not accompanied by any physical illness; generally speaking I was never ill, but I think that when I am dying—if I am still conscious—it is unlikely that I will encounter anything new; and already now, it seems to me, I could describe my own death, the gradually fading noise of life, the slow disappearance of flowers, colors, smells, and ideas, the cold and irrevocable estrangement from all that I loved and that I would no longer love or know. And because this state was so familiar to me, I experienced, I suppose, all those things which were, though contradictory, equally characteristic of my life: relative indifference to my own fate, the absence of envy or ambitions, and alongside these a violent, sensual existence and profound sadness that every feeling was unrepeatable and any attempt to go back to it, though seemingly just as strong, found me already changed and had a different impact than it had ten years, or ten days, or ten hours ago.

Sometimes after one of these episodes I would fall into an almost deathlike state of being, and then I would frequently lie for days in my room without leaving it, seeing nothing and taking no interest in anything; then I would sink into a deep sleep, as if turned to stone, and when I woke again, I would begin to live again as before.

Then on one such day Suzanne came to see me once again. I had not seen her for a relatively long time, roughly since the time when Vasiliev's unexpected death, which she was genuinely glad about, brought a certain tranquility into her existence. She even seemed to recover her health a little and to have put on weight, but as far as I could discern in the semidarkness—the shutters on my windows were lowered—she had the same wild and agitated expression in her eyes. I was only beginning to come round after my prolonged spiritual prostration, and I needed a certain amount of time to recall the whole story of Suzanne, Fedorchenko, and Vasiliev. But even when with a certain effort of the will I had forced myself to return to it, it still seemed to me that none of this merited the slightest detailed attention.

"What is it now?"

"It's started again," said Suzanne.

She sat down in an armchair and began complaining that Fedorchenko was once again leaving her on her own for entire days, and often nights, too, that once again he was no longer himself, was drinking a lot, was spending time in cafés, and often went— she had followed him there—to a Russian late-night restaurant in Montparnasse.

"Leave him alone," I said. "I don't think there's anything I can do. Obviously you no longer interest him; there's nothing you can do about that."

"If you only knew how he worshipped me before we had the misfortune of that lunatic showing up."

"Well then, the worshipping is over."

"It's because he's ill."

"With what?"

"It's the same thing again."

"But no generals have been kidnapped since then, as far as I know."

"The general's only a detail," she said, vehemently, "only a detail, the general."

"Detail or otherwise, you've gone back to the same crazy stuff as before."

"He's your old schoolmate; you've got to do something."

"What, for instance?"

"Talk to him, explain to him."

"I'm not a priest."

"Don't abandon me like this—at the whim of fate," she said, sobbing. "I'm a poor woman; I don't have anybody. Who can I turn to?"

It was evident that she had placed some kind of fantastic and impossible hope in me: it was something close to a mania. I shrugged my shoulders and promised to speak to Fedorchenko, and after this she left, unexpectedly though mistakenly calm.

It did not take me long to find him; I met him that same night in Montparnasse. I was struck by how much thinner he was; his face had acquired a permanent expression of alarm and tension. There was a glint in his eyes, and I did not know whether to put this down to the effects of alcohol or some other, more serious cause. When we sat down at a little table in an empty nighttime café, then after his first few words—as before, when talking to Vasiliev—I sensed that now things were hopeless and that nothing could stop him. He began by singing in his deep voice—he had no ear and sang out of tune—two gypsy romances. With a look of indifferent astonishment on his face, a waiter looked into the room we were sitting in, but Fedorchenko did not notice him. Then he said, "Today we are alive, tomorrow we die, isn't that right? Do you remember what we sang when we finished high school? What was it? Yes, '*nos habebit humus . . .*' and then '*nemini parcetur.*' "

And I thought from what depths these words from a forgotten song in a foreign tongue must have come to him, words which, if he had carried on living as he had done before, he would not have remembered until he died. He was speaking now in Russian, without inserting French words, and this was also a worrying sign: until then he had avoided Russian.

In the café, as always, there was the dull drone of peculiar nighttime voices, which are so different from those heard in the daytime. Some of these sounds distantly recalled those snatches of conversation one hears in the darkness when a train stops at night at some small railway station, and then out of the cool dark of the fields come words exchanged by railway workers with their strange and unforgettable intonation. We sat in my café, and even though the bar was separated from us by a partition, I could see it clearly before me: Madame Duval with her false teeth, the immobile figure of Plato with a glass of white wine in front of him, the yellow face of the waiter who was so happy to be earning a living, and alongside them the slow, brainless movements of the elaborately dressed pimps and prostitutes who came here like animals drawn to the trough. Fedorchenko was silent, propping up his head on his hands. Then he said two words: "It's hard."

"Why?"

He looked up at me with his eyes full of alarm, and for a second it seemed to me that it was some other person looking at me, whom I had never known and who had nothing in common with Fedorchenko.

"I keep thinking about the same thing," he said. "You remember, what I talked to you about at the Champs-Élysées. You didn't want to answer me back then."

"Ah, I remember. But I don't think any answers to those questions exist, and maybe the questions don't exist either."

"Good," he said. "Say you open a shop. You know why you do it: to make money and have enough to live on. Is that right?"

"Yes."

"Now something else. You are alive, and that's more difficult than running a shop, and more important. Is that right?"

"That's right."

"Why do you do it?"

I shrugged my shoulders.

"If a shopkeeper finds out that running a shop isn't worth it and that money is a complete load of rubbish, then he'll close the shop down, then he'll go away and, let's say, go fishing. But if you don't know what you're living for, then what do you do? What can you do?" he repeated. "Well, fine, so I go and get drunk every two days, and then I don't understand anything. But that's no way out of the situation."

"It's a bad way out, at any rate."

"I want to know. I want you to explain to me. First: why am I here on this earth? Second: what'll happen to me when I die, and if nothing will happen, then what the hell's the point of everything else?"

"What exactly?"

"Everything: the state, science, politics, Suzanne, commerce, music—especially music. Why is there a sky over our heads? And what's it all for? Surely it can't all be for no reason?"

"I don't know what to reply to you."

"And why did Vasiliev have to die? I can't stop thinking about that."

"Of course, that was a terrible thing. But don't forget he was mad."

"Do you think so?"

"I'm sure he was."

"Yes, but if there's no God, state, science, and so forth, then that means there's nobody mad, either."

I was astonished not just by him talking about these things, but also by what he said about them. Up until now his conversation had touched exclusively on material questions, and now for the first time he had succumbed to this fateful abstraction, which he was not strong enough to stand up to. It had penetrated his mind, poisoning his unprotected consciousness, and defeating it was a thousand times more difficult than defeating hunger, or illness, or demanding physical work. He carried on sitting there without raising his head and then began to speak again, slowly and softly: "I recently read the Gospels again."

I nodded.

"I remember one thing I read."

"What?"

"'Come unto me, all ye that labor and are heavy laden, and I will give you rest.' So there is an answer to it all somewhere."

He looked at me once more, and again it seemed to me that I was looking into some person's eyes which I had not seen before that night. This impression was so strong and vivid that I began to feel uncomfortable. It was like the feeling I would have experienced if I had suddenly seen a ghost or a corpse slowly getting up from its coffin. At that very moment it became clear to me that this man was doomed no less irrevocably than Vasiliev, because with those eyes it would be impossible for him to carry on living as before—with his business, Suzanne, trips to the country on Saturdays. It seemed to me as if silence had suddenly fallen on the café, even though I could still hear the din of voices coming from the bar, and it would have been quite natural for this state to be resolved by some kind of catastrophe. But, of course, nothing happened. I tried to keep up this painful conversation and became more and more convinced that the person sitting opposite me had lost any resemblance to Fedorchenko, whom I had known so long and so well. He spoke about things which previously could never have entered his head. The questions he could not stop thinking about and the answers to which seemed so vital to him that without them it was not worth living—all these questions were long familiar to me, and since I had slowly and gradually grown used to the tragic absence of any solution to them, I had developed a sort of immunity against them. Fedorchenko, though, was defenseless against them. It seemed as if I were watching over some cruel and imaginary experiment, that I was seeing the futile struggle of an organism with a rapidly spreading illness which it did not have the strength to overcome. It was so painful that being alone with this man became almost unbearable.

On my way home after taking leave of him, I thought about what could be done. It was clear that only a miracle could bring Fedorchenko back to the way he was before; he was like a man falling from a sheer wall, and thinking of this, I remembered Plato and our conversation about the chair above the abyss.

A little while later I went to the Russian nighttime cabaret that Fedorchenko often frequented and that Suzanne had told me about. In my life there were a number of things I could never resist: these were several books—I was unable to tear myself away from them if they found their way into my hands—and a woman's face which for many years would unfailingly, wherever I was living and however I was living, appear before me the moment I closed my eyes, and the sea and snow, which still held an irresistible attraction for me, and then, finally, there was singing at night, a guitar or a band, a café or cabaret, and the piercingly sad lurching sounds of a gypsy song or a Russian lament. I knew by heart these often ridiculous and comical combinations of words, which would have been impossible in any remotely tolerable poem, these separations, dreams, chains, partings, flowers, fields, tears, and regrets, all of them unacceptable for almost anybody's tastes; but through these words there came through a Slavic sorrow that was invincible in its musical conviction and without which the world would not have been the way I made it for myself. It was a particular and irresistible charm, which moved endlessly along a sonorous musical spiral, and with each new circle it passed by the same feelings it had brushed against earlier and which seemed to be trying, in a tortured and fruitless effort, to follow the fleeting, slowly retreating melody. There was something similar, I felt, in those slender trees which bent in the wind and seemed to be constantly trying to fly after it—when there is a storm and when all that is not built to be immovable is borne away by the irresistible movement of the wind. In it there was also a reminder of another, vanished world, of the end of the last and the beginning of the present century when time still moved so slowly and when the story of one essentially trivial feeling could fill a whole life. It was also a vision of distant things: summer fields and gardens beneath the moon, the smell of flowers and new-mown hay, the blue-white gleam of snow as resonant as glass, coachmen, horses, shafts, sleigh bells, and sound shadows which transported to us other people's memories of those who were long dead and whom we had never known. But the most important thing was that after hearing this music there came minutes of a particular sensual lassitude and a vague, wild emotion unlike anything else. After this one could commit actions that should not be committed, speak words that never should have been spoken, and make some tantalizingly alluring and irrevocable mistake.

The cabaret I had come to was just like many other Russian cabarets, which differed only in the greater or lesser opulence—or poverty—of the décor. There was the same band—violinist, cellist, pianist—the same waiters with clean-shaven and melancholic faces, the same small stage set at a slight angle, as if it had moved a little from its usual place. There were two male and two female singers, all with resonant surnames, but the top name was Katia Orlova, a lady no longer young, heavily made up, in a black, tragic, very décolleté dress—while at the front table, from eleven o'clock in the evening until five o'clock in the morning, there would sit a broad-shouldered, heavily built man in a dinner jacket and tortoiseshell glasses, a Dutchman, her current lover, with his customary bottle of champagne. By chance I happened to know this woman; she had had a stormy and fickle life; she astonished me, when I met her and began talking to her, by quoting from Annensky and Rilke and generally knowing a great deal which, ordinarily, a cabaret singer would have no notion of. She was drunk that morning, openly frank and confiding, and she told me about her life—about her schooldays, Petersburg, Florence, Dresden, about prewar Paris, the boarding school in England where she had been a pupil, and much more. She was ugly; only her eyes were very pretty; she had a low, small voice which she used with an instinctive and unerring talent; she had never studied with anyone. Later on she forgot both the early morning when she and I had met—it was in a café after a late-night restaurant, there were at least ten people there—and the verses she had recited for me, and my face, and she never recognized me during my visits to whichever cabaret she was appearing at.

In her there was something akin to an inexplicable and, as is sometimes the case, almost electric charm, and I remember one time someone completely drunk and whom I did not know saying something about her that astonished me with its fortuitous accuracy, that is, that when she began to sing, one had the impression that the current had been switched on. Later I found out that he was an engineer, an electrical specialist, and that, far from wishing to find some special way of defining her, he was simply using the term which was most familiar to him.

If one had to say in one word what it was that Katia always sang about, in all her songs and in all languages, then it would be hard to find anything that suited better than the word *regret*. I think that for her this summed up all her personal experience, as with the majority of people who are sufficiently developed and intelligent to understand abstract things but who do not have the strength to construct new systems of sensibility—a strength that is often to be found in other, more primitive people. At all events, this was the constant meaning of all of Katia's songs, their "key," as one of my friends put it when speaking of her. And it was this, in the chain of spiritual catastrophes, that Fedorchenko, who was one of her devotees, could not understand. And so gradually, as a result of this strange and irresistible chance, every other night he would plunge into this minor-key, musical mist and each time involuntarily begin to live the loss of all the things Katia sang of and which had never happened for him, since he had never known either those *troikas* in the snow, or avenues in an old park, or lost love, nothing of that sad and foolish world. I saw how he sat, heavily propping up his head with his hand and with his eyes fixed on the stage and Katia's black dress.

All of this—the unanswerable questions and always-ready Gypsy longing—would not perhaps, on their own, have been able to have such a fateful effect on him if they had not been a part of that precipitous and immense spiritual ailment of which he was the victim and whose meaning seemed to me clear, just as it seemed clear to me why my conversations with Fedorchenko about philosophical problems aroused only feelings of discomfort in me. It was a result of his monstrously late spiritual development. Those things with which our consciousness—mine and that of the majority of my friends and contemporaries—had come into contact very long ago, when we had only just learned to think and which then invariably continued their unceasing, gradual work, losing their initial acuteness and painfulness and becoming almost habitual— these things had emerged for him only now, after he had lived a whole life, in which they had never played any role. So that now this had revealed itself in all its tragic and unavoidable complexity. He resembled a corpulent, forty-year-old man who has never known physical effort, who was suddenly being forced to perform acrobatic exercises designed for a sixteen-year-old youth; and from this his muscles are torn, his bones cracked, his sinews strained, his limbs which have long since lost their suppleness are aching, his heart hammering, unable to stand such a strain.

And the first of these things was the beginning of an under-standing of feelings which he himself had never experienced and an involvement in other people's distant lives, in sum that work of the imagination which he had never known before. He began to read books; he took an interest in the fate of the heroes as if it was closely connected to his own personal destiny. This man, who had been remarkable for his robust peasant good health and who had no conception either of ailments or of even a second-long loss of consciousness or of that state between reality and the imagination which is familiar to nearly all people who are involved in art, now began to exist as if in a state of continuous inner delirium, a mixture of memories of the theories and death of Vasiliev, the contents of books read for the first time, and questions, always those same questions, without any possibility of finding an answer to them. This was for him something especially unbearable because by his nature he belonged to that category of people for whom, at best, logical constructions represent the maximum of their intellectual attainments and for whom the existence of irrational things is inadmissible.

Over the past year he had seen and absorbed more than over the whole of his life. The more I thought about it, the more I was struck by the astonishing and fortuitous resemblance of his current condition with purely physiological phenomena, of which I had read descriptions in medical books—the very same desperate struggle, condemned in advance to failure, with an irresistibly spreading poison. And the more time went on, the more evident became the obvious and tragic divergence of Fedorchenko's fate from the path it ought to have followed. This was all the more apparent as his business was flourishing and bringing in income that increased with each month. There was, finally, one additional deciding factor in this life of his, something that Suzanne had first told me about when she had been to my flat and fainted there: she was pregnant. She had changed for the worse, and her childishly delinquent face had acquired an uncharacteristic seriousness, and through all the layers of makeup that she applied to it, her human features suddenly began to show through, just as on an old painting, after a first attempt at restoration, unexpected details show up, revealing its earlier meaning, which has remained hidden up to now. "Now people say 'madame' to me," she said to me, "and give up their seats to me, and my customers give me pieces of advice and ask me how I'm feeling."

But nothing could stop Fedorchenko now. It seemed to me that if he had gone away to the other end of the earth, completely changed his life, and then forgot about what had happened to him, even then this whole terrible world, this air in which he was gasping for breath, even then it would have come back to haunt him.

I remember in particular looking at him for a long time when I had come one day to the cabaret; he was not aware of my presence. He was sitting with his eyes closed, with his head thrown back on his sinewy neck, and I noticed then that his face had the capacity to turn pale—up until then it had always been a reddish color. And in that darkness—he never once opened his eyes—through the musical fog, came Katia's low voice, singing of regrets and farewells and about lost possibilities of happiness—and Russia once again, an almost unknown and distant Russia, along with the same snow, and coachmen, and sleigh bells. I became aware at that point, amid this singing and sobbing Gypsy melancholy, of the irremediable wrongness of a life like this and all that was going on, and at the same time it was one of those mistakes after which a person's previous existence, happy and calm, forever loses its seemingly preordained and deserved attractiveness. It was an irrevocable mistake; a person who committed it and who now fully understood this simple and fragile mirage could no longer find what had gone before it.

All this time the fate of Fedorchenko—although my attitude to him was always, it seemed to me, one of complete indifference occupied me greatly; I had the impression that I was witnessing the death agony of his soul, while incapable of helping him in any way at all. I searched a long time for an explanation for this involuntary and unexpected sympathy of mine toward him. All the same, I think that it arose from Fedorchenko becoming, in these last months of his life, as a result of his precipitate and fateful evolution, something close to the type of person who had always interested me and with whom, up to then, he had had nothing in common. All this time I could not rid myself of the feeling that I, too, in some oblique and illicit way, was a participant in his misfortune. This was a result of one unfortunate quality of mine: I had involuntarily accustomed my imagination to excessively strenuous and intense activity, and once begun, this activity would carry on, and I was not always able to stop it. And just as, so it seemed to me, I understood Plato, following him as much as I was allowed to in all his deliberations and his delusions, made deeper by his constant intoxication, just as with unexplainable and intense interest I almost experienced Raldy's stormy existence or Alice's life, recreating virtually every tiny detail in my imagination, so was I now surrounded by the air in which Fedorchenko was gasping for breath and dying.

Reasoning logically, I had no business with all of these people, but as always, I was troubled by the distant sadness of others, just as I was pursued by another's death—my whole life long. I almost did not belong to myself at such times, when these things reached a particular concentration and when some chain of events was approaching its end. My own personal fate had worked out in such a way that I had often found myself present during unavoidably tragic dénouements; this had been repeated so many times and in such varied circumstances that I had begun to seem to myself in some measure like a representative from an undertaker's. As a result of this lengthy experience I had come to the conclusion— it was being reaffirmed one more time now through the example of Fedorchenko—that my normal view of people and their inner makeup was almost always wrong, and this became apparent in the last months or weeks or years of their life. I would then ask myself the question: what was more true—my established idea about this man or this woman or the complete alteration in it, which occurred later? Thus it was with Fedorchenko. He had lived his life, and all considered him—having, it would seem, sufficient grounds for doing so—a dull and limited person who was interested in nothing other than things of a material order. And now here he was dying, having completely forgotten about his income and his business, and how he was dressed, and when it would be Sunday, and sincerely tormenting himself over that same spiritual and abstract world of which his entire previous existence was a denial.

I remember that summer especially well. What was special about it was that when I recall other periods of my life, the past emerges before me slowly, but when I recall the stifling June, July, and August of that year, everything appears all at once, hurriedly and simultaneously, like some inexplicably complex entity that combines within itself heterogeneous and dissimilar things, and the chaotic nature of this improbable combination remains unchanged and always the same. I see the small, quiet street in Paris on which I lived and the cracked, folding wooden shutters of my window, spots of sunlight on the roadway; I see the street singers who came here every day, I hear their broken, uncertain voices; I feel the heavy, stone Parisian heat; I see against the smoky and hot sky on a neighboring red-brick building a circular terrace with a chaise longue on which there sat a woman in a dark red dressing gown— I could never make out her face—reading a book; the last weeks in the city before people left for the south, Sundays and Sunday crowds of people, nocturnal turnings, displacing streetlamps, and the murmur of car tires on the silent surfaces of wood and stone, the tired nocturnal faces of my passengers in the uneasy hours before dawn, and as well the particular feeling of ennui, unlike any other, which did not go away and was not susceptible to oblivion. I remember the sound of the rain on my wooden shutters in those early morning hours when I returned from work and lay down to go to sleep; it evoked in me memories and sensations so profound that, however hard I searched in my memory, I could not find a time in my life when these sounds did not represent for me something as familiar as the feeling of my own prostrate body. And now I would listen to the rain as I had done ten or twenty years before, and then I could dimly sense my subconscious animal connection with infinitely remote ancestors with whom there remained nothing in common save these few purely physical recurrences, each one of which, however, carried within itself the idea of something close to immortality.

In those days and weeks the final events of Fedorchenko's life took place. They unfolded so distinctly and with such certainty—their course was so predetermined—that from the outside it seemed that nothing could be simpler than to turn away from them. In other words, Fedorchenko need only have given up his unnecessary and futile philosophy and simply gone about his business for any thought of danger of whatever kind to have seemed foolish and without any foundation. But in the unfolding of this spiritual catastrophe there was something resembling the direction of a dynamite explosion—the line of greatest resistance.

I hardly met him in the last weeks of his existence. Two or three times I noticed him in the cabaret where Katia sang, and even then it seemed to me that in his face there was an intense alienation from what was going on; it was the most absent face that I had ever seen, it was an improbable abstraction of Fedorchenko. However hard I tried to understand what exactly it was, what specifically physical signs created this impression, I was obliged to return to one and the same conclusion—that it was as elusive as it was unquestionable. I learned later on that he had been writing a great deal recently, and all of it in Russian; Suzanne told me about this. But no one managed to find these papers.

What happened then, and which I witnessed, took a long time to penetrate into my consciousness, although I remembered all the details of these events. But for some reason I did not want to think about it; and every time I tried to recall that day, some tune would come into my head, or a film I had recently seen, or the particular intonation of a female voice I had heard on the street—but not that day. And only a couple of weeks later, in the south of France, beside the sea, one morning I remembered it all clearly and in detail.

I lay on the beach with the sea in front of me, particularly smooth on that windless day, and the scorchingly hot red pine trees that came right down to it; the air shimmered transparently above the surface of the beach, the cicadas screeched, and cars passed occasionally on the road nearby. Everything that had happened in my life up to that moment seemed extraordinarily far away, almost nonexistent; there remained nothing but this sea, this as-ever cloudless and remote sky. I turned over from my back onto my stomach and saw a scrap of newspaper that someone had thrown there. It was an old issue of *Paris-Soir,* crumpled, torn, and half trampled into the sand, so that all I could see were the large letters of a headline: A STRANGE STORY . . .

And when I read these words, there immediately rose before me, with the instantaneousness that is most characteristic of memories associated with some kind of smell, the final day on which the most important events in the life of Fedorchenko concluded.

It was a rainy, sultry day; I awoke with the same feeling of causeless and insurmountable ennui with which I had fallen asleep, glanced at the portrait of a woman that hung on the wall—and which had so interested Suzanne—and looked for a long time at that face, which that morning seemed to me distant and alien, even though I knew all of its expressions, and all the movements of those lips, and all the alterations of those eyes; but that day even it almost ceased to exist for me. I had only just finished getting dressed when the doorbell rang and Suzanne entered. The expression on her face was just as troubled and helpless as during all that time. She was in the final month of pregnancy, her belly stuck out a long way, and her features were drawn and dull.

"You don't look too good, my dear," I said. "Has something else happened, or have you just come to annoy me as usual?"

"I've come to annoy you, as you put it. Let's go to my place; we can have breakfast there. I can't stay there alone."

"And your husband?"

"He's asleep; he only came back this morning. I don't know where he's been."

I went off with her. I would not have done so if I had been my normal self, but then I didn't care where I went or what I did. She livened up a bit, and we talked about when and how this would all finish. Suzanne told me that after Vasiliev's death she had hoped that everything would go back to how it had been before, but there had been no improvement. She felt more and more with each passing day that the person whom she had married no longer existed, and in place of him there was another, who still retained a physical resemblance to the first but whom she did not know and did not understand. She put it differently.

"I don't recognize him; sometimes I think that I've never seen this man before. Do you know?"

"So you say you don't recognize him?" I mechanically repeated her sentence, thinking about something else. It had seemed at the time I was thinking about something else; lying beside the sea I could easily recall my thoughts at that time: they had been of Fedorchenko's face in the cabaret and his astonishing, deathlike absence—essentially, the same thing that Suzanne was talking about.

"I'll just go and wake him up," she said, getting up and walking over to the closed door of his room. "You look at him, and then you can tell me yourself if it's the same man."

"Of course he's the same," I replied. "Only he's in a different state, that's all."

She pulled the door toward herself, but the door did not give.

"Well!" she said in astonishment. "What's this?"

She pulled harder, leaning with one hand against the wall—I had the impression that on the other side there was some kind of weight attached to the door. Finally, with an effort, the door opened; that very second Suzanne cried out with such a wild, animal cry that I leaped up from my chair and rushed over to her.

Fedorchenko's contorted body was half hanging and half sitting on the end of a short, thin strap which was tightly wound around the door handle. The strap had cut deep into his neck, his face was a purplish crimson color, and his dead, open eyes looked directly and blindly in front of him.

People were already coming up the stairs; they began ringing and knocking outside the flat; I opened the door for them. Suzanne, who had not stopped crying out, was writhing convulsively on the bed. After a while the police appeared, and then nurses dressed in white, who took Suzanne away: she had gone into labor. I had to give an explanation for my presence there. The concierge told the police inspector that the tenant had returned home after five o'clock in the morning. The doctor who had been sent from the police station declared that the death had occurred several hours beforehand. I was able to leave only toward evening. Outside, the same sultry, warm rain, which had never stopped, was falling.

The following morning I went to the hospital to see Suzanne. She had changed greatly over one night: on her face, unusually for her—and new to me—was an expression almost of solemn calmness. She was unrecognizable, as if she had understood certain unusually significant things which she never would have known had they not been preceded by this incomprehensible tragedy and had it not been for that corpse that hung so awkwardly and heavily on her door. Her hair was neatly combed; her gold tooth glinted beneath her slightly raised upper lip.

"I have a boy," she said. "Quite a drama, wasn't it? At least we can say it's all over now."

"Yes, it's over," I repeated.

A couple of days later I told Plato all of this, the way I told him about much that I witnessed or took part in. He was very drunk that evening, I saw him home, and this took us more than half the distance that separated our café from the little street he lived on. On the way he said that it really was all over and that Suzanne had no idea how right she was. Before saying good-bye we stopped for a minute under a streetlamp. He looked straight into my face with his cloudy and unmoving eyes, then suddenly seized my hand, squeezed it hard—it was the first occasion in all that time he had done this—and said, "I don't understand how you can bear all of this when you're a nondrinker. You need to drink, I assure you; otherwise you've had it; and when your own end comes, it'll be even more tragic than all the stories you tell me."

I parted from him on the Avenue du Maine. He walked away making little gestures with his right hand, and I imagined he must be repeating, "You need to drink, you need to drink, you need to drink, you need to drink, otherwise it's impossible to bear it."

And as I made my way home at dawn that day, I thought about the night roads and of the vaguely terrifying meaning of all these last years, about the deaths of Raldy and Vasiliev, about Alice, about Suzanne, about Fedorchenko, about Plato, about that wordless and powerful flow of air that traversed my path through this sinister and fantastical Paris, and which bore away with it other people's ridiculous tragedies, and I understood that in the future I would see everything with different eyes, and however I ended up living and whatever fate had in store for me, behind me, like some burned-up and dead world, like the dark ruins of collapsed buildings, this alien city in a distant and alien land would always stand as an unmoving and silent reminder.

Notes

11   *sortie de bal*   A fur jacket worn over a ball gown.

21   *Les Halles*   The central market in Paris; it was later pulled down and today is a large shopping mall.

21   *Boehme*   Jakob Boehme (1575–1624) was a German religious mystic.

24   *Gérard de Nerval*   Nom de plume of Gérard Labrunie (1808–55), a French Romantic poet whose works are characterized by metaphysical and esoteric themes and references; after a series of mental breakdowns, he hanged himself from a window in Paris.

37   *Blok, Annensky*   Aleksandr Aleksandrovich Blok (1880–1921) was a major Russian symbolist poet; Innokenty Fedorovich Annensky (1855–1909) was a Russian symbolist poet, classical scholar, and translator. Together with Dostoevsky, these authors represent the spiritual, antimaterialist tendencies of the Russian intelligentsia that Gazdanov's fellow worker seeks to embody.

42   *My darling, my beloved*   Lines from Liza and Polina's duet in Tchaikovsky's opera *The Queen of Spades* (1890).

51   *amant de coeur*   French for, literally, "lover of the heart" (i.e., someone with whom one is romantically, rather than merely sexually, involved).

53   *L'Aiglon*   In English, *The Eaglet*, a historical drama by Edmond Rostand (1868–1918).

53   *La Dame aux Camélias*   In English, *The Lady with the Camelias*, a well-known play by A. Dumas, fils.

56   *maisons de passe*   In English, house of assignation, a more discreet establishment than a brothel or *bordel*.

75   *Auguste Comte*   (1798–1857) French philosopher, proponent of positivism (the belief that the only true knowledge is based on sensory experience), and founder of modern sociology. Comte suffered

from mental illness and was admitted to an asylum in 1826, only to be released without having been cured.

75   *Stirner* Max Stirner (nom de plume of Johann Kaspar Schmidt, 1806–56) was a German philosopher and precursor of nihilism, existentialism, and anarchism.

75   *I immediately recognized him* Aleksandr Kerensky (1881–1970) was head of the provisional government in Russia in 1917.

77   *Peter's reforms* Reference to the reforms of Peter the Great (1672–1725, ruled Russia from 1682), who attempted to modernize and Westernize Russia, including building a new capital city—St. Petersburg, in northwestern Russia—and creating a modern navy and government service.

84   *gospoda* Russian for *gentlemen*.

93   *mairie* Mayor's office or town/city hall, the administrative center of a French town or village, which is run by an elected mayor.

109   *dans cette monde* The grammatically correct form of this phrase would be "dans *ce* monde" (in this world), the word *monde* being masculine in French and requiring the masculine form *ce* (this) to agree with it; *cette* is the feminine equivalent of *ce*.

115   *Savinkov* Boris Savinkov (1879–1925) was a Russian writer and revolutionary terrorist. Exiled after 1917, arrested in 1924 after attempting to enter Russia clandestinely. Committed suicide in prison.

119   *some Russian general had been kidnapped* Probably a reference to the kidnapping in Paris in 1930 by OGPU (Soviet secret service and forerunner of the KGB) agents of former White Army general Alexander Kutepov (1882–1930), leader of the exiled Russian All-Military Union, an anti-Bolshevik group.

157   *peau de chagrin* Reference to the novel of this name by Balzac in which a young man finds a magic piece of shagreen that fulfills his every desire. With each wish, however, it shrinks and consumes a portion of his physical powers.

169   *Edmond Dantès* The principal character from Dumas, père's novel *The Count of Monte-Cristo* (1844).

171   *an oak tree as in Lermontov's poem* Reference to the final lines of Mikhail Yur'evich Lermontov's poem of 1841, "I go out alone onto the road . . ." Often interpreted as expressing the poet's death wish.

173   *Pigalle* District of Paris below Montmartre with numerous nightclubs and cabarets (including the famous Moulin Rouge); it is the center of the red-light district.

182   bliny, golubtsy, pel'meni, *and the inevitable* borshch Russian dishes: *bliny* are yeast pancakes; *golubtsy* are stuffed cabbage leaves; *pel'meni* are a type of filled pasta; *borshch* is beetroot soup.

183   *Petushok* Literally: cockerel.

183   *rasstegai* an open-topped Russian pie.

185   *chanteur à voix* Literally: singer with a voice.

192   *We met, and there was a tremor in our hearts . . .* In a 1947 journal publication of this section of the novel, the song text appears in French as a quatrain and then a couplet:

On s'est rencontré le coeur plein de fièvre
Le front durci de rêves ardents,
Et le même sourire nous venait aux lèvres,
Dans les doux soupirs des premiers serments.

Votre passage a laissé dans mon cœur
Une empreinte profonde réclamant le bonheur

217   *Proudhon* Pierre-Joseph Proudhon (1809–65) was a French political philosopher, one of the founders of anarchism. He is famous for the assertion "Property is theft!" made in his first major work, *What is Property? Or, an Inquiry into the Principle of Right and Government* (1840).

217   *Carpeaux*   Jean-Baptiste Carpeaux (1827–75) was a French sculptor and painter.

218   *Tino Rossi*   Also known as Constantino, Rossi (1907–83) was a popular French singer and film actor, originally from Corsica.

222   *nos habebit humus . . . nemini parcetur*   Words from the Latin hymn *"Gaudeamus igutur"* ("Let Us Then Rejoice"), widely used as a graduation song in European universities and colleges. *"Nos habebit humus"* ("the earth will have us"); *"nemini parcetur"* ("none shall be spared").

224   *Come unto me, all ye that labor and are heavy laden*   From Matthew 11:28.